MURDER IMPERFECT

Neal Sanders

The Hardington Press

MURDER IMPERFECT

Murder Imperfect is a work of fiction. While certain locales and organizations are rooted in fact, the people and events described are entirely the product of the author's imagination.

Second printing, March 2010

for Betty, who believed

MURDER IMPERFECT

1.

You can call this a confession if you must. Last year – on June 27 to be specific – I murdered my husband. I did it with malice aforethought – a premeditated, cold blooded killing.

No. On second thought, let's not call this a confession. A confession implies some acknowledgement of guilt or remorse. I don't feel the least bit guilty and I certainly have no remorse. The bastard got what he deserved. If I may be permitted a lone dip into melodrama, he was a man who needed killing. I was the one who did it.

So, let's just call this my story.

Killing him wasn't my original plan. I was just going to divorce him. The usual grounds: he was cheating on me. Cheating, hell. He was addicted to twenty-six-year-olds and was carrying on affairs with a string of them. And it wasn't like I didn't have evidence.

But then I discovered he had squirreled away nearly five million dollars, all of it obtained quite illegally. He didn't think I knew about it. In a divorce, he would have denied its existence and, once I proved otherwise, the SEC would take notice and lay claim to all of it. George would go to prison, of course, but I'd never see a dime of that five million and the government would start looking at our legitimate assets as well. The IRS or the SEC might well decide that they would make excellent punitive damages to dissuade others from following through with scams like George's. It was entirely possible that I could end our marriage and wind up broke.

The notion of George in prison was gratifying, but not so much so that I was willing to become poor for the sense of satisfaction.

So, murder it was.

Maybe I should introduce myself and give you the standard background. My name is Katherine, better known as Kat. I am thirty-six now, considered quite attractive and I take care of myself. My complexion is fair, my hair is brunette and I have green eyes, or at least green contacts. Where I live now is of no consequence to this story but, last June, I lived in Wellesley Hills, Massachusetts.

At the time of his death, George was also thirty-six. In the eight years we were married he went from athletic and reasonably good looking to middle-aged with a budding double chin and a thickening waist that he hid by sucking in his stomach when he thought someone was looking, as well as with pleated pants and too-tight belts. He was employed as a securities analyst by the Boston firm of Peavy, Jensen & Beck.

'Securities analyst' is one of those job titles that cause peoples' eyes to glaze over. In the right firm and the right industry, though - say, Goldman Sachs and biotechnology - it's a very high-powered and prestigious occupation that pays extremely well. In a regional firm like PJ&B (whose clients invariably call it PB&J) and in an industry sector like food, beverage and lodging, it's a snoozer of a career move, which made it perfect for a dullard like my late, unlamented husband.

My job description since the age of twenty-seven has been housewife, perfect hostess and slave. It wasn't always like that. I had a career, once. I graduated with honors from Syracuse University with a Masters degree in English. I was a copywriter at Hill, Holliday in Boston. At twenty-three, I moved to Boston to be with the guy I thought I was going to marry. He was my college sweetheart and I was going to be happy with him for the rest of my life.

Mark and I were engaged, or at least I thought we were. I even remember the day he proposed. He got down on one knee, told me he loved me, and said he wanted us to be together always. I had followed him after college to a city that was not exactly my first choice of places to live, but Boston was where he had found a job. I thought we were going to settle down, have kids and be a family.

In three years I never got an engagement ring, though. Mark had a perfectly logical explanation, of course. 'A down payment on a place of our own is a lot more meaningful than some overpriced diamond,' he had said. Except that in those three years, we also never got around to finding that place. Instead, one day he announced he had taken a job in Houston and that 'we needed some time apart'. So much for getting married. So much for being engaged. Suddenly, I was twenty six and all those plans for a happy life had evaporated.

If marriage and a home are part of your life vision, twenty-six is a terrible age to be college-educated, female and unattached. It's an even worse age if you have nearly a hundred thousand bucks of student loans outstanding. Back when I was eighteen, mom and dad gave me the choice of a free ride at Mankato State University – ten miles from the house I had lived in all my life – or the same amount of money toward any other college I could get into. I frankly thought they were bluffing – have me close to home where they could keep an eye on me.

I was wrong. Three months after graduation, I received a big package stuffed with handy payment envelopes to begin remitting $492.78 each and every month for the rest of my life.

So, at twenty-six, I had a crappy copywriting job at an agency that was the big fish in the fetid, advertising backwater that is Boston, trying to think of clever new things to say about donuts and car dealerships. And I had those student loans as this ticking time bomb. And Mark's parents had thoughtfully sent me an engagement announcement for their son's forthcoming nuptials to someone named Audrey. I'll bet she got the ring up front.

Which explains why, when I caught George's eye at a wedding, I didn't mind him sitting down next to me at the reception and listening to his bullshit pickup line. He was a year older than I, had an MBA, and worked at PJ&B as an assistant to the firm's retail analyst. The job and the firm meant nothing to me but the letters 'MBA' caused me to pay much closer attention. MBAs were hot. MBA's were smart. The letters MBA made something in my mind go 'ka-ching'.

Today, I know better. At a cocktail party a few years ago, I met the head of graduate school admissions at an extremely prestigious local university that will remain nameless. He had three or four too many Grey Goose martinis and told me how the MBA admissions process really works. Graduate schools are fairly selective about who they let in. Their entering classes are full of bright over-achievers. Just as in undergraduate education, however, a few places are reserved for what are called 'legacies', the progeny of wealthy alumni who are already showering the university with donations. For these legacies, the admissions committee turns a blind eye to grades, GREs, and IQ.

Once someone gets into an MBA program, he said, the school isn't in the habit of throwing out the student, no matter how poorly they're doing. Colleges aren't in the business of creating resentful dropouts with chips on their shoulders for might-have-been alma maters. The role of the university is to put a degree in that person's hand, send them out into the world and then, starting ten years after they graduate, begin raking in unbelievable amounts of money from grateful alumni in the form of appreciated stock options to swell the university's endowment.

But I didn't know that at the time. I assumed the guy whose eye I had caught was some future corporate CEO and I was about to come into his life in a big way. And I was desperate as only a 'senior copywriter' (only six steps removed from 'creative director' where the real money starts) in hock up to her belly button could be.

At this point you're saying to yourself, 'She went after George strictly for the money. She married him because he could repay her student loans. No sympathy.' Maybe that was some small part of my thinking that lovely Saturday afternoon. Maybe I was wondering how, on my pathetic $30,000 copywriter's salary, I was going to swing a loan repayment of nearly five hundred dollars a month on top of my share of the fifteen hundred bucks for a one-bedroom apartment I was suddenly sharing with two unwanted roommates. So, yes, some part of my mind was contemplating how unfair life was.

But you'd be wrong about the rest of it. I still bought into that 'one day my prince will come' baloney. I was a dark-haired maiden waiting in the tower to be rescued by a knight in shining armor. Preferably, by a knight who looked like Kenneth Branagh, or what Kenneth Branagh looked like around the time he did '*Henry V*' and '*Much Ado About Nothing*'. Six weeks after our breakup, I had convinced myself that Mark was a mistake from which I could learn. I had invested five years in him and gotten a lousy return, but I had also gained Wisdom, or at least that's what some self-help book told me.

And George was good looking with dark wavy hair and a great chin and a smile that melted your heart. He spoke in educated tones and looked sincere, with a way of cocking his head when I spoke that made me believe he was both listening and interested in what I had to say. What's more, he made it clear from the outset that he was actually *looking* for Miss Right – weddings are a great place for separating the lookers from the buyers. He was the marrying kind and had decided at twenty-seven it was time to tie the knot just as soon as he found the girl of his dreams.

So, yes, I went after George with every trick in the whole self-help section and we had a whirlwind romance and I overlooked a couple of things like his preening in the bathroom mirror for fifteen minutes every morning or the humming sound he made while he ate Frosted Flakes for breakfast. Maybe I overlooked some things that ought to have been warning flags that George wasn't the most debonair man on the cruise ship and that those academic credentials were suspect. But I was twenty-six and I desperately wanted happiness.

We made it to the altar nine months after we met, including a four-month engagement and no, I wasn't pregnant. I was just determined that George wasn't going to get away and marry some other nubile cutie. *Cosmopolitan* was a big help. I bowled him over with my nine-step plan, or maybe it was eleven or eight steps. Anyway, it worked. On a Saturday morning in October at a tiny Episcopal church in Ipswich, a minister said, 'you may kiss the bride' and it was all official.

Are we destined to marry our fathers? There's a school of thought that says all women are programmed, for better or worse, to seek out daddy. As for me, I was consciously trying to stay as far away from mine as possible in choice of dates, boyfriends, paramours, fiancés and husbands. My father was rotten to my mother, through and through. For as long as I can remember, he had a standing Thursday night poker game that was a poorly disguised rendezvous with his mistress-secretary at her apartment. When one secretary would quit, he would take up with the next one in a continuing stream of infidelities that lasted decades.

My mother bore it in stoic silence except that she would break down and cry when she washed his clothes and there was makeup on his dress shirts, undershirts and underwear. She took to drinking sherry when I was twelve. I wasn't about to tell her to stop. I just wrapped my arms around her and told her I was on her side. Incredibly, after forty years they are still married. Watching my mother fall apart was killing me, though, and it explains why I had no desire to get my college education within commuting distance of home.

So, I was looking for 'happily ever after' and I was convinced I had found it in George. Did I love him? Oh, yeah. I got goose bumps just from kissing him. He could smile at me and I would feel like that princess. He could put his hand on my face and I'd glow.

But I was a realistic princess. Once burned, twice shy and all that stuff. I had married for love but I also understood that marriage is also an economic union. 'Happily ever after' was going to take some work on my part. By the time we were married, I had figured out that a) George wasn't the brightest bulb in the chandelier, and b) he would advance in the business world only with a great deal of help from me. I set about to manage his career.

George's genetic makeup said lying there and doing nothing was a perfectly acceptable career path. If people were animals, George was a catfish. A sluggish, bottom-dwelling catfish that does the absolute minimum to get by and eats whatever is even slower than it is. That was my George. He had fallen into PJ&B because he had an MBA from the 'right' university (and he had gotten into that MBA program because he was a 'legacy' admission). He had accepted the job of assistant to the retail analyst because it was offered and, given his druthers, he would stay in that job until he retired or was fired.

Which meant I had to learn the investment banking business. I discovered that being a securities analyst could be a great job, provided you did a couple of things right. One of them was being a pilot fish (my apology for another fish analogy, but it's the same one they use in the industry). A pilot fish is a small, nimble little creature that doesn't get eaten by the bigger fish because it is constantly on the move and has an uncanny knack for finding stuff that bigger fish want to eat. It hangs around just long enough to make certain that the big fish see what the pilot fish sees, then it gets out of the way before it becomes part of the lunch.

I had to turn my George from a catfish into a pilot fish. Or at least make him look like one long enough to get a promotion.

It took a year. While George was happily passing his working days proofreading dreary copy no one would ever read produced by the marginally competent retail analyst and filling in numbers on his spreadsheets, I was looking for deals. A good analyst always looks for deals, no matter what industry they're in, because deals are the lifeblood of investment banking. Bring in deals and you'll be inundated with money by your firm. Don't bring in deals and you'll eventually be asked to leave.

I looked for deals everywhere. Because George's analyst boss followed the 'retailing industry', I chatted up sales clerks at every small chain store in the Boston area, all to no avail. No one was looking to buy, or to be bought. Or, if they were, they weren't sharing that information with their sales staff. I identified a couple of good prospects of stores that ought to be candidates and I filed them away for the future.

I also listened for deals at work. It was the main reason I kept my copywriting job at Hill, Holliday. Ad people love to gossip. Clients love to gossip and, when they've had enough to drink, they'll tell you all manner of strange and wonderful things.

One evening in November, just after George's and my first anniversary, I was at a campaign launch party for one of those 'celebrity' restaurants named for a quarterback who was still trading on his Heisman Trophy fifteen years after his glory days. The quarterback had opened eight of these restaurants in the Boston area, all stuffed with football memorabilia. Hill, Holliday had been hired to 'freshen up' the chain's image.

As I sipped bad California 'Chablis', I overheard two guys next to me talking about 'discounted cash flow' and 'multiples of book value'. But they weren't talking about the quarterback's restaurants. They were discussing another restaurant chain, one named for a famous baseball pitcher. And they were talking about the pitcher's restaurant chain and their frustration that its management wouldn't talk to these two guys because the quarterback's chain was smaller even though the baseball player's chain was less profitable on a per-restaurant basis.

They weren't the ad guys, or even the marketing guys. These were financial types, horning in the campaign launch party to score free booze. And the more they drank, the more they talked.

I stood within earshot as they commiserated about their problems getting a foot in the door of their rival. I started making notes on cocktail napkins. The next morning, I started doing my homework.

Two weeks later, PJ&B held its Christmas party, a swank affair at the Ritz-Carlton, or what used to be the Ritz-Carlton. And I made my move. I had met the head of mergers and acquisitions at the firm's summer get-together at one of its founders' oceanside estate on Cape Cod. I had worn a cute little halter dress that had annoyed George but caught the eye of a number of PJ&B's dirty old men. The head of mergers and acquisitions – a good looking guy in his forties - had, at the time, given me a conspiratorial wink. I walked up to him with two glasses of Champagne in my hands.

"You probably don't remember me," I said. "I'm Kat, George's wife." Always put the 'wife' word up front if you want the conversation to be about business instead of about the Patriots or Christmas or sex.

"Kat, sure," he said, probably not remembering me from Adam, but flashing me a white-toothed smile all the same.

"The summer party. On the Cape. I was wearing a bright red dress." And then, with a little blushing and lowering of my eyes, I added, "It was a little inappropriate for a company function. I was a little embarrassed…" I made a curving 'vee' down my chest to indicate how low cut the halter had been.

"Kat. Of course." And he did remember. God bless men, their predictability, and their one-track minds.

Looking back up, straight into his eyes and dropping all pretense of modesty, I said, "I have this bet with George." I handed him a fresh glass of Champagne. "George says the firm won't be interested because food and beverage really isn't PJ&B's thing and it's probably worth only a million in fees, but I told George…"

I had him hooked at, 'million dollars in fees.' Fees are all that count. An investment banking firm will do a deal for elephant manure if it pays a modified Lehman formula and the fees get into seven figures.

So I explained to the head of mergers and acquisitions how George had cultivated a contact at the quarterback's restaurant and there was a lightly leveraged stock-for-stock deal to be done to buy a chain half again as large but with quantifiable cost savings that would make it a win-win deal, but the quarterback's in-house financial guys couldn't get their foot in the door because the Merrill Lynches and J.P. Morgans of the world looked down their noses at 'little deals'.

Like I said, I had learned the investment banking business.

Over Christmas, the quarterback's chain acquired the pitcher's chain. It merited only three paragraphs in the *Wall Street Journal*, but it netted PJ&B a little over a million in fees. And it got George a handsome bonus, which he took without the slightest embarrassment despite the fact that I had to explain the deal to him at least twice the following morning when he was sober. But for a catfish, George proved he could rouse himself long enough to gulp some food.

On January 1, George also became PJ&B's first-ever restaurant, food and beverage analyst. The bonus plus the new salary meant we could move out of his South End condo. I had already looked at the home addresses of every senior manager at PJ&B and plotted them on a map. There was a nifty cluster of them in Wellesley Hills, a rarefied corner of a snooty suburb. George's idea of upgrading his living arrangements would have consisted of buying a bright red Porsche. Instead, in the cold winds of January, I dragged him out house hunting.

Wellesley Hills has a number of streets – Abbott Road is the showcase - with huge, fancy houses on them. They were built in the twenties when Boston bankers must all have had ten children. The houses were gorgeous, but they were out of our reach financially and, anyway, I wasn't going to spend my life cleaning one of them. North of those fancy digs is another area with slightly more modest homes, but you get the same zip code and ride the train from the same commuter rail station.

We moved in March. For a housewarming present, I outfitted George with a new Burberry coat and a spiffy briefcase so he wouldn't look out of place on the platform.

I also quit my job. It was time, I thought, to start that family. I had my heart set on a boy, to be followed after eighteen months by a girl. That's how much I was into the family thing.

My going-away party at Hill, Holliday was a tour-de-force of false modesty on my part. The women envied me my move up in the world and ogled the fancy bracelet George bought me with that first bonus check. The men, who would miss staring down my neckline when I leaned over to edit their copy, ogled my sweater. I gave a tearful speech about this having been the best four years of my life. Yadda, yadda, yadda. Farewell career, hello to the good life.

It was the late 1990s and the markets – especially Nasdaq – were going crazy. Just having the sign 'investment banker' on your door brought you business, and PJ&B prospered. Deals came George's way just because he proved he could breathe. George brought half a dozen deals to the firm for restaurant chains going public. He did this by answering the phone or, more specifically, by having his assistant answer the phone. None of those callers, unfortunately, were Starbucks. They were ludicrous concepts for restaurants – think waitresses dressed as aliens - with hallucination-driven earnings forecasts. But in 1999 or the first few months of 2000, anybody could go public and put a hundred million in the bank. We paid off my student loans from George's 1999 bonus and had plenty left over.

The Nasdaq crossed 5000 in early 2000 then fell on a 'temporary pullback'. By July the market was in the tank. George squeezed in a couple of more deals before the window slammed shut completely, but the party was over. By early 2001, everybody realized to their shock and amazement that it had all been a bubble.

In February 2001, a year after the market peak and with the Nasdaq barely above the 1000 mark, PJ&B axed half of its staff, including all but one technology analyst from what had been a staff of ten. George survived. Not because he was especially good, but because he was the sole incumbent. The market for semiconductor chips crashed with a thud but potato chips held up nicely. When PJ&B let go its hotels and lodging analyst, George picked up coverage on those companies, furthering his job security.

For the next several years, we all laid low. I played housewife and George dutifully brought home a paycheck. Not a huge one, but sufficient for our needs. Then, the market turned up. Deals started getting done again. There were bonuses for the first time in what seemed like forever.

But things had changed. I had changed. And unexpectedly, George had changed though, in his case, it was not for the better.

Which is not to say that George had been a perfect husband to that point. My knight in shining armor fell off his horse about eight months after we got back from our honeymoon. George had gone to an analyst's conference put on by one of the companies he covered. He was away four days and suspiciously not answering his cell phone at night.

I had offered to pick him up at the airport on his return and he had pointedly declined. But I was still being a model wife and decided to surprise him by meeting him at baggage claim. I was getting ready to wave at him when I saw him coming down the escalator, but something about the tableau made me stop.

He was holding hands with a woman.

I didn't know her. She wasn't my best friend and it wasn't his secretary. But she was young and pretty and well-dressed. I faded into the background and watched. They giggled as they talked and waited for their luggage. And when they parted at the door out to ground transportation, there was a kiss that told me this was not some boy-just-met-girl sort of thing. He had his hand on her ass and she was enjoying it.

Hello, daddy.

I didn't confront him. Maybe that was a mistake. Maybe I was too shocked. More likely, I was in denial, even after I checked and found that the analyst conference he had attended was a day-and-a-half event. I didn't want to believe that less than a year after he said, 'I do' to me, he was doing it with someone else.

Maybe I didn't want to admit that marrying George was a mistake.

I watched him closely thereafter. I monitored his supply of condoms. I sniffed his shirts for the tell-tale signs of an errant spouse. Over the intervening years there would be other times. Quite a few of them, actually. Always on business trips and not with the same woman. George apparently believed in the Boarding Pass Compact: once you've handed the gate agent your boarding pass, anything that happens thereafter doesn't count.

Somehow, I adjusted. And maybe that was my real mistake.

But starting a little over a year ago, things really changed. The first thing was that George became sneaky. He had always brought home his office computer – your basic Dell laptop - and spent an hour each morning and another each evening in the study with the door closed, making phone calls and plugging numbers into spreadsheets. I left him alone. One day while looking for some note cards in the study, I stumbled on a second laptop – an identical brand and model - rife with password protection, stashed behind the Monopoly set we hadn't played since before we were married. George was doing something with that computer and I made it my new years' resolution to find out what it was.

The second thing was that George changed his habits. For eight years, except when he was attending conferences (with or without something on the side) or visiting companies, he was invariably on the 6:04 and at home with a martini in his hand before 6:20. Suddenly, he was seldom home before 11 p.m., when he wasn't mysteriously out of town at trade shows I had never heard of. He was, he said, checking out restaurants and hotels, doing 'due diligence' and coming up with merger candidates.

This was not my George. My dull, unimaginative George was up to no good. My second new years' resolution was to find out what he was really doing with his time.

The first rule of being a suspicious wife is to ask no questions of her spouse. You can observe, poke, and ferret out information by any methods available, but under no conditions can you ever let on that you're suspicious. When people know you're suspicious of them, they start trying to throw you off the scent. I wanted George to believe I was blissfully ignorant.

Because George was tedious and predictable, but nevertheless a male, the secrets of the changes in his schedule revealed themselves first. George was stepping out on me. And, this time, he was doing so seriously. No furtive trysts between analyst meetings in St. Louis. This was going on in my back yard.

Was I surprised? Well, yes. George had no reason to complain about his sex life or about me in general. I had more than held up my end of the bargain. I had reached my mid-30s with an unlined, bag-free face. I had kept my figure and I was enthusiastic about sex even when I knew it was going to be one of George's ninety-second specials. I was an asset to him in business and I ran our house efficiently.

Was I angry? The surprise was that I was not. I may have started off truly in love with him but somewhere along the way – say, between his 'due diligence session' in San Diego and the 'food and beverage convention' in Atlanta, I had enough.

And, let's be completely honest: I had gotten bored with George. I knew everything there was to know about him. When you got down to the root of everything, my husband was completely predictable and not especially interesting. He had also – and I don't apologize for pointing this out again – gotten prematurely middle aged.

I was, however, annoyed at George's choice of companionship. She was twenty-six, single, and in need of a sugar daddy. She was also a brunette. In psychological terms, George was repeating those heady early days of his relationship with me, except that now he was definitely the one in charge. He had the money and the power. Put in less psychologically acceptable terms, George was seriously warped.

He broke it off with that first 'she' six weeks after I learned about her, but immediately moved onto a second mistress. She was also twenty-six, also brunette and sported a hair style remarkably similar to the one I had worn nine years earlier. How many times did George have to re-live his twenties? It was freaky. He was repeating that halcyon courting process he had followed with me, though at much nicer restaurants.

I found out these things by discreetly following my husband. And in the process, I uncovered a disturbing question to which I did not know the answer. How, exactly, was George paying for all this?

His paycheck was being deposited directly into our joint checking account. As part of my household management duties I kept the account balanced. I knew of his ATM withdrawals and they were for the usual amounts. I also paid the bills including the credit cards, and there were no charges for the places he was squiring these chippies to.

George had an outside source of income. One I didn't know about.

I watched this going on for several months. George dropped brunette number two and took up with brunette number three. Of course, she was twenty-six. He probably dumped them on their twenty-seventh birthday. Gave them a swell piece of jewelry and their walking papers.

By this time I had all the evidence I needed. It was time to confront him with the whole string of infidelities going back to the one eight months after our honeymoon. I knew to the dollar what we had in the bank, our IRAs and in our brokerage accounts and I did enough research to understand what kind of settlement I was going to get and what level alimony I could expect in a community property state like Massachusetts. On the whole it would be quite satisfactory. I was going to be a thirty-something divorcee with a million-dollar cushion plus most of the proceeds from the sale of our home, which was now worth at least half a million dollars more than we paid for it eight years earlier.

I hadn't yet gone to see a lawyer, though that was the next step. Before I did anything, though, I wanted to know where George was getting all that money he was throwing around.

Then, one evening in early May when George was supposed to be in New York at a trade show but was in fact at a hotel in Boston's financial district planking brunette number three, I cracked the code on his laptop.

He had been reasonably cute about the passwords, which is what took me a while. But once I was in, it was a revelation.

George was a thief. And not a small-time thief. Over the previous eighteen months, George had surreptitiously accumulated just short of five million dollars.

He had gotten it in several ways, none of them legal. First, he solicited payments to provide coverage of companies. Second, he had accepted bribes to upgrade recommendations. Third, he had received payoffs to tip off certain institutional investors in advance of changes in his ratings. And fourth, he had traded in the stocks of companies that were acquisition targets of PJ&B clients.

The securities industry is a clubby world. Once you're in, you're golden. It's a lifetime deal – if not with one firm then with another - unless you really screw up. It is also a world built on trust. As an analyst, you sign a million forms swearing you will never accept payment for anything under any circumstances, except from your employer for the services you render to the firm. Every research report that goes out contains a sworn statement that the analyst has no financial interest in the company about which the report is written. The SEC files those forms by the bushel basket but no one goes out and audits analysts' brokerage accounts. Unless someone says something that causes the SEC to start issuing subpoenas, persons within securities firms are deemed to be good little boys and girls.

Why does an analyst choose to follow the Amalgamated Cookie Company? Once upon a time, it was because Amalgamated Cookie was an investment banking client of the analyst's employer. You hire PJ&B and you're guaranteed coverage from a specific analyst, starting with a table-pounding 'buy' rating. No one put that sort of thing in writing, but it was understood by everyone concerned.

After the market melt-down in 2000, everything was supposed to change. Too many analysts had kept up those 'buy' ratings on banking clients even as Amalgamated Cookie's earnings were crumbling. New laws took away the unspoken promise of coverage for banking and the perpetual 'buy'. Analysts gained new respect and new freedoms.

Freedoms which analysts like George used to become entrepreneurial. Or, in his case, a crook.

The computer spelled out the payments George had received, especially those from hedge funds. These funds raked in obscene amounts of money and paid out a pittance to analysts like George to give them advanced warning of market-changing events like rating changes. Except that to these hedge funds, a pittance amounted to nearly three million dollars over two years.

George had also pocketed half a million dollars for agreeing to cover three companies that desperately wanted Wall Street brokerage reports on them. George didn't inform his superiors at PJ&B that there was a financial reward for him. He just used his 'discretion' to add companies to his coverage universe. He had added two hundred thousand dollars more for a couple of unwarranted upgrades.

The hedge-fund payments and the pay-for-coverage deals were Bad Things that would get George barred from the securities industry for life if and when he were caught. But George hadn't stopped there. He had also done the ultimate no-no. He had set up half a dozen internet brokerage accounts to purchase stocks and options on stocks of companies that were targeted as takeover candidates by PJ&B

clients. Of all the dumb things to do, this was the dumbest because the SEC routinely scrutinizes all trades for the period prior to an announcement of a merger or acquisition, and singles out those 'lucky' trades that make people lots of money. George had made more than a million dollars in 'lucky' trades in the preceding six months. One of the deals had already been announced, the other were in the pipeline. It was only a matter of time before he got caught.

Plan 'A' – which I had been following up until that day in May when I cracked the passwords on George's computer - had been to confront him with his infidelities, file for a divorce and settle for half of the marital assets plus a reasonable alimony. Once I unlocked the secrets of that computer behind the Monopoly set, I determined to add a demand for most if not all of the five million, with the expectation that George could cheat his way into another five million on his own and bed all the twenty-six-year-old brunettes in Boston in the process.

However, the more I looked at the implications of what George had done – using the computers in the Wellesley Free Library to do my research, of course – the more I realized that Plan A wasn't going to work. The companies that had paid George to follow them were unlikely to go public with what they had done, but hedge funds were making all the wrong kinds of headlines for just such shenanigans. George was on the payroll of four different hedge fund managers – all cloaked by code names - and there was a reasonable prospect that someday, one of those funds was going to implode. When it did, all that dirty laundry was going to get aired.

And the inside trades were the most unstable element of all. It wasn't a question of whether the SEC was going to investigate; it was a matter of when. And, when they did, the SEC was going to want 'disgorgement' of the gains, plus a penalty.

I was technically an 'innocent spouse', a term that showed up in several IRS documents. George had done this conniving without my knowledge and I sure as hell wasn't going to admit that I had figured it all out several months earlier and kept my mouth shut about it. However, all that an 'innocent spouse' meant was that I wasn't going to join George in prison. The SEC and the IRS were going to seize the five million. And then, to dissuade the next analyst from contemplating such a get-rich-scheme, they were going to make an example of George by taking a couple million more in penalties.

Those penalties would wipe out our joint financial assets. I was going to be the penniless ex-wife of a jailed and disgraced securities analyst. And let's not forget the astronomical legal costs of defending him while he professed his innocence. I wouldn't just be broke – I'd be in hock for his attorney's fees.

I was going to be indigent, homeless and living on food stamps. All because George was stupid.

All of which suddenly made divorce impossible.

If I was going to get my hands on that money, there was only one way I was going to get out of the marriage and with my well-deserved share of our true net worth.

I was going to have to kill George and make it look like an accident. And, at the same time, I was going to have to liquidate all those accounts of his without calling attention to what I was doing. Once it was done, there was a very real possibility that I might have to disappear for a very long time.

That realization came, like I said, in May. At the time, I figured I had about four months to pull it off. But timetables change with events. And in just a few weeks time, I had more than my share of events.

2.

When you're contemplating the murder of an unfaithful spouse – and especially one whose stupidity, left unchecked, is going to ruin your life – it's good therapy to let your imagination run wild for a few minutes.

Mine did. My perfect fantasy was for George to die in the bed of his current twenty-six-year-old mistress and for her to have his blood on her negligee and the murder weapon in her hands when the police arrived. It was an appealing vision, but I had trouble figuring out a way to make the details work.

Down the scale of fantasy options was running down George with a large truck or having him fall under the wheels of a commuter train. They were satisfying in a vicarious way but I knew they were destined to remain daydreams.

The problem with all of them was that they involved lengthy police investigations. Maybe I've watched too many re-runs of *Law and Order*, but my view of the police is rooted in the late Jerry Orbach's portrayal of Detective Lenny Briscoe. He may take his time, but he always gets to the right perp and, in the process, finds all the motivation a prosecutor could ever want. And he does it while making talk-show-worthy wisecracks.

I didn't want Jerry Orbach or his Wellesley counterpart to come knocking at my door one afternoon. I didn't want anyone looking for motives and finding phony brokerage accounts. I didn't want an autopsy and I didn't want wisecracks. I wanted to open the door one afternoon and find a cute, young and inexperienced Wellesley policeman at the door. He would be ashen-faced because he would have never done this kind of thing before. He would take off his hat, revealing curly blonde hair, and say, "I'm sorry ma'am, but there's been a terrible accident…"

That's what I wanted.

And, if I was going to get what I wanted, I had to choose a suitable cause of death.

The problem is that men in their thirties don't die. Statistically, if you make to it thirty, you'll make it to forty. Medical issues head the list of the few who do succumb: heart disease, cancer, chronic liver disease, diabetes and stroke account for 36% of deaths. Such deaths don't get investigated but I had no inkling of how I could give George a heart attack. Suicides represent about 11% of deaths, but suicides get investigated to determine the 'why' and would inevitably lead back to hedge funds and on-line brokerage accounts. Killing George and making it look like a suicide was definitely out.

Homicides are just 2.8% of white males in George's age category and there's no such thing as an un-investigated homicide. Kill a well-paid securities analyst and the investigation would go on forever. Even if I managed to put the bloody knife in his mistress' hands, the police would keep at it until they had a satisfactory, wrap-it-up-with-a-bow motive.

Which left the number one killer of middle aged men: 'unintentional injuries': 22.8% of deaths.

George was going to have a fatal accident.

* * * * *

If the first rule of being a suspicious wife is to betray no evidence of your suspicion to your husband, then the second rule is to have no accomplices. I knew from the start I was going to have to carry this off completely on my own.

I had made my share of friends in Wellesley Hills. The town has a fairly sizeable contingent of stay-at-home wives of various ages. Many of us had spouses in the financial services industry – brokers and money managers mostly. We would bump into one another while shopping at Whole Foods or sipping a latte at Quebrada. We'd then spend a few hours at one another's houses drinking coffee and chatting about the things that women have in common.

It's frightening how quickly women let down their emotional defenses with one another. An hour after you've met someone, you're sharing stories about stretch marks and irregular periods. A week later, you're discussing details of your mortgage and home equity loans. Fantasies about former co-workers or personal trainers are never far behind. Women have the innate urge to share, and they bond by putting the details of their personal lives out on the table.

I had three especially close friends with whom I had shared nearly every detail of my life. On the afternoon that I made my final visit to the Wellesley Free Library and concluded that George had to go, I also realized that, if anything went wrong, those close friends were the ones that the police were going to visit when they started looking for clues about George's accidental death. They could not know what I was really thinking. I could trust only myself.

If I had a mind to enlist anyone as my accomplice it would have been Trish. We were the same age and had comparable outlooks on life. She was a redhead with a tanned, athletic body who never missed a chance to show off her long, glorious legs. She, too, had a career in advertising before 'retiring' to take care of her husband, a broker at Merrill Lynch. I had confided my boredom with George to her some months earlier after she had said she was contemplating a fling with the tennis pro at her club. She had started questioning me closely thereafter, waiting for the next chapter in my boredom saga. She assumed that my malaise with George would play itself out in the form of adultery and was eager to get enough of a psychic boost from my infidelity to launch one of her own.

When I inexplicably became closed-lipped on the subject, she began to suspect that something had started and that I was being uncharacteristically discreet to protect the name of my lover. My protestations to the contrary got me nowhere.

Finally, because I was following George to better establish his patterns and was away from the house far more frequently that I had been in the past, I broke down and 'confessed' my affair.

I told her his name was Phil and he was one of George's co-workers at PJ&B. We were meeting secretly in Boston for a few hours here and there. Phil was married so there was no chance that it was going anywhere. It was just release; something new and different and would burn itself out after a few months. Phil was an actual guy at the firm and, under different circumstances, he and I might have gotten something going. But I wasn't going to provide any police detective with any scintilla of a motive.

So, I told Trish about luscious encounters with Phil under 500-thread-count sheets at the Four Seasons when, in fact, my sex life had come to a whimpering halt because George was apparently too exhausted from keeping up with Brunette Number Three to even give me my ninety-second quickie on Saturday night.

It got Trish off my back – except that I had to keep coming up with new details. Having an imaginary lover is hard enough. Creating romantic, inventive sex scenes gets to be onerous when what you're really spending your time doing is tailing your spouse, looking for an elevator shaft he might fall down one afternoon. I finally provided sufficiently enthusiastic detail that Trish took the plunge with the tennis pro. From there on in, I had to listen to *her* tales of terrific, athletic sex in the afternoon.

I began to wonder if she was planning to murder her husband.

A second close friend, Nancy, was too ethical a person to have been considered a co-conspirator had I taken one on. But Nancy, too, had to be placated. She had been a child psychologist in one of the suburban school systems before 'burning out', but her senses were undiminished. Every time we were together she would discern moods and issues that were in the back of my mind. She kept her hair in a practical bob, and wore wire-rim glasses that emphasized the intelligence in her eyes. She would push her glasses to the top of the bridge on her nose, rest her chin on her hand, and stare intently at me. It was only her friendly, honest face that prevented the habit from being annoying.

"Something's going on with George," she told me one afternoon as we sat by her pool.

I must have looked startled. "What do you mean?"

Up went the glasses. "George and his annoying habits are almost always the second or third thing you talk about," Nancy said. "You didn't mention them last week and we've been talking over an hour today and you haven't mentioned him once. What's going on?"

I sputtered and thought fast. I nearly blurted out that I knew he was having an affair. Instead, I said, "I'm thinking about having a baby."

I went on to expound to Nancy on how being a stay-at-home wife had left me with this guilty feeling and the world needed a higher-grade gene pool and my biological clock was ticking. I made it up as I went along.

And Nancy took it in stride. She had a ten-year-old son she doted on. "You shouldn't have a child out of guilt," she said, "but if now feels like the right time, then go for it."

I broke down in tears and thanked her for supporting me.

Thereafter, Nancy would wait for me to raise the subject. While I was providing Trish with details about my torrid affair with Phil, I bared my child-conceiving progress to Nancy. I had to make certain never to have the two women in the same room with one another.

Why I chose a potential pregnancy is beyond me. As I noted earlier, one of the reasons I chose the house in Wellesley after George got his promotion was that I wanted to start a family. I went without birth control for about six months, expecting that I might get pregnant. I didn't. When the market fell off the cliff and the bonuses evaporated, I did the math and concluded we could either have our house or children but not both. I went back on the pill.

Then came the string of infidelities. Children were supposed to save marriages, but I told my mom when I was fifteen that if she was staying with daddy because of me, she had my vote to pull the plug. She just looked at me with those sad eyes and said that I'd understand when I was older.

Well, I was older. And I hadn't lost myself in bottles of Tio Pepe, either. I had my own ways of coping with George's wayward ways. But by about the fifth year of our marriage, I could no longer imagine him fathering my child. My feelings went from love to tolerance to annoyance and, finally, to fatigue at the whole idea of staying married to him. And, of course, once I decided to murder him, a pregnancy would have been downright inconvenient.

My third close friend, Patsy, lived in one of those huge old houses on Abbott Road. She filled it with three blonde children, a live-in maid, nanny, and cook. She kept a landscape architect busy moving around shrubs and creating garden 'rooms' and a contractor and crew on retainer as she continually renovated her house.

Patsy was the golden girl living the golden life. Petite, blonde and freckled, she still had the enthusiasm of the cheerleader she had been at Ole Miss. With a staff of three and God only knows how many other helpers-for-hire on her speed dial, she lived a life that consisted largely of shopping, spa-going, and dining at whatever was the restaurant of the moment.

Money was no object because her husband, Peter, was a hedge fund manager. Quant Four Capital had several billion dollars under management and Peter and his three buddies took two percent of that money off the top every year as a 'management fee', plus twenty percent of the fund's annual gain. With that kind of money rolling in, Patsy could have burned down their house every year, rebuilt and re-decorated from scratch and it wouldn't have made a dent in their financial condition.

Behind the free-spending veneer, though, Patsy was remarkably down to earth. Like me, she had started with little and so felt that what had happened to her over the past few years was ephemeral. She chartered jets to take the family on weekend jaunts to the Caribbean but inwardly knew that there would come a time when she would be flying economy class to Disney World.

"It isn't real," Patsy told me one afternoon as we were getting facials at a spa – her treat, of course. "Peter tells me not to treat it as a permanent condition, but to enjoy it while it lasts."

"Then why aren't you saving like crazy?" I asked. "Why not salt away half of what he's making so you can go on living like this for the rest of your lives?"

I remember Patsy sitting up on her elbows, a mud pack on her face and cucumbers in her eyes. "Peter says not to," she said, somberly. "Peter says that when the hedge fund industry blows up, everyone's going to want their money back. He says the only protection we've got is to say that we've spent it all."

It was the most chilling advice I had ever heard. But most likely the most prophetic.

3.

You may wonder what it's like to live with a serial philanderer. In truth, it was easy. I just had to keep my mouth shut, smile and never call attention to the loony inconsistencies in my spouse's stories.

The key to retaining my sanity was to make every day productive – the end result of that productivity being a foolproof plan to kill George, while collecting a mountain of evidence to aid in a divorce proceeding should murder prove to be impractical or should I chicken out. My husband helped me immeasurably by being a creature of habit.

George was up every morning at 5:30. He would pad downstairs to the study, close the door tightly behind him, and get on his computer - either the firm's or his own or both – and emerged at 6:45 to shower and shave. While he showered, I crept around and went through his briefcase, wallet and clothes looking for receipts and other incriminating evidence from the previous evening. I then went downstairs, appeared sleepy and yawning, and made breakfast. George read the newspapers and was out the door at 8 a.m. to catch the 8:15. On a good morning, we exchanged perhaps fifty words:

George: "I see the BMW needs its 30,000 mile service."

Me, smiling: "I'll call for an appointment this morning."

George: "I'm flying out to Phoenix tonight for a conference."

Me, smiling: "Are you leaving from the office or will you be home first?"

George: "From the office."

Me, being efficient: "Do you want me to pack you a suitcase?"

George: "Ummm, it's just an in-and-out thing. I won't need one. I'll just send out my shirt and underwear from the hotel."

Me, smiling: "OK."

I loved that 'in and out' reference. How Freudian could you get? And the jerk didn't even think to pack a suitcase. Of course, he didn't need to because he had two changes of clothing at his girlfriend's apartment. But I said nothing. Instead, I smiled and gave him a goodbye peck on the cheek.

Every morning he was home, George caught that 8:15 from Wellesley Hills to South Station. The minute he was out of sight I was in the study, pulling out his second computer and scanning his latest work. I regularly backed up everything on the computer onto CDs just in case the laptop disappeared one day. I would note any new transactions, additions to his accounts, or changes to earlier documents or spreadsheets. In the space of a few months, I knew his scam at least as well as he did.

Payments from the hedge funds were made monthly, credited into Internet-based banks and accounts opened in a made-up name with a phony social security number. George used different names on different accounts – most of them Hispanic. He didn't know it, but I – or rather, Benito Morales – had become a signatory to each of those accounts with wire transfer privileges to yet another bank. When the day came, I could clean out those accounts in under five minutes.

Once I had completed my review of George's crooked deals, I would putter around the house for the day and do housewife things. My assumption was that, in order to stay employed, George would give PJ&B his more or less undivided attention until after the market closed.

I use the conversation from the mid-June morning that George was ostensibly headed for Phoenix because it changed the timeline of my decision when to murder him.

Let me explain. By this time, I had my husband's routine down to a science. On nights when he said he was going to be late on the pretext of doing due diligence on some restaurant or another, it meant he would spend the evening with his mistress at her apartment, then have a cab take him to Back Bay Station. There, he could get a train as late as 11:30 and be in Wellesley Hills before midnight. For him, it was a sweet deal: a couple of hours of nooky and be asleep in his own bed at midnight, keeping me awake with his snoring.

When George was 'going out of town', it meant he and his sweetie would stay the night at a swank hotel in Boston. I already had plenty of photos of George going into apartments with his mistresses from my 'Plan A' period, but there was always a need for more documentation of hotel shenanigans. And, besides, I loved to snoop.

That particular afternoon, I caught an afternoon train into Boston and was positioned discreetly near the entrance to One Financial Center where PJ&B had its headquarters. George emerged at 5:15, positively skipping out onto the building's plaza, oblivious to me and everyone around him.

Where would he go? Being a Tuesday, my guess was that things would start with drinks and dinner before repairing to the hotel room for dessert. For reasons Nancy could likely have readily explained had I chosen to confide in her, he never stayed overnight in his mistresses' apartment. Apparently that was a mistake he had made with me – the first step in getting caught in my web - and was one he wasn't going to repeat.

His current mistress had a name, of course. Susan Perkins Booth – Susie Perkyboobs, I called her. I knew she was a management trainee at the Langham Hotel. Because she had a Facebook page, I also knew she was twenty-six, had graduated from the Cornell School of Hotel Management, and professed to love jazz. In my opinion, anyone who says they like jazz, the Eagles, or French Burgundies is trying to score with an older man. Susie was also a Leo, which suggested that, while she did not know it, her affair with my husband had only a month or two left on the meter.

George skipped into 15 Beacon, an ultra-hip hotel on the edge of Beacon Hill. I took a cell phone photo of his entry for the record. A few minutes later, Susie Perkyboobs also went into the hotel, a fake Louis Vuitton overnight bag swinging by her side. She, too, was photographed for the record. She was attractive, no question. Her long hair had the gleam that youth and a good conditioner provides and her face showed nary a line. Her makeup was spare and emphasized her blushing youth. She completed the picture with a pert nose, slightly upturned. She was also dressing much better these past few weeks and I wondered if George's largesse now extended to providing his mistresses with a wardrobe allowance. This afternoon, she had on a very short, deep blue dress, cut in a 'vee' in front to show a lot of cleavage. Her hair was a little different than usual, shaped in a mid-shoulder style much like my own. Maybe she was trying to look older for George. If so, it was a mistake.

I gave them half an hour for drinks, then went inside to make certain they had gone into the dining room. It didn't take much, just a glance and the hostess didn't as much as inquire if I was waiting for my party. I snapped a quick cell phone photo of the two of them, canoodling over linguini. Mission accomplished.

Because this was an all-nighter, I went from the hotel to her apartment. Susie Perkyboobs had a crummy walkup in the Fenway area, the kind that appealed to students at Northeastern. But she lived alone, which likely meant she was getting some kind of stipend from mom and dad while she climbed the hotel management career ladder or until she landed her man.

Susie's building offered a wealth of accidental death opportunities and it was too bad George invariably called for a cab instead of walking to the train. There was a potential fall into a basement window well, the railings were loose, and the interior stairs were extremely steep. Because of George's growing paunch, my guess was that he increasingly had to have faith that his feet found the next stair down. It would be a piece of cake to follow them in, wait in the second floor landing, and give him a helpful shove either down the stairs or over the railing.

There were two problems: he would scream as he fell, bringing multiple tenants out of their apartments to ascertain what had happened, and there was that pesky cab driver waiting for him outside, who would undoubtedly see me enter and leave. The death would be ruled accidental, but only until the first person stepped forward to say an attractive thirty-ish woman had fled the building. Jerry Orbach wouldn't be far behind, wisecracking.

Along about now you're thinking, "She's obsessed with the 'other woman'. Otherwise, what is she doing creeping around her apartment and following them into hotels?"

It wasn't like that.

I still wanted evidence. Solid evidence of infidelity and betrayal that he couldn't worm his way out of. I wanted my lawyer to be able to lay every photo on the table; spread out like a deck of cards. I wanted a judge to gasp at how despicable George was and award me whatever I wanted. Although I had worked out a good plan to kill him, there was a chance I might chicken out, settle for a divorce, and take my chances that the SEC didn't catch George in his net until the settlement was final and my half of the assets were safely beyond the government's reach.

But I also admit I had been at this for seven months. And, yes, I had all the photographic evidence I needed. I had made George fill out a calendar so it would be his own handwriting saying he was in Phoenix or Dallas or wherever. My photos all had date codes proving otherwise. I had the bastard nailed dead to rights for adultery.

So maybe I did go over the top a little bit. I broke into Susie Perkyboob's apartment multiple times and nosed around. Where did I get a key? Easy. She gave one to George so that he could wait for her if she were running late. I noted the extra key on George's key ring one morning and copied it.

Based on my multiple visits to her apartment, I understood Susie Perkyboobs. She had one or perhaps two shots to find her guy and she was loaded for bear. Naughty nighties by the drawerful. Satin and lace underthings, all designed to lure the right kind of man. She was far from perfect: she achieved that admirable 34C chest with the help of a dozen 'lightly padded' (are they ever anything except 'lightly padded'?) bras. She wore extra-control-top pantyhose and her kitchen was a host to every diet concept ever pitched on late-night cable television.

I also understood – by poking around - that Susie had bought into the wedding thing ever since she got her Bride Barbie at age ten, and had been planning her Big Day for the better part of a decade. She had refined her list of bridesmaids and had selected their outfits and had a binder full of perfect wedding reception ideas. She was torn between getting married on a beach in Hawaii at sunrise and having everyone fly in to a castle in Ireland. The role of Ken was still being cast. It was getting the perfect mix of spring flowers for the bouquet that really mattered.

But why did she have to go after a married man ten years older than herself? Her emails to friends (yes, I read her email; so sue me) told the story. She wanted it all and she didn't have the patience to wait her turn. George was the right age and the right income. The only impediment to her happiness was that dumb old wedding ring on her boyfriend's left hand.

On the night of George's 'trip to Phoenix' in mid-June, I was reading Susie's appointment diary and checking her email. I was especially interested in the cryptic entries for 'G' that coincided with his late-evening investigations of investment banking prospects. The ones with 'G' all had little red hearts next to them.

'G', however, wasn't the only initial to rate a red heart in that appointment book. Last night, when George had been home at his regular time, there was an 'R'. Somebody else was dipping their wick in little Susie. Today's entries showed 'G' at 6 p.m. There was no heart yet, so it meant she added the data only after the fact. There was also an entry for 5 p.m.: 'JP – POSQ' with an exclamation point. I would have to make a point of checking the next time I was in her apartment to see if Susie played a double-header: two hearts in one day.

I was reading her latest email when the hair on the back of my neck stood straight on end and I got goose bumps. The previous evening, Susie had written a friend:

For the first time, George is talking divorce. I want it to be his idea, so I'm playing it cool. But I did suggest that he needs to think about grounds. If he just breaks the news to her over coffee one morning, she'll screw him over royally. So I asked him what does she do all day and on those nights he's with me? What if she's got something on the side? Like shagging the UPS delivery guy or having at it with the service rep at the Lexus dealership? When I mentioned those as possibilities, he got really excited and said he might not even have to do a 50-50 split. Anyway, I planted the seed.

Holy crapola, I thought. She's got him thinking about divorce.

That was the first thing I thought. The second was, how quickly might George place a call to a detective agency and get them cracking on a dossier on me? And how quickly might that agency put someone on the case? In other words, could I have been followed this evening?

I decided I had poked around Susie Perkyboobs' apartment long enough. I downloaded her emails onto a memory stick and got out of there. Outside her apartment, I looked carefully for the idling car or man under a street lamp with a camera. Nothing.

I went home and re-did my timetable. Until that evening, I had planned on killing George in September. We would go away on some romantic vacation to the Caribbean – some place where the police work is shoddy from the get-go and, where tourists are concerned, accidental death is an infinitely preferential finding to murder, not to mention a lot less paperwork.

I even had a cause of death worked out. Though George had no formal certification, he fancied himself a scuba diver. There was always a chance he'd drown himself though stupidity, but I had intended to help matters along by holding his head underwater for four or five minutes with his air regulator turned off. Idiot tourists drowned all the time, especially in places like the Bahamas. I had planned to book us that getaway and surprise George with it for his birthday. Now, that was too far away.

It was mid-June. Events had indeed altered the timetable. I figured I had less than a month.

4.

The weekend after he 'went to Phoenix' and I discovered my husband was contemplating divorce, we drove up to Ipswich for George's father's seventy-fifth birthday.

You should know that George comes from a wealthy family. Not filthy rich and not even hedge-fund rich, just old money wealthy. His father lives in a rather large old colonial house on fifty acres overlooking Essex Bay. It would be idyllic except that the greenheads – nasty biting flies that are unfazed by insect repellent - are so thick in mid-summer you don't dare go near the water.

You should also know that George doesn't stand a chance in hell of inheriting any of this. George is the fifth of five children and the third of three sons. His eldest brother, the patent attorney, will get the bulk of the estate. Carl is the apple of dad's eye and the perfect son. George's eldest sister, Celeste, will get the rest. She was the docile child who didn't rock the boat and married someone acceptable and dull.

You may wonder what happened to the inheritance prospects of children three, four and five. Well, the answer is, wife number two. George's father has been married three times. Wife number one, Cecilia, was a saint who bore him two perfect children. Then she died of some incredibly righteous disease. In the oil portrait that still adorns the wall of the library in the family home, Cecelia is a radiant thirty with her two children gazing up adoringly at her, puppy-like. That is how she is permanently enshrined.

After five years, George's father remarried.

Wife number two was a shrew and a harridan who connived to spend every dollar of the family's money in a vain attempt to buy her way into respectable society. She was resoundingly rebuffed and snubbed by every decent social group in eastern Massachusetts. After five years, she left in a huff to the relief of everyone and the regret of none. Even her name was erased like the cartouche of some discredited Egyptian pharaoh: she was simply, 'wife number two'.

Now, there may be another side of that story. It may be that she was in over her head and couldn't live up to the standard of perfection of wife number one staring down from the library paneling, and so gave up rather than bang her head against that wall any longer. But no one has ever told that other side of the story: the family is united in the 'wife from hell' version.

The funny thing is, wife number two managed to produce three children in her five-year reign. Granted, one of them was in the oven at the time of the nuptials (something never even tacitly acknowledged by anyone in the family but that I figured out by comparing birth certificates to marriage licenses), but that still leaves a lot of evenings spent in ways other than crossing off names in the Blue Book. I once raised the question of how wife number two could have been so reviled yet fecund and got such a cold look in return that I beat the hastiest retreat on record.

Wife number two decamped when George was just six months old, which is really sad for George. A boy deserves a mother during those formative years. Instead, George's father swore off matrimony for ten years, leaving the raising of his five children to a succession of nannies. The collateral question is why wife number two didn't take the three children with her. I have lots of theories about that, none of which square with the united front legend that had been allowed to grow.

Wife number three – Jill – arrived to a house with two nearly-grown adolescents away in college and three children at home being treated like a cross between bastards and orphans. She had been a friend of Saint Cecelia and knew her smartest move would be to become the Keeper of the Flame. She wisely chose not to bond with these kiddies, instead doting on her new husband and showing proper deference to the sainted first wife.

This was the lay of the land as we arrived for the birthday boy's celebration.

We were the last to pull into the long gravel driveway. Ahead of us were an assortment of Mercedes and Lexuses. George's father may have stinted on love for his offspring, but he had ensured that each of his children received a first-rate education at his alma mater. As noted earlier, a professional degree from a name-brand university is a ticket to a comfortable existence, however tenuous the academic or intellectual claim to the sheepskin.

Carl, the patent attorney, was nearly fifty and had a placid façade that masked an interior with but one function: a clockwork mechanism counting down the days to his inheritance of all this. Carl was already subdividing the farm and naming the resulting streets. He and his vapid wife sat smugly on the broad front porch, polishing off gin and tonics. Their children were in boarding schools from September to May, and beefing up their college resumes at summer enrichment programs the other three months. In a good year, Carl and Laura crossed paths with their children maybe half a dozen times.

Carl was plump – an unwanted preview of coming attractions for George – and the slick mane of black hair he had when I first met him nine years earlier had thinned alarmingly. The gene pool on George's father's side appeared to have about a thirty-year warranty, after which it was *caveat emptor*. Laura had not matched his weight gain, but you could spot her at a distance of a thousand feet by her Lily Pulitzer outfits, which she wore incessantly. A continuous diet of pink and green sweaters and skirts is barely tolerable in a child of five. In an adult, it shows at best a lack of imagination and, at worst, a whiff of psychosis.

Celeste, the eldest daughter and the only other child slated to inherit anything, dutifully carried around a tray of canapés from group to group. She was three years Carl's junior – maybe 47 – but looked a decade younger. Of course, she also packed on fifty extra pounds, which helped conceal the lines and wrinkles. Her husband, Fred, having carelessly wandered onto the rear lawn, was engaged in an energetic game of swatting the first of the seasonal greenheads.

Rachael, the one who was substantially more advanced than a gleam in her father's eye at the time of his marriage to wife number two, contemplated the day's unfolding events from the living room, where she sat alone. Rachael was forty and had recently shed her umpteenth paramour. She was the family's designated free spirit, albeit a bit long in the tooth to bear such a title. The first time we met she proudly told me she had never worn a bra. At thirty-one it had been a defiant political statement. Still holding true to her beliefs nine years later, the results were just painful to look at. She had also never been given the basic mechanics of makeup and her hair was a black and gray frizz that looked as though it belonged to an Old English Sheepdog. All in all, not a pleasant sight. Rachael taught political science at a small, undistinguished college in Boston and it was best to avoid her rather than give an incorrect answer to one of her litmus-test-gender-supremacy questions.

Which left Paul, two years older than George. Paul was the family aberration. He was gorgeous. He had the build of a tennis player and the bearing of a yachtsman – he was both - with a chiseled chin, a natural tan and a smile that dazzled like the June sun. Paul was an acknowledged star in biotechnology. Paul had already founded and sold two biotech companies and had just started his third. Needless to say, Paul was wealthy – far wealthier than his father who barely acknowledged his existence.

Paul was one the reasons I had married George. George had brought me to 'meet the family' on our fifth date. George's father barely looked up from his *Barron's* upon being introduced. Carl and Celeste, upon learning that not only did I hail from Minnesota, but came from an undistinguished family, promptly lost interest in me.

Rachael gave me a fifteen-minute-long Rorschach test that ended with her declaring, with a sneer, that I was 'hopelessly bourgeoisie'. It was only Paul who made me feel welcome. By the time that first afternoon had faded to sunset, he knew my tastes in music, art and cinema and we had jointly dissected the works of Philip Roth and Tom Wolfe. Before I left, he pulled me aside and said I was 'just what the family needed'.

"You're a gem, Kat, a breath of fresh air," he had said to me. "It isn't just George who needs someone like you. We all do. Stick around and be the catalyst that gets this family out of its long-running rut."

I should add that Paul was also gay. Not flamboyantly so, just gay. But Paul's sexual orientation pained his father no end, on top of which Paul was already the fruit of the evil woman. Over the years, George and I were invited to Paul's home in Cambridge for dinner or parties and I had met Paul's partner, Jerry, a biophysicist and all-around nice guy. We all got along quite well, though George couldn't resist a few fraternal, homophobic barbs on the way home. Paul came solo to the birthday party out of respect for his father's prejudices, which I thought was nobly self-sacrificing.

Other than setting the background for the depressingly dysfunctional family that produced George – and it still gave him no excuse for being who he was – I recount that weekend because it yielded my murder weapon.

We were three hours into the party, Rachael was berating Celeste and Laura for their failure to acknowledge that marriage was contractual subjugation and that her research showed that marital rape was endemic. Celeste looked overwhelmed, Laura looked bored. Carl and his father were deeply into an assessment of the abysmal state of the Massachusetts Republican Party which they both supported. Fred was watching the Red Sox in the family room. George was asleep in the library and Jill was cleaning up in the kitchen along with the staff.

Which left Paul and me, on the porch, chatting in oversize white wicker chairs about Paul's new company.

"You know what a protease inhibitor is?" Paul asked.

I was as reasonably well read on the subject as a housewife could be expected to be. "An AIDS drug," I said.

Paul nodded, the equivalent of giving me a passing grade. "The problem has always been drug interactions. There's no one pill to control HIV. Instead, it's multiple drugs - a cocktail. The cocktail carries its own set of problems, many of them serious, just because it's a mix of drugs developed at different times for other purposes. You introduce another drug into the mix and it's like a hand grenade. Take Viagra. A gay man with HIV takes Viagra at his own peril because of the contraindication of Ritvin and Viagra…"

Up to this point, I had been listening to be polite. Suddenly, Paul had my full attention.

You see, George had a secret supply of Viagra. He was apparently taking it to keep up with Susie Perkyboobs.

"What do you mean, 'contraindication'?" I asked, suddenly very alert.

"The drugs can't be mixed for one reason or another," Paul explained. "Ritvin enhances the potency of Viagra something like tenfold, which could kill a man…"

I listened to the rest of Paul's business plan, which was to create a new class of protease inhibitor without side effects, ultimately leading to a one-pill drug for the control of HIV. I nodded in all the right places. I called his work equal parts humanitarian and genius-inspiring. I asked him to bring Jerry to dinner at our house and we agreed on a date two weeks hence. He, in turn, invited me to see his company's new digs.

And I put Ritvin on my shopping list.

5.

I had acquired a tail. I first saw him on the Monday following the birthday celebration in Ipswich. He was parked in a lawn service truck three doors down from my house. Nearly everyone on the street had a lawn service but, in our neighborhood, the trucks came, disgorged half a dozen swarthy men, and then disappeared after two hours. This one stayed all day and no one got in or out.

I obliged my tail by going through a perfectly unmemorable day. I bought groceries and went to the drug store. I had lunch with Nancy and we chatted about books. I puttered in the garden. It was one of those nights when George wasn't doing 'due diligence' and so was home on the 6:04. I met him at the station and brought him home for steaks cooked on the big outdoor grill we almost never used. Day one of being tailed was a breeze.

But it wasn't getting me my Ritvin. I was aware from the New York *Times* that devices existed that allowed eavesdroppers to monitor not only people's conversations, but their computer use – knowing what web sites they visited and what keystrokes they made in writing emails. Presumably these tools were known to private detectives and one might already be installed on my computer. So, using my PC to read about Ritvin became impossible. Nor could I go to the library as I had for the past several months. Why would I be using the library's computer for research instead of my own? Without research I didn't know how much I needed. Was it one pill or twenty? Would it work the same day or did it take a week?

Three days went by and I was frustrated both by being watched and by my lack of progress in implementing my plan. Monday's lawn service truck became Tuesday's plumber's van and Wednesday's contractor's pickup truck, but the occupant remained the same. On Wednesday, however, George announced that he was 'checking out an investment banking lead' and would be home late. I remained visibly at home that evening, watching television or on the phone with girl friends while my husband cavorted naked in Susie Perkyboobs' apartment. Meanwhile. the dossier on Kat remained dull and uninteresting.

Thursday morning, however, brought a jolting call. Terry Dupree, my old creative director called me at home. "We should have lunch," he said. "We miss you back at the agency." He then asked if I might be free today.

You have to understand that Terry and I hadn't spoken to one another in more than five years. For him to give me a call out of the blue – and to be cryptic – got my attention and I quickly agreed.

Terry was also how I met George lo those many years ago. It was six weeks after Mark had dumped me and I moped around the agency wondering if life would ever again be worth living. Terry was my male buddy and, yes, he was gay. The percentage of male agency creative directors who are gay is off the probability charts. It probably has something to do with working with all those buff male models.

The only one who didn't know Terry's sexual orientation was his mother. As a result, I was Terry's beard to any number of social events to which his mother might also be present. One of them was a January wedding at the Four Seasons. I tried to beg off but Terry convinced me that not only did he need me, but that there would be a bevy of eligible men to help me forget Mark. It was at that reception that I met George. The rebound can be a wonderful thing, or at least I thought so at the time.

Terry and I had lunch at Legal Sea Foods. I took the train into Back Bay Station, my tail nonchalantly reading the Boston *Globe* at the other end of the car. He was there in the restaurant, sitting at the bar, taking photographs with his cell phone. I was much better than he was at not being noticed.

Terry chatted about old times and changes at Hill, Holliday, then came to the point.

"People are asking questions about you," Terry said. "Someone was making calls into the agency this week looking for people who worked with you."

"Did they find anyone?" I asked, my stomach sinking.

"Maybe," Terry said. "He got me on the phone and said he was doing a 'routine background investigation'. I didn't let him get any further. But other people said they also got calls."

"Anyone with a particular axe to grind?"

"Marcia Kelly."

I uttered a number of very unladylike words, some under my breath but others audible enough to cause Terry to flinch. Marcia and I had joined Hill, Holliday at the same time. She was competent and creative but homely in a way that no amount of makeup or hair styling could cure. She had a large, protruding nose and a neck wattle that, along with a chunky build, made her look like a chicken. Though managers swear on their grandmothers' graves that it is not the case, ad agencies are built around sex appeal. Attractive men and women get pushed front and center to pitch accounts and call on clients. Everyone else stays in the office and creates. Marcia never left the office.

Her resentment of me – and she took out that anger on me rather than on the agency – knew no bounds. Every time I was invited along to a client lunch, she fumed. Every time I was added to a pitch team meeting with a prospective account, she hissed. I was the cute young thing in short skirts and form-fitting sweaters. Marcia was the poultry-faced copywriter who cranked out great storyboards.

A better person would have sued the agency for bias, collected a fortune, and used the proceeds to open their own shop. Marcia didn't do that. Instead, she found petty ways to get even with me, like stealing things from my desk and spilling drinks on me.

"Any idea what she may have told them?" I asked.

Terry shook his head. "I just know she had a look like the Cheshire Cat when she told me this guy had called her."

Marcia could bad-mouth me, I thought, but everything she knew was eight years old. A divorce attorney couldn't use stuff from before a person was married. And I had left Hill, Holliday right after George got his bonus and he was made an analyst…

Holy crap.

All right, so I'm not perfect. I'm human, just like everyone else on the face of the earth. And, eleven months after I married George – and three months after I spotted George at Logan playing grab-ass with another woman – I allowed myself to get even. It was also about this time that I was becoming convinced that he would never change his catfish ways, even with my help. My overheard conversation about sports-themed restaurants was two months in the future.

So, I explored my options. One particular option. Edward DeVries, a very handsome manager at one of my accounts. He was single, he flirted with me even though he knew I was a newlywed – or maybe because he knew I was a newlywed – and I kind of flirted back. We had lunch a couple of times. Had I met him before I met George, he was the guy I would have thrown myself at with Cosmo's nine-step plan.

The flirting got more serious until, one day, I told George we had a crash project at the office that would occupy me all weekend. It was a week after our first anniversary, a day we had 'celebrated' by eating out at TGI Fridays. There hadn't even been an anniversary present.

To my saying that I would be gone two days, George just replied, 'uh, huh' and kept filling in spreadsheets with numbers from a 10K.

It was a spectacular weekend. Two brilliant October days at a huge beach house in Watch Hill. I took off my engagement ring and my wedding ring and left them in my purse along with my inhibitions. My clothes, for the most part, lay on the floor where I dropped them. Edward DeVries and I made the most of that weekend and I fell head over heels.

On Monday, he sent me flowers.

It was a big bouquet and, while the card made no mention of the weekend, it did bear his name. Marcia noticed it immediately and went straight to Human Resources. That afternoon, I had a very uncomfortable meeting with Jack Connors, the third name on the door of the agency and the man very much in charge of the place. Jack never accused me of anything and he asked me no questions. Instead, he talked about the fine line everyone was expected to walk in agency-client relationships between the business and the personal. Billings were the lifeblood of an agency and nothing could ever be allowed to jeopardize those billings.

He didn't fire me. He didn't even suggest that I 'pursue other career avenues.' He just let it be known, without ever saying a word on the subject, that he knew exactly what had happened over the weekend. And if it ever happened again, my career in advertising was toast.

Marcia, of course, figured it out. She was the one who had tattled. I was gently removed from the account that had brought Edward DeVries into my life.

A month later, I overheard the fateful conversation about pitchers and quarterbacks. Two months later, I resuscitated George's career. Three months later I was house-hunting in Wellesley Hills. Four months later, Hill, Holliday threw me a going-away party, which Marcia did not attend.

"I thought you ought to know," Terry said.

"Does Marcia still talk about me?"

Terry shook his head. "She moved onto other game after you left." Then he added, "But she has a memory like an elephant. And that look on her face told me everything I needed to know."

"She had many animal-like qualities," I said. On a different day and in different circumstances, it would have been a great zinger. Instead, it just hung in the air.

"Better in person than on the phone or through an email," Terry said. "I'll keep my ears open for anything else."

Terry gave me a kiss on the cheek which I assume was captured via cell phone by the person tailing me. All the way back to Wellesley Hills, I kicked myself for having been so stupid. Marcia had handed George a giant brick for his wall of evidence.

No, Marcia didn't hand George the brick, I did. I was the one who had flirted with Edward DeVries. I was the one who played footsies with him during lunch. And I was the one who beamed and said 'yes' when he suggested a weekend for 'just the two of us' at a friend's beach house. I was the one who was young and stupid. I was the one who had decided to fight infidelity fire with infidelity fire, rather than with sherry or forgiveness. I was the one who needed to get back at George.

I had to get my hands on some Ritvin.

*****

When I got home, I called Paul. I told him I was so excited from our talk over the weekend that I just had to take him up on his offer to see his new company and could I come over and look around?

Paul laughed. "For my favorite sister-in-law, anything," he said. "Tomorrow at ten, though I warn you there isn't much to see yet."

I was worried about phone taps and what might be recorded in that truck down the street, but a call to your husband's brother – and especially to one who is known to be gay – didn't rise to the level of suspicious. And besides, I was just accepting an invitation previously extended.

When George came home, I told him Paul had invited me to see his new company the following morning. In case someone had hidden microphones in the house, this was a clue that my visit was of no interest to them.

"Remind him that PJ&B would love to take this one public if he doesn't flip it first," George said. "And what's for dinner?"

* * * * *

The company didn't even have a name yet. "We just call it 'Rev 3' for now," Paul said.

We were in a converted factory or warehouse – it was hard to tell what it had once been – near Kendall Square. It had beautiful exposed brick walls, high ceilings, recessed lights everywhere, and a three-story atrium with skylights. Paul had leased a floor - "Twenty thousand square feet or so," he shrugged – though there were still fewer that twenty people on staff.

"It's the same crew," Paul explained. "We all know the drill, we all understand the risk-reward. If it flies, these guys all get a cut of the proceeds. If it doesn't…" He shrugged again. "They've gotten pieces of two other deals. They're not starving. In three months, if everything goes right, we'll have over a hundred people in here."

Computers were everywhere, most still in boxes, awaiting the employees who would use them. Paul patted one that sat in an area of things that looked like gray filing cabinets but were computer storage, I was assured. "This is the heart of it all. This is where we design the drug. This is where we prove it."

Then he showed me the pharmaceutical room. "Samples of everything we need. The pharma companies view us as alternative R&D. If it works, they'll be banging at the door looking to make a deal. If it doesn't, all it cost them was some pills."

The pharmaceutical room was unlocked. It didn't even have a door.

"George said to tell you his firm can take you public," I remembered to say.

Paul gave a small laugh. "PB&J," he said, deliberately switching the letters as so many clients did. "PB&J shouldn't be allowed anywhere near an offering memorandum. PB&J should stick to touting municipal bonds to rich little widow ladies in Cohasset."

Then he looked at me. "I'm sorry, Kat. That's not called for."

I looked at him in the eye and shook my head. "You're not telling me anything I don't already know. When I told George I was coming, he made me promise to say something."

"Poor George," Paul said. "It's a good thing he's got you because…"

Someone came up to Paul and touched his arm. "Telephone," the person said. "I think you'll want to take it."

"You'll be OK for a few minutes?" Paul asked.

I nodded. "Take your time. If you're not back in an hour, I'll show myself out."

As soon as Paul was out of sight, I backtracked to the pharmaceutical room. Most of the drugs were still in shipping cartons. I crossed my fingers and went through those that were shelved. On the second drug rack I found eight bottles of Ritvin, each with a hundred tablets. Using a shipping invoice to avoid leaving fingerprints, I opened the bottle at the back of the shelf and shook out six, yellow, aspirin-sized tablets. I had brought along a baggie and slipped them into it.

It had all taken under a minute.

I had my murder weapon.

Paul was back in ten minutes, I was admiring the drug design computer and its appendages.

"I promise I didn't turn it on," I said, smiling.

Paul had a wary look on his face and, for a moment, I wondered if someone had observed me running my fingers across pill bottles. Instead, he guided me to a small, plain room with a half-dead philodendron seeking light, water or both. It was only when I saw the photo of Jerry that I realized this Spartan office was Paul's.

"This is the second call I've gotten like this," Paul said when he had closed the door. He paused for a moment, either trying to find the right words or the courage to break some bad news.

"On Tuesday, I had a call from someone saying they were

conducting a routine background investigation. They didn't say who they were with and I typically ignore those calls. You should know they were asking about you."

He let that sink in.

"I was polite but declined to answer their questions, which called for opinions rather than facts. Anyway, that was Tuesday. Just now, I had another call. Different person, this one requesting an appointment for an interview. He said he was aware I had declined to speak with the first person who called, and said perhaps the problem was that the first caller hadn't made clear that the request was official."

"Official?" I said.

"He says he's with the Securities and Exchange Commission."

"Why would the SEC want to talk to you about me?"

Paul shook his head. "When I said they were asking about 'you', I meant you and George."

I just stood there with my mouth open.

"Kat, is there something about George I ought to know?"

*****

I drove home in a daze. All of a sudden, everything had been turned on its head. The guy outside the house in a lawn service truck wasn't some private investigator out to build a case for George's divorce. In all likelihood, George had never called any detective agency and telling Susie Perkyboobs he was thinking along those lines was just part of his patter to keep his mistress's interest. The person calling Hill, Holliday and the man in the van were with the government. And they either were keeping tabs on George or else were trying to determine whether George was doing all this alone or if I was his accomplice.

I thought I still had a month. It was beginning to look like I had a few days.

6.

In the hours between Paul's bombshell and George's arrival home, I made a set of decisions.

First, I would listen very carefully for any clue from George that he knew he was under investigation. Usually, my husband was sufficiently lost in George World that I doubted he would have noticed anything short of handcuffs being slapped on him, but I would listen anyway.

Second, I would say nothing. If our house was bugged, I wanted to remain the 'innocent spouse'. George wasn't going to rope me into his stupidity at this late hour.

Third, I planned to liquidate George's accounts just as soon as I could get a safe internet connection. If George found that all his money was gone, he wasn't exactly going to come crying to me about it.

Fourth, I would keep George off that duplicate Dell laptop at all costs. Our eavesdropper showed up each morning at 7 a.m. - about the time George logged off and took a shower. I didn't want any keystrokes being captured that gave access to account numbers or passwords. Ensuring that George got nowhere near his computer required a separate stop on my way home from Cambridge.

And fifth, I would spike George's Frosted Flakes at the first opportunity. I had ground the Ritvin into a powder and had it at the ready. As soon as George said, 'I'm going to be late', in it went. To hell with getting the right dosages. I just wanted that ten-fold Viagra reaction.

When George came home – the 6:04, this not being a hanky-panky night – I greeted him with a big hug and a kiss. I wrapped my arms around his neck and asked if he preferred a martini or a beer.

"Martini," he said, somewhat mystified.

"I went to see Paul this morning," I said, handing him his drink. "It's all still very small, but he has a floor of a building in Kendall Square. And I put in a pitch for PJ&B doing the underwriting, as you requested."

"How did he react?" George asked.

"He laughed," I said. That much, at least was true. "He says they're a long way from thinking about an underwriter."

"He'll probably just flip it like he did the first two," George said. "Which reminds me. I've got some investment banking duties tomorrow night. We're taking a prospective IPO to Fenway Park. It's a 7:05 game."

"Who's in town?" I asked, smiling my best.

George shrugged. "Not the Yankees. I know that much."

What George knew about baseball would fit neatly on a 3x5 card with room left over for a cake recipe. I knew the Orioles were in town. George had probably been offered tickets and now found them a perfect excuse to spend an evening screwing Susie Perkyboobs, unless 'flip it like he did the first two' was another of those Freudian slips – this one announcing that Susie was getting perilously close to her twenty-seventh birthday and so was about to get thrown over for someone more age-appropriate.

Either way, George was going to the office in the morning with an unhealthy dose of Ritvin in his system.

"How's everything at the office?" I asked.

"Same old, same old."

* * * * *

On a typical evening that George was home, we watched television or something we had gotten from Netflix or Blockbuster. I didn't want George near the computer and so I laid out three James Bond films on the dinner table. That had been my 'separate stop' on my way home from seeing Paul's company.

"I thought you might like these," I said.

George gravitates to James Bond the way felines do to catnip. He especially believes that Roger Moore is the 'real' James Bond and I offered up *The Spy Who Loved Me*, *For Your Eyes Only*, and *Live and Let Die*. He caressed them, he salivated. He vowed to watch at least two out of three.

I also took the liberty of grinding up three Excedrin PM along with the pepper over his salad. As a result, at 10 p.m., George was having trouble keeping his eyes open. Once he was in his pajamas and sound asleep, I turned off his radio's wake-up feature.

I awakened at my customary 7 a.m. the next morning and roused George. "Do you have today off?" I said. "Don't you have investment banking clients to see tonight?"

George looked at me and at the clock and started screaming obscenities. I got him into the shower and laid out his toiletries. Breakfast was waiting for him downstairs and I said I'd drive him to the train station to save time. George wolfed down his Frosted Flakes and a cup of coffee. The coffee had one Ritvin tablet ground up into it, the Frosted Flakes, two. Given that George barely chewed his food, I doubt that had there been a taste difference he would have noticed. At 8:03 we left the house and made the five-minute dash for the train station. His heart was still racing, hopefully from his truncated morning schedule and not from the effects of the drugs he had ingested.

I kissed my husband goodbye for what I hoped would be the last time and handed him his *Wall Street Journal*.

"Have a wonderful day," I smiled.

If he said anything in return, it was not memorable.

* * * * *

I went back to the house and thoroughly cleaned everything with which the Ritvin could conceivably have come into contact. The extra Ritvin tablets were flushed down the toilet. George's coffee cup and cereal bowl were thoroughly washed by hand and then went through the dishwasher for good measure. The kitchen counter and table were scrubbed repeatedly. I had a cleaning lady in twice a week and I already suspected her of taking shortcuts. This time, I was going to make certain it was done thoroughly.

At nine o'clock I peeked out the bedroom window and saw my tail, today in a plumber's van.

I needed to access George's computer one last time, but I needed a safe internet connection. So I called Trish and invited her out for lunch. I told her we'd meet at the Blue Ginger at noon, and that I had something special to share with her. 'Something special' had come to mean a code word about my pretend sex life with George's co-worker, Phil. Trish giggled and said that she, too, had something to share.

Working on the assumption that my phone was tapped, I was reasonably certain I had telegraphed my important movements for the morning to those who watched me.

At 10:30, I popped George's secret Dell laptop into my largest handbag, where it made no visible impression. For once, the gods of fashion were in sync with my needs. When those oversize handbags first made their appearance I couldn't fathom why anyone needed so much space, though I bought one just to be *au courant.*

In theory, I could have done what I needed to do from any computer. I was taking along George's Dell only because it had all the right 'cookies' in its digital memory to allow me to get onto George's brokerage and banking websites without being challenged.

I headed for the Mall at Chestnut Hill, home to the biggest Bloomingdale's outside of Manhattan. The plumber's van tailed me at a safe distance.

I knew a couple of things: first, that on a weekday morning, the ratio of women to men inside the Mall might be something like fifty to one. Chestnut Hill is a 'chick mall'. Every store is dedicated to things that women want. You cannot buy a high definition television or a power drill in the Mall of Chestnut Hill. You can buy several hundred different perfumes and facial products, as well as clothes from all major designers.

So, knowing that first thing, I made a guess about two other things. The first was that my tail would be loathe to stand out in a crowd of women. And, second, if I turned my car over to valet parking, there was a reasonable chance that my tail would wait for the car, knowing I had a noon appointment to exchange girl talk. If he followed me inside, I'd figure out a different way of getting on that computer.

I was right. The plumber's van stopped a safe distance from the valet line. As I was sashaying inside, the van was looking for a parking place where the driver could keep an eye on the valet lot.

Inside the Mall, I made two quick purchases to prove I had been shopping, and then headed for a coffee shop called the Café Au Lait that had a sign promising 'free internet'.

Over the next twenty minutes, I calmly went about the process of liquidating George's accounts and transferring them to those of 'Benito Morales'. It was amazing how simple it was. In less than half an hour, $4,877,252.39, all in the form of electrons, slipped out of seven accounts and into one. It would take three days to clear, after which the money would go to a third account. I would have to interrupt my grieving widowhood to make that shift and, by then, the exchange could be done by any computer. I sipped the last of my iced coffee and snapped closed the lid of the computer. I still had the computer to get rid of, but I also had a plan for that.

At 11:40 I retrieved my car from valet parking and made the drive back to Wellesley. My faithful tail was three cars behind me. I met Trish for lunch at noon and I showed her what I had bought. My tail had a table for one on the other side of the restaurant. Trish's affair with the tennis pro was going full speed ahead. She was so anxious to share her passion that she barely elicited a few comments from me about my wild afternoons with Phil. I offered that Phil was feeling pangs of conscience about his wife sitting at home with two teenage children and Trish looked at me with alarm.

"Women don't sit at home with teenage children," she said. "The teenagers aren't home to begin with and their mother will do anything to get away from them at that age. Kat, he's going to dump you!"

"It wouldn't be the end of the world," I said with a hint of sadness. "The whole thing had kind of run its course."

"Poor Kat," Trish said and insisted on paying for lunch.

When I left the restaurant, I opened my purse and found a message on my cell phone. I may have many faults, but one of them is not interrupting a lunch with a friend to take a call. My phone gets turned off. My friends get my undivided attention.

The call was from Patsy. She was in tears and sounded close to hysteria. I couldn't understand the message but I knew she needed to see me.

Patsy greeted me at the door in a to-die-for Donna Karan sweater set and skirt, the perfect upper-middle-class housewife in her perfect home. Her appearance, though, was the only thing that was normal. Her house was the quietest I have ever heard it. The gardeners were gone, the contractors were nowhere in evidence. Even the children were missing.

"I told Consuela to take them to the club for the day," Patsy said when I looked around the parlor and saw no evidence of life.

Patsy had fortified herself with several martinis. She offered me one and I declined.

"Peter's firm has blown up," she said calmly when she had a sip of her drink. "Quant Four Capital has just announced that it lost six billion dollars of its clients' money because of a bad bet on copper."

"How can you lose six billion dollars on copper?" I asked, incredulous.

"They apparently owned every futures contract on the face of the earth and kept bidding up the price. This morning, Chile flooded the market with copper to cash in on the high price, and the market cut the price of futures in half. Four hours and 'poof'. It's all gone." She took another drink.

"Where's Peter?" I asked.

Patsy started crying. "The SEC was in Quant Four's offices within an hour of the announcement. Peter is 'cooperating with the authorities', according to the radio. He talked to me for about three minutes. All he said was, 'you'd better send everyone home. Just tell them to stop what they're doing and go home.'"

"Oh, poor Patsy," was all I could say.

"It's stuffy in here," Patsy said. "Let's go out in the garden."

Actually, the room was pleasantly cool and it was getting humid outside. But I followed Patsy out into her garden.

When we were outside, Patsy began walking beside me, pointing at the perennial border. "Just listen and nod occasionally," Patsy said. "I'm pretty sure there aren't bugs out here."

I had a queasy feeling she wasn't talking about mosquitoes. I nodded and pointed at a rose bush.

"I know some things," Patsy said. "When the radio says Peter is 'cooperating', my guess is he's telling them what he knows in exchange for a deal."

"Why does Peter have to make a deal?" I asked. "They made a bad bet on copper contracts."

Patsy kneeled down to inspect the rose. I did the same. "Copper made it all come undone. And it didn't really all happen today. It's been unraveling for weeks. Chilean copper was just the final straw – they couldn't hide it any more. For the past year, Peter's firm has been rigging the market – lots of markets. It's been everything from naked short selling to paying off analysts for inside information."

I froze at 'paying off analysts'.

"Kat, I'm pretty sure one of the analysts Peter was paying was George."

*****

To my credit, I didn't throw up right there in her garden.

"But George covers hotels and restaurants, not copper," I said.

Patsy gave me a pitying look. "Quant Four had its fingers in anything that can make money," she said. "If they could short a restaurant stock down to zero and then have an analyst in their pocket ready to issue a 'buy' rating, they'd do it in a heartbeat."

"Peter told you all this?" I asked.

Patsy shook her head vigorously. "I figured it out. I'm not stupid. When Peter told me to 'spend the money', I started nosing around…"

I took Patsy by the shoulders of her size two sweater. "Patsy, listen carefully: you don't know anything. Peter never told you anything. You never suspected anything."

Patsy looked me in the eye. "The innocent spouse rule?"

I nodded.

"Six billion dollars," Patsy said with tears in her eyes. "Peter and his buddies lost six billion dollars in about four hours. And they've been doing illegal stuff for years, most of which made billions. When you lose that much that quickly, nobody's innocent."

"Does Peter have a computer at home?" I asked.

"You mean, like the ones I'm not supposed to know about?"

I nodded. "Would it help Peter or hurt him if they disappeared?" I asked.

"I don't know," Patsy said, sounding slightly frightened.

"Pretty soon, people are going to come here with a search warrant," I said. "Before they get here, you need to know whether you're helping Peter or hurting him by people finding those computers and what's on them."

"Did you know George was taking money from Peter?"

The question caught me completely off guard. Until that moment, I had assumed Patsy had called her closest friend, looking for a shoulder to cry on and perhaps some advice. I suppose a question like that, out of the blue, could have been asked from a position of complete innocence, a frightened woman looking for an ally or at least someone who knew she was in the same boat legally.

It could also have been a coached question with a hidden microphone capturing the answer. I kicked myself for having asked about computers.

"No," I said. "And I can't believe George would do anything like that. He'd never jeopardize his position or his family. He's a good man."

* * * * *

George is a big fan of *NCIS* and I've watched that ditzy woman with the tattoos on her neck resurrect data off of computers that have been dropped off cliffs. I assume the show's writers root their scripts in some degree of facts. The best way to make a computer unusable is to make it disappear permanently.

My original plan had been to take the sledge hammer in the garage to George's laptop, then lose the plumber's van at a traffic light along Route 9 or, if necessary, out on Route 128, drive to some place in Dover or Sherborn where a quiet road crosses the Charles River, and drop the pieces of the computer into the river.

If Patsy's husband was busy 'naming names' in some SEC conference room in Boston, the very act of my trying to lose my tail might engender some Amber Alert for a white Lexus driven by an attractive, thirty-five-year-old brunette. They'd get me and the computer intact.

So I went home and down into the basement and smashed the computer as planned. And then I swept up the pieces and potted them.

I have a trio of big containers on the back patio filled with gorgeous flowering plants and vines. A very talented woman comes out every May and does them for some ungodly amount of money. They're lovely to look at, though I'm not really big on flowers. But I do own a pair of gardening gloves and I took one of those containers apart and buried the pieces of the computer down in the soil underneath the masses of roots.

By the time I was finished, it was nearly five o'clock. George would be skipping out of PJ&B, ready to boink Susie Perkyboobs. I understand Viagra takes a while to be effective, so he might have taken his dose before he left the office. He might have heard about the crash of Quant Four Capital; he might even have talked about it with co-workers. But George was basically stupid. If he even knew that Quant Four was Peter Brandt's firm – a questionable assumption – he would never guess that Peter was ratting him out to get a lighter sentence.

So George would be taking a taxi to the Fenway area, though certainly not to Fenway Park. And he would be climbing those stairs, his bloodstream full of Ritvin with a Viagra chaser. On Sunday, Paul had spoken of a 'ten-fold effect' of combining the two drugs. It shouldn't be long.

I wanted to be with Patsy, who desperately needed someone to hold her hand. But that question about whether I knew that George was on Peter's payroll had spooked me. I had to stay away from Patsy for a while.

Instead, I went over my list. Yes, I had a written to-do list. Don't murder your husband without one. I had cleaned and vacuumed all surfaces that might have had a trace of Ritvin. I had transferred the money from George's accounts in a way that required no use of the internet from my home. I had disposed of George's computer, albeit not in as complete a way as I had planned. But I had also vacuumed the basement floor, eliminating even the tiniest screw from the computer, and then changed the vacuum cleaner bag, burying the old one in the garbage that would be picked up in the morning.

All those back-up CDs I had made of the data on George's computer were hacked into pieces and thrown in the garbage. My duplicate key to her apartment was bent with a pair of pliers until it was barely recognizable as a key.

As to my own computer, I had erased everything having to do with George's infidelities. All the photos, lovingly catalogued by me, of him with his various mistresses were deleted. So, too, were my trove of Susie Perkyboob's emails as well as my notes on his comings and goings. I erased my history of web sites I had visited and those pesky 'temporary files' of web pages. When I was done, all that was left was a very impersonal computer telling of the dull life of a suburban housewife: cheery emails to my parents and friends, photos and stories sent to me over the years. Yes, a person examining this computer would yawn.

All I had left to do was rehearse my story. And I was starting to do that when the doorbell rang.

I opened the door to find a Wellesley policeman. Not young, cute and blonde. Instead, he was chubby and in his fifties. He was also sweating.

"There's been an accident, ma'am," he said. "Involving your husband."

"Is he all right?" I asked, clutching at my heart.

"I don't know, ma'am," he said. "I've just been asked to take you to the hospital."

The hospital? I thought. *No, he's got to be dead.*

Then, I theorized that they wouldn't leave him lying where he died. They'd move him to a hospital. Sure. It made sense.

But what was next to the Fenway area? All those hospitals. The Longwood Medical Complex. Eighteen hospitals. Half of them advertising that they had the best patient care in the world. Great, George has a heart attack and they save him.

The police car, siren blaring, zoomed toward Boston. It wasn't hard to keep crying when I was worried sick that my damned husband might still be alive.

7.

The police car came to an abrupt stop at the entrance to the emergency room of Beth Israel Deaconess Medical Center, one of the biggest, fanciest hospitals in the Longwood Medical Complex, and one that ran radio ads touting its expertise in heart care.

"Just go in and tell them who you are, ma'am," the policeman said. "They'll take care of you. And good luck. I hope it's not serious."

To which my irrational first thought was, *fine, how am I going to get home?*

I gave them my and George's name at the information desk, a properly hysterical look on my face and sound in my voice.

Go on, I thought. *Break the news to me. Tell me he's in the morgue.*

The woman at the reception desk waggled her arm in the air and pointed at me. A moment later, a tall, forty-ish woman, pants-suited with short black hair, was at my side. She asked me my name.

She took me by the shoulder. "We need to find a place to talk," she said. "There's a coffee shop down the hall…"

"Where's my husband?" I cried. "The policeman said he was in an accident."

"Your husband has had a heart attack," the woman said, gently. "They're still working on him and you can't see him yet."

Yet? You mean the bastard's going to live?

I allowed her to guide me down the hall, but instead of a coffee shop we went to a small room set up with tables and chairs. *Family Counseling Office* the sign over the door said. Inside was one of those single-cup brewing systems. The woman chose a vial of coffee and inserted it in the machine.

"French roast OK?" she asked.

"When can I see my husband?" I replied.

"They'll call me as soon as it's OK," she replied.

She returned with two mugs of coffee. "I'm Detective Sharon Tucci," she said. "I'm sorry to be meeting you under these circumstances. I need to ask you a few questions."

I took a close look at Ms. Tucci. Definitely a policewoman or someone who lived on what I imagined was a policewoman's salary. The short black hair was passable but looked like the kind of thing you get at a SuperCuts or some such chain. Her hair was dyed to mask the first hints of gray but the color was off slightly – something from a shelf at the drug store, not a custom color job. The pantsuit was well chosen but of a ubiquitous style, something you'd probably find at Macy's. She wore just enough makeup to show she thought about it. Underneath it all was a tall, attractive woman with a round, intelligent face. She wore no wedding ring, in fact no jewelry at all except for a tiny gold cross on a chain around her neck.

She took George's driver's license from out of a jacket pocket. "First, this is your husband, right?"

I nodded. Talk about vain. George had gotten a haircut and trimmed his nose hair before going to the DMV to get a stupid driver's license photo taken.

"Do you know where your husband was this evening?"

"He was going from the office to Fenway Park," I said. "He's a securities analyst and was entertaining some investment banking clients. He said something about a prospective IPO."

Sharon Tucci wrote that down.

"Do you know a Susan Booth?"

I waited exactly one and a half beats before answering. "No."

"Is your husband on any medications?"

I paused two beats this time. "Lipitor – for cholesterol. Aspirin and vitamins, but they're all over-the-counter medicines.

"How about Viagra?"

I made my face register disbelief. "No!" It was great acting.

"I hate to have to ask this, but is your husband HIV positive?"

"No!" I spat out. "And I think I'd know if he were HIV positive, or on Viagra."

Detective Tucci wrote it all down and nodded.

"Please tell me what's going on," I asked.

Her cell phone rang.

She answered it, gave a few cryptic 'yep's and glanced at me, a look somewhere between pity and scorn on her face.

"Let's go see your husband," she said.

*****

The walk down the hospital corridor was the longest I've ever taken. They had drawn blood. They found the Viagra. They had also found the Ritvin. George was going to 'fess up to the Viagra but swear truthfully he had never knowingly taken any protease inhibitor. And because no one was stupid enough to knowingly combine the two drugs, they'd start examining my comings and goings, and then they'd start counting the numbers of pills in Ritvin bottles at Paul's nameless third company in Kendall Square. What's the penalty for attempted murder? Ten years?

There were four men, two in white coats and two in suits in the curtained-off table of the emergency room where George lay. At least I assume it was George. There were so many tubes and wires attached to him that the human form underneath was indecipherable.

Detective Tucci cleared her throat. The men stopped talking among themselves and looked at the two new people.

"This is Doctor Lohr," Detective Tucci said to me. "I'll let him explain."

Doctor Lohr looked like a doctor. Serious-faced, tortoise-shell glasses and a white coat with his ID badge hanging askew. He might have been ten years either side of fifty. This evening, he looked tired, with bags under his eyes and deep lines in his forehead.

"You husband has suffered a massive heart attack," Doctor Lohr said. "It appears there has been very serious damage to his heart muscle. At present, his heart can't beat on its own. We're using a mechanical device to assist his heart as well as one to aid his breathing. We're also concerned that his brain may also have sustained damage due to a loss of oxygen for an extended period."

"My husband had no history of heart trouble," I said. It seemed like the right response.

"The attack wasn't brought on by a pre-existing condition," Doctor Lohr said. "Rather, the attack was the result of two drugs – sildenafil citrate and a protease inhibitor – administered improperly. Your husband's heart was no match for the drugs."

"But he's going to live, isn't he?" I asked. I tried to keep hope in my voice.

"He's in grave condition," Doctor Lohr said, keeping his voice uninflected. "For the moment, he's on a heart and lung bypass system. Were we to remove them at this time, it's very doubtful that his heart could or would function on its own. These gentlemen would like to talk to you about certain other options." He nodded at the two men in suits.

One of the men – youngish, sandy blonde with a forgettable face and wearing a suit and tie that could only have come from Wal-Mart - took a step toward me and offered his hand. "I'm terribly sorry to meet you under these circumstances. I'm Jason Whitburn and this is Rich Cordell." He indicated a much better dressed African American man who nodded his head. "We're with the SEC – the Securities and Exchange Commission."

"What do you have to do with my husband's heart attack?" My voice was slightly incredulous.

"Your husband has been under investigation by our office for several weeks," Whitburn said. I put his age at thirty. His voice betrayed some sort of New-York-area upbringing. "We've been observing him for some time and were about to bring him in for questioning. We believe he has information related to several securities fraud investigations we have underway…"

"My George?"

"Yes, ma'am." Whitburn shuffled his feet slightly and looked down. "If he dies, we lose that potential source of information…"

"You want to keep my husband alive on some heart-lung machine so you can question him?" This time I didn't have to fake it. The indignant tone was real.

"That's not what we were suggesting, ma'am…"

I turned to Doctor Lohr. "Is there any hope he'll recover? Could he get a heart transplant?"

The doctor stammered. "We-we have no way of knowing. His condition is grave and I said there might be brain damage…"

I turned back to Whitburn and Cordell. "So my husband's life is hanging by a thread and all you care about is when you can question him?"

A second doctor who had been silent until now spoke. "There's minimal brain activity."

"What does that mean?" I asked.

The second doctor – his ID badge said 'Chang' and the man was an elderly Asian – took a step forward into the conversation.

"The EEG shows only very slight voluntary motor activity. He's not brain dead, but it's also not good."

"So he could be like this for months – or years?" I said.

"I'm afraid so," Chang said. "If he lives past the next few hours."

I turned to Detective Tucci. "I need some time. Can we go back to that room?"

She nodded. "Give us some time, please."

We went back to the room. Though she was uninvited, Detective Tucci stayed with me. She drew another cup of the execrable coffee from the machine. I declined with a shake of my head.

"That's a lot to absorb in a few minutes," she said.

I had my hands behind my neck, trying to relieve the tenseness I felt. "Why would someone take – what did he call it – siden…"

"Viagra and Ritvin," Detective Tucci said. "Super Viagra, they call it. Viagra will give a man an erection on demand for a couple of hours. Add a touch of Ritvin and the erection is rock hard all night – or so they tell me."

"You mentioned a name," I said, looking up at her.

"Susan Booth."

"I take it… my husband wasn't… watching the Red Sox," My words came out as one long sigh.

"Do you really want to know?"

"I'd find out eventually. I'm sure those SEC guys were smirking."

"He had the heart attack in bed," Detective Tucci said, very matter-of-factly. "With Miss Booth. She called the 911 and was fairly hysterical. She's sedated. You don't sound too surprised."

The lies began slipping out easily. "I suspected. I wondered why he suddenly had so many out-of-town trips. He started getting mysterious on me."

"What about that SEC stuff?"

I looked at her blankly and I went back to rubbing my neck. "I have no idea what they're talking about," I said. And it sounded convincing. "Of course, George never talked about work. He said he never wanted to put me in a position of accidentally revealing something important to one of my friends. Of course, he also said I wouldn't understand that stuff, anyway."

"Do you know what you want to do?" she asked. "About your husband."

I thought for a second, framing the answer. "I just found out my husband has had a massive heart attack and he may die regardless of what I decide. I also just found out he was cheating on me, and that the SEC was going to bring him in for questioning. I don't want to leave him in some purgatory, but I want him to live. I love him and I want him back. I'm going to ask if some mechanical heart or transplant would bring him back to anything near normal."

And then I mentally crossed my fingers.

Detective Tucci nodded and gave a little tug at the cross around her neck. "It's what I'd do," she said.

But at that moment bells and buzzers went off down the hall and the loudspeaker announced a 'Code Blue in Emergency 4'. Detective Tucci and I raced out of the room and down the hall to where three doctors converged around George and pulled the curtain so that we could not see.

A minute later, George's gurney and half a dozen pieces of equipment pushed through the curtain and down the hall to an elevator. I clenched Detective Tucci's hand. This time, the sweat on my face was real.

8.

So I got away with murder. And it all sounded so noble. No sooner had I announced to Detective Tucci that I would authorize any heroic lengths to save my husband than a popped blood vessel deep in his brain let me off the hook. The bleeding inside his head was too severe and the EEG showed a flat line, anyway.

I made a scene at his bedside and told the SEC ghouls to get out of the hospital – which they did, or at least out of sight. And I kissed George tenderly on the lips one last time before they unplugged him.

And I cried real tears. The tears were of relief rather than grief but they were just as salty and stung my face just the same.

I signed papers, not really knowing what they were. I was asked what funeral home I preferred and I shook my head at the person who asked. I had only gotten as far as planning his murder. I hadn't gotten around to planning the funeral.

Sometime around midnight we were done and Detective Tucci offered to drive me home. She asked if I had friends I could call. I said I did and she asked if they were close enough to help out in a situation like this. I told her they had been my best friends for years and they would help to see me through this. She said that was good.

We rounded the turn onto my street and I was surprised to see the light on in my house. There were cars in the driveway including a police car.

"What's going on?" I asked, incredulous that my grieving widowhood was being interrupted so callously.

"We're going to find out," Detective Tucci said, grimly.

We parked as close to the house as we could. She got out of the car and started up the sidewalk yelling, 'What the hell is going on here?"

I was met at the door by Jason Whitburn and Rich Cordell. With them was a Wellesley policeman. This time, their looks of sympathy had been replaced by cold stares.

"We have a warrant to search these premises," Whitburn said, the New York-ese in his voice becoming much more pronounced. "Here is a copy of the warrant. We are looking for paper or data files related to your husband's suspected receipt of funds for exchange of illegal insider information, and for suspected trades based on insider knowledge."

"You creeps couldn't even wait until he was buried?" Detective Tucci sneered.

"We offered an alternative," Whitburn said. "We believed that her husband would have cooperated. He was a relatively minor player in all this and we could have spared his family – exactly this kind of treatment." Whitburn nodded at me with an icy look. "When he died, it left us no choice. You should know that a simultaneous search is being executed at his office."

Why did that sound strangely rehearsed?

I watched as my computer – a clunky desktop – was taken away, together with copious boxes of papers. I went inside my home and found every drawer in every room pulled out. The one with our household financial records was now empty. It was all done neatly, but it was thorough in a scary way. These guys weren't kidding around. I glanced out the French doors that led onto the patio. The stone containers were intact. The kitchen garbage, however, was gone.

Whitburn came over to me when it seemed they had finished. "Ma'am, while we're sorry for your loss, we're going to have to ask you to come in and give us a statement regarding your husband's affairs." He caught himself. "His financial affairs. You are advised to bring an attorney with you as what you say will be on the record. If we don't hear from you in three or four days, we'll be in touch to arrange a time."

Detective Tucci – I hadn't taken her up on her offer to 'please call me Sharon' – stayed with me, unbidden. She demanded that every drawer be put back in its proper place and made Rich Cordell vacuum the carpets to get rid of the footprints from the hordes of investigators.

"I've never seen anything like this," she fumed. "Your husband's body isn't even cold and they're tearing the place apart." I still wasn't certain if she was trying to be a friend or if her interceding on my behalf with the SEC guys was feigned in order to gain my confidence for her own investigation.

"Do you want some coffee?" she asked. "I don't think they took the coffee maker."

"It's late," I said. "I need some sleep."

It was supposed to be my shining hour. I was supposed to be a young, good looking widow with a new chapter of my life about to open. My bastard, cheating husband was dead. He had died in the bed of his mistress of what I hoped was a very painful heart attack. No one had uttered the phrase 'foul play'. Instead, I had learned of a wonderfully useful thing called 'Super Viagra' in which men, in order to impress their girlfriends, willingly spiked their little blue pills with a potentially fatal enhancer. It was like freebasing cocaine – ultimately stupid in pursuit of a better high or, in this case, a heightened sexual experience. From a woman's perspective, though, it seems like it would go from 'wowee' to 'put it away, already' after a couple of orgasms. George would never have thought of such a thing on his own, and so I'm glad that the police jumped to the conclusion on his – and my - behalf.

However, it didn't feel like any damned shining hour. My house had been searched and my privacy invaded. Depending upon George's stupidity, he may have left all manner of incriminating evidence in his office. If he did, of course, it would deflect attention away from the lack of such papers in his home. I didn't think the SEC could resurrect information off those shredded CD-ROMs and, even if they did, who was to say that I did it and not George early that morning?

But I was still feeling lousy. The SEC thing would hang over my head for weeks if not months, making the creation of a new life difficult if not impossible.

It's a real downer when you kill your husband, get away with it, and you can't even gloat.

*****

The next morning's Boston *Globe* – not to mention the *Wall Street Journal* - led with *QUANT FOUR'S COPPER MELTDOWN.*

The whole gruesome story was there. Peter Brandt and his hedge fund buddies had set out to corner the sleepy copper market and drive up its price into the stratosphere. It had worked for a while. Copper soared and the firm's clients made nearly a hundred million dollars while users of copper paid dearly for access to that most basic of utilitarian commodities, all because one firm owned most of the contracts for future delivery and so set their price.

But the invisible hand of Adam Smith does indeed work. Copper sitting in idle inventories began to be meted out, first in a trickle and then, finally in a flood. Quant Four's traders had mopped up the first new supplies and used precious capital to keep pushing up the value of contracts for future deliveries. But there is more to commodities than the futures market. There is also the 'spot' market where traders can go to buy copper for immediate delivery. And on that market, copper was getting downright cheap. There were fewer and fewer takers for Quant Four's pricey futures contracts. When the Chilean government opened up the spigot on its multi-million-ton reserves, the futures market teetered and then collapsed in the space of a few hours.

A resourceful *Journal* reporter with well-honed contacts in the SEC got the rest of the story:

QUANT CAPITAL PRINCIPAL
TIPS SEC TO INSIDER TRADING

The story was less thorough than the one on the firm's collapse, and it omitted crucial names. But the gist of the story was there: in

Quant Four Capital's quest for every-higher returns for its principals and clients, the firm had 'knowingly engaged in insider trading and exchange of information' in multiple industries. The firm had cultivated investment bankers and gained the names of takeover candidates. The firm had also paid analysts for advance copies of research reports and, especially, of ratings changes.

The name of the person who was cooperating with the SEC was not given nor were there any names of tainted firms. Despite the absence of specifics, it was clear that someone with a conscience – or looking for a shot at a suspended sentence – was singing to the feds.

Two sentences in the *Journal* article jumped off the page:

"Search warrants were issued and raids carried out last night at multiple securities firms and analysts' and investment bankers' homes, the SEC official said. One was conducted at the home of a Boston-area research analyst who had died just hours earlier of a heart attack."

It did not take long for the phone to start ringing. Reporters had also read the *Journal* piece and the enterprising ones had started calling hospitals asking for names of heart attack victims. I responded to the first few callers with, 'yes my husband died last night and yes, he is an analyst; but no, I do not wish to say if the SEC carried out a raid on my home.' The Caller ID showed the *Financial Times*, New York *Times* and Washington *Post* all wanting to verify that my husband was a crooked analyst. I unplugged the answering machine and then, eventually, all of the telephones.

I needed to bury George. I also needed a lawyer.

There are several fine old, established funeral homes in Wellesley. I picked one at random and called. I said I wanted a funeral as soon as possible. I presumed George's family had some kind of a plot or a mausoleum up in Ipswich.

Ye gods, I also had to tell George's family. I needed to add that to my list.

And then I froze. *The list.* What in the hell had I done with my list?

I went into our bedroom – my bedroom – found my purse, closed my eyes, and turned my purse upside down on the bed.

Out came my wallet, hairbrush, keys, makeup, pens, appointment book… and my list. It was in my purse when I went to the hospital. It was three feet away from where Detective Tucci questioned me. It was in my lap while the SEC raided my home. I tore the list into tiny pieces and flushed them down the toilet.

I called George's parent's home, got Jill – wife number three – and explained that George had died the previous evening of a heart attack.

Jill wasn't sure whether she should be devastated. On the one hand, no parent or step-parent should ever have to bury a child. On the other hand, George was one of the three evil spawn of wife number two. I left it to her discretion how to handle it with George's father, and asked her to get back to me on my cell phone with burial instructions.

"Why your cell phone?" Jill asked.

"It's complicated," I said.

The funeral home was on hold when I hung up with Jill. They had called Beth Israel Deaconess to arrange to pick up George's body.

"They can't release it until after the autopsy," the funeral director told me in his most sincere voice. "You didn't mention an autopsy in our earlier call."

"Is there usually an autopsy?" I asked.

"Not for a heart attack," the funeral director said.

Boy, did I need an attorney.

* * * * *

How do you find a top-notch criminal attorney when the only thing that has happened so far is that the SEC has asked you to come in and give a statement, and your husband's body is being autopsied?

Isn't hiring a criminal attorney tipping your hand that you're guilty of something?

The yellow pages are of no help. The big ads scream either DIVORCE! or else BEEN IN AN ACCIDENT? WE CAN GET YOU THAT SETTLEMENT!

Fortunately, the Boston *Globe* came through. On the front page of the City/Region section was the headline, *JURY CLEARS WINSTEAD IN WIFE'S MURDER*. 'Winstead' was a Billerica accountant accused of stabbing his wife to death in a jealous rage. The case had been a staple of the evening news for weeks. After reading the first article summarizing the district attorney's case, I had concluded that Winstead was guilty as hell and I had ignored the case thereafter. Now, I ran my finger down the article, looking for the name of the attorney who has successfully planted the seed of reasonable doubt in a jury's mind.

Attorney Lewis Faircloth called Winstead's acquittal a 'victory for common sense'. "The state should never have brought this to trial. It was a case, from the beginning, of a rush to judgment."

Lewis Faircloth was my kind of attorney.

The kind who defended guilty people and got them off.

9.

Getting through to Lewis Faircloth required only instructing his secretary to look at the lead story in the morning's *Globe*. "My husband died of a heart attack last night," I said. "He has been implicated in the Quant Four Capital meltdown. The SEC raided my house last night while his body was still warm and today, someone is autopsying my husband."

"I'll put you through," the woman said.

I briefly explained my predicament to attorney Faircloth.

"Stop," he said.

I stopped speaking.

"You're on a cell phone?"

I said I was.

"Drive to this address, he instructed me. I'll see you when you get here."

* * * * *

"Here" was a classic colonial in Weston and, by 'colonial', I mean a house complete with a wooden plaque on the façade saying 'Harrison House 1735'. It was hard to tell where the old Harrison home ended and its modern extensions began. The house was architecturally seamless on the exterior.

Weston, for those not familiar with Boston, is one of the handful of communities that Wellesley grudgingly recognizes as a peer. In fact, the per capita income of Weston is probably twice that of Wellesley, but it's a case of whether a town is simply filthy rich or is stinking rich.

Phoebe Faircloth greeted me at the door. She was a cheerful, sixty-something woman who looked as though she gardened or played golf regularly. She wasn't a tall woman but she had stature, if that makes any sense. She had an amazing tan that I instantly knew had nothing to do with either tanning lamps or trips to Virgin Gorda. Her face had lines, God bless her. She had never had a botox treatment. Her ensemble made her look like she had been about to leave the house to be part of a foursome at Nashatuck Country Club.

"You got here quickly," she said cheerfully, walking me through the house, done very tastefully in yellows and whites. "Lew can't wait to meet you." I believed her.

We walked down a half flight of stairs into a sunny library, with book shelves lining one wall. Lewis – I guess he was Lew from now on – was reading the *Wall Street Journal*, stretched out on a divan done in English roses. He had on khakis and a white polo shirt. When he stood up, I thought I had stepped into an episode of *Law and Order*. The man could be a stunt double for Fred Thompson, the DA and fleeting presidential candidate. He was in his sixties, avuncular, with jowls and a thin crop of gray hair on his head. He was solid, his face exuded intelligence and his eyes were penetrating.

"Something cold to drink, dear?" Phoebe Faircloth asked. "We have lemonade or sodas."

"Oh, lemonade," I said. This was surreal. There might be a murder charge hanging over my head, but I'd bet the lemonade would be fresh-squeezed.

Lew took my hand in both of his. "I'm terribly sorry to hear of your husband's death," he said, and it sounded quite sincere. The face was Fred Thompson but the accent was pure educated Boston. "Hear" came out 'heah'.

"Thank you," I said.

Phoebe came back in with a tray on which was a pitcher of lemonade and three glasses. She poured. Then she picked up a steno pad and waited. Lew's wife was apparently also the 'secretary' with whom I had spoken half an hour earlier.

"Tell me everything," Lew said.

And so I told him my 'official' version of the story. At various points in the telling, I saw looks pass between Lew and Phoebe. There was an uncanny timing to those looks in that they passed right after I told a lie.

"So you didn't know your husband was seeing this Susan Booth?" Lew asked.

"Maybe I did know," I said, shifting my story. "After he started coming home late, I followed him a few times."

"The status of Miss Booth to be explored at greater length another time," he said.

"And you never suspected that your husband might have been accepting… no, that's not a question I want you to answer."

But he quizzed me repeatedly on the events of the previous evening. He asked for the search warrant that had been served on me and I pulled it out of my purse. He passed it to Phoebe who read it quickly.

"Not a word about anything except files and documents," she said.

He nodded.

I went through the sequence of events from the time the Wellesley policeman showed up at my door until Detective Tucci had hugged me good night and wished me luck.

"I've crossed her in court," he said.

"He means cross-examined her," Phoebe added.

"She is one canny…" Lew looked up at his wife. "Person," he continued.

"Bitch," Phoebe corrected. "She was a bitch in the Willie Loomis trial. Lied on the stand repeatedly trying to save the state's case. The jury didn't believe her, though. They came back in three hours."

"You can bet she's interviewing every one of your friends right now, looking for the dirt," Lew said. "And if she can't find the dirt, she'll start inventing it. So we need to know the real dirt from the invented kind, and we need to know it all. Not today, but soon."

Finally, he said, "Let's talk about money."

"I've got money," I said. "We're well off."

Lew shook his head. "Have you used an ATM this morning? Made a credit card purchase? Those SEC bastards move fast. They're going to squeeze you three ways from Sunday to get your cooperation. They want your husband's money and they don't mind cutting off your electricity to get it."

I nodded.

"Depending on how far this goes, my fee will be somewhere in $300,000 range," he said, looking at me for a reaction. "There will also be out-of-pocket expenses for things like depositions, paralegals, brief preparations, and that will be anywhere from another $50,000 to $100,000. I'm sure you could get cheaper representation, but you're going to need the best. You've got the SEC howling outside the front door and the corrupt Boston PD outside the back. They've made some stupid mistakes because the SEC never figured on a murder investigation, but they'll recover."

"Do I need a separate attorney for the SEC?"

"I'll let you know if you do and, if that's the case, I'll bring in the right person. But we don't need a phalanx of lawyers. Let's cut out the heart of the state's case, which is going to be this: you found out your husband was cheating on you. You also found out he was on the take. You killed him either by spiking his Viagra or some other way. You've hidden the money in hopes the SEC and the IRS can never find it. You're a greedy woman who got even with her husband and got rich in the process."

Which was, of course, exactly the truth.

"What we're going to say is, every bit of the evidence against you is tainted and what isn't tainted is predicated on circumstantial evidence. Whatever money your husband may have stolen disappeared with him, and good luck finding it. We don't have it. We've also got the sob story of all time: government agencies raiding your home just hours after your beloved husband died, and two-faced police detectives pretending to be your friend even while they're planning to indict you for murder."

"You think there will be an indictment?"

"To Sean O'Connell – he's the Suffolk County DA - this is pure heaven," Lew said. "Rich Wellesley lady poisons husband in girlfriend's bed. It's the three M's: murder, mistresses, and money. It will be on the news every night. TruTV is going to televise it. It's a lousy case but he doesn't know it yet. I will try to educate him. If I am successful, my fee will go down substantially. But I wouldn't count on it. If he wins it, it's a big step toward the AG spot, which is what he's dying for."

"Attorney General," Phoebe added. "And one more thing, dear."

What now? I thought.

Phoebe turned on a television set in the corner of the office. She pushed a button on a Tivo-like recorder.

There, on screen, was Patsy's beautiful house on Abbott Road. It was surrounded by TV trucks and cameras which, in turn, were trampling her immaculate flower beds. A reporter soundlessly said something very serious into his microphone. A scene flashed up, apparently from earlier this morning, of Patsy opening the door, shielding her face, and immediately retreating into the house.

"You want to stay as far away from this woman as possible. You should have nothing to do with her under any circumstances."

"That's one case I wouldn't take on a bet," Lew said. "They're going to hang that guy from the tallest church steeple in New England."

I nodded one last time. Being a widow was turning out to be a real bitch.

10.

It took a week, including an eerie fourth of July holiday, to get George's body released and a funeral scheduled. It would have been a fine funeral except for all the television cameras.

By now, everyone had the story – carefully leaked by the Suffolk County DA – that George's 'heart attack' was under investigation and that George had been hours away from being led away in handcuffs by the SEC.

Susie Perkyboobs had turned into a media darling. That she was carrying on an affair with a married man seemed not to matter, particularly to Fox News or the Boston *Herald*. She was this sweet young thing dressed in black, in mourning for the man she loved who had been taken away from her. George had been a wonderful man, caught up in a web of intrigue far beyond his control. Evil hedge fund managers had used him and possibly blackmailed him. She, in turn, was a Victim.

Of course, there was the titillating fact that she and George had been in bed at the time and that George had been doing his studly duty with performance enhancing drugs. People want to get a look at a woman like that, especially if she's well-built and young. Susie became adept at giving interviews in profile so that everyone could ogle those boobs, even partly hidden under black silk.

For me she had nothing but vitriol. I was, on the one hand, the shrew who spent every dime George made so that he was driven to be ensnared by the hedge fund boys. On the other hand, I may have been the evil genius behind the whole scheme. "I find it curious that the common thread in all this is her close friendship with Patsy Brandt," she told reporters, tipping her head to one side, the better to reveal that shiny hair. "I hope the investigators thoroughly explore that link." Spoken like someone conceived and born during the Reagan administration.

The SEC was also doing its part to leak the juicy parts the story, the better to put pressure on me. The Boston *Globe* printed charts showing the amazing good luck that Quant Four Capital had with trades just before George's upgrades or downgrades of companies. The SEC also supplied them with charts for 'Hedge Funds X, Y and Z' showing similar fortunate trades surrounding George's opinion changes. Rather than being called a 'small fish', as Whitburn had tried to portray George when he was making his pitch to keep him on life support, George was now a 'major figure' in their investigation.

And everywhere there was talk of money. Before Peter Brandt stopped cooperating – his partners virtually clubbed him into seeing that he was losing all leverage by continuing to be helpful - he implied that half a dozen analysts were on Quant Four's secret payroll and that George had confided to him that he had similar deals with multiple hedge funds. How much had Quant Four paid out in bribes? "Three or four million," Peter had said. He couldn't be sure, however, because "we were making so much money, the payments were just rounding errors."

George's father attended the funeral – after a fashion. He, wife-number-three Jill, son Carl and his wife Laura circled the church in a Town Car until everyone was inside and the media had stowed their cameras. Then, just as the service was beginning, they slipped in the door and took a seat in the back pew. While everyone else took communion, they made a stealth exit through the rector's office.

Jill made a statement that George's father was 'too distraught' to face reporters. It was a better explanation than saying that George had disgraced the family name by going out in such a spectacular fashion just as he had disgraced the family tree by being born in the first place.

George's mother – wife number two – never appeared. Decency ought to have required that someone reach out to her and let her know one of her children had died. I had offered to make the contact but didn't know where to start. I asked Paul if he knew how to contact his mother. He was silent for several long moments before saying he 'would do his best to make certain she knew about the funeral.'

Paul and George's two sisters did come and sat with me in that front pew. Paul sat by my side, holding my hand throughout the service. If Paul suspected that his pharmaceutical room was the source of the Ritvin that had turbocharged George's Viagra, he never let on anything to me. Paul also spoke to the reporters outside the little church in Ipswich where the funeral was held. He said George was a decent man who, like us all, had failings.

"Judge a man as you would be judged," Paul said in his eulogy. "Dwell on the kindnesses and the acts of decency. George was my brother and my friend, and I can find no fault in the way he treated me throughout my life."

Pretty good stuff, I thought.

"He was a good husband and a good provider, and he was a good son," Paul said.

Well, two out of three ain't bad, I thought.

"Today, there are clouds over his last days, but I believe the passage of time will show us the true George," Paul concluded.

Uh huh, I thought. A white-collar criminal of the highest order with a meritorious citation for adultery.

Susie Perkyboobs was at the church. I couldn't very well keep her out and I wasn't going to get into some kind of a cat fight with the cameras capturing the hair pulling and fingernail scratching. While I sat in the front pew with the family – well, the family except the *pater familias* and his contingent – Suzy was shown a seat somewhere in the wings, where she cried inconsolably through the service to everyone's annoyance.

It was a high Episcopalian funeral, not that George or I had set foot in a church since we were married. The young rector had never met George and had been hesitant to officiate over the mass of someone who had not been part of the congregation in two decades. His qualms were allayed, however, right after Paul wrote a check that made up the shortfall in the church's roofing fund.

I took the communion only because everyone would notice if I didn't. I'm not big on the heaven and hell thing. If I were, I would have settled for a divorce. But I took the wafer and the wine and told myself that someone out there was capturing the moment with a digital camera, and a headline of 'Widow Finds Solace in Faith' looks a lot better than 'Murderess Unrepentant'.

* * * * *

George was buried at noon in the corner of the farm that had held the remains of his family since before the Revolutionary War. Brother Carl probably fumed that it was one more impediment to the subdivision process. He had probably planned on moving the family plot lock, stock and barrel to a site without a view. A fresh grave would give the town selectmen pause.

At 2:30 p.m., and with me still in my funeral clothes including a somber black veil, Lew and I drove into Boston to the SEC's offices for my 'preliminary statement'. There were television cameras there, too, and I cut a sympathetic figure on the six o'clock news, the attractive widow lady being hauled in to be questioned about her late husband's crimes on the day of his funeral.

Lew has, of course, already made certain that his media buddies had the story of the midnight raid on my home, and how I had kissed my hubby goodbye only hours earlier. The Feds' *faux pas*, coupled with having just buried my husband, gave me the high moral ground in the proceedings.

We were in a small, plain, windowless conference room. In one corner, a woman with a transcription keyboard sat at the ready. An SEC lawyer I had not previously seen - a thirty-ish thin-faced woman with horn-rimmed glasses and mousy brown roots at the base of her styleless red hair – sat at the table opposite a chair which I suppose was mine to occupy.

In a corner, trying to look inconspicuous, was Jason Whitburn, the asshole who had wanted to keep George on life support and then wrecked my house looking for evidence a few hours later. This was my first real chance to look at him in something approaching natural conditions, and I didn't like what I saw. He had beady eyes, and pointed teeth, as though someone had, as a practical joke, given him a mouth full of canines where there ought to be molars. The word *weasel* kept going through my mind. It wasn't helped by his off-the-discount-rack suit with its bad collar roll and too-tight sleeves. Who knew the government paid its lawyers so poorly?

"I'm here unofficially," Whitburn said by way of introduction. "Just an observer."

I stated my name and address for the record, and the lady lawyer launched into her questions.

"We were told this was an opportunity to provide a statement," Lew objected as soon as the first question was out of the SEC's attorney's mouth.

"Change of plans," Whitburn said and shrugged. Some 'observer'. He was doing a thing with a rubber band in his hands, idly pulling it and making circles but doing them just in my visual range. "We found some interesting stuff in our search of your client's premises. We thought it might be nice to cut to the chase and save the taxpayers some money."

"My client will decline to answer any question for which she does not feel she had been fully prepared," Lew said. I think he was saying that I would keep my mouth shut unless he said it was OK to speak.

The lawyer with the mousy roots asked her first question. "Do you own a Gateway desktop computer…" She went on to provide a model and serial number.

"I owned a Gateway computer until you took it away," I said. "I have no idea of the model or serial number."

"Did your husband ever use a Dell notebook computer belonging to Peavy, Jensen and Beck in your home?" she asked.

"He brought home his laptop from work every night," I said. "It was black, but I don't know if it was a Dell."

"Do you or did your husband own any other computers?"

I scrunched my nose and appeared to think for a second. "There may be another one in the basement," I said. "It's pretty old and we tried to donate it to a school but they wouldn't take it."

The lawyer didn't feel my answer merited a follow-up question. "Do you have Comcast internet service?" she asked.

"Yes."

Whitburn, who had been fidgeting in the corner, finally stepped up to the table, pulling a chair after him. He sat down and faced me.

"Are you aware that each computer on an internet service has a distinctive IP address?" he said, glaring at me.

"I have no idea what an 'IP address' is," I said, "so I guess the answer is 'no'."

"Every computer has a signature that the network recognizes called an internet protocol address," he said, moving in for the kill. He sat down next to me and put his face about three inches from mine. "According to Comcast, your home had three IP addresses. Where's the third computer?"

"Stop!" Lew said. "Client conference." He motioned to the transcription person who had been taking down every word of the exchange. "Time out."

The transcriptionist's fingers went from her machine to her lap.

"Kat, you are not obliged to answer any of these questions and it's clear to me that they're on a fishing expedition. We can give our statement and walk out of here."

"I don't know anything about another computer," I said. "Unless they found one in the house during their search."

Lew turned to Whitburn. "Did you find another computer?"

"I don't have to tell you that," he said.

"You'll have to tell me in discovery," Lew shot back. "If you want her answer on the record, you'll answer my question – on the record – now."

Whitburn looked annoyed. "No, we didn't find another computer. But we found bits of plastic in the garbage that are consistent with a computer."

Lew nodded at the typist. "Put that on the record – and everything else unless one of us says otherwise." To Whitburn he said, "Bits of plastic?"

"Like someone smashed a computer to smithereens, carried off the major pieces of the computer, and then swept up the debris and put it in with the kitchen garbage," Whitburn said.

"And your office had surveillance on my client for – what? – four days before her husband's death? And you swooped down on her home while she was still saying goodbye to her husband, certainly before she ever could have known you were going to execute a search warrant. During those four days, did she ever carry a computer or pieces of a computer out of her home?" Lew was at his courtroom best and the transcription lady's fingers were flying.

"We suspect your client knew she was under surveillance and took measures to…" Whitburn caught himself. "This is ridiculous. If your client wants to go on the record as saying she knows of no third computer, then let her do so. And when we find that computer or any evidence that she used it, we're going to use her statement to hang her."

"You'll just have to produce the evidence in discovery," Lew shrugged. "Why don't you ask us after you've found something?"

Whitburn's irritation showed. He glared at me, then turned to the typist. "Off the record until I say otherwise." He then turned his full, nasty gaze on me. "We have resources you can't imagine. We can look at every stock trade in every brokerage account in the country," he said.

"We can look at every bank deposit. And what we know is this: your husband took bribes. And if he took bribes, then I'll also bet he did other stupid stuff like trade on inside information from Peavy. Our computers are going through every one of those transactions right now and we're going to flag everything that looks even remotely suspicious."

He shifted his weasel face with its sharp, pointed teeth back to be within a few inches of mine. "And here's what else we know: when we find those accounts, we're going to see your fingerprints on them, too. Because you're a smart woman and your husband was dumb. There's no way you didn't know he was cheating on you. There's no way you didn't know he was breaking the law. He probably didn't tell you, but you're smart and you figured it out. And do you want to know how I know?"

He didn't wait for an answer. He took a small recorder out of his shirt pocket and pushed a button. From the tinny speakers came a conversation:

"Patsy, listen carefully: you don't know anything. Peter never told you anything. You never suspected anything."

"The innocent spouse rule?" Then there was a moment's silence. *"Six billion dollars. Peter and his buddies lost six billion dollars in about four hours. And they've been doing illegal stuff for years, most of which made billions. When you lose that much that quickly, nobody's innocent."*

"Does Peter have a computer at home?"

"You mean, like the ones I'm not supposed to know about?"

"Would it help Peter or hurt him if they disappeared?"

"I don't know."

"Pretty soon, people are going to come here with a search warrant. Before they get here, you need to know whether you're helping Peter or hurting him by people finding those computers and what's on them."

Whitburn snapped off the recording.

"Like I said, you're a smart lady," he smiled. "You can tell us about the accounts and help us find the money, and maybe we can work a deal. But if you wait until we find your husband's computer and then we find that you handled the funds or moved them…" He let the thought linger in the air for a moment. "We can't go after your husband. But we can go after you with everything we've got. And it isn't going to be a pretty sight."

11.

"I guess that didn't go very well," I said as we left the SEC's offices.

Lew waited until we were on the street to answer. "Oh, you'd be surprised. An inexperienced litigator – or a zealot on a crusade – always gives away too much. Mr. Whitburn is both, and he just previewed his case such as it is."

We went into a Starbucks, largely deserted on a hot late afternoon. "Right now, those guys at the SEC have squat. Excuse me… they know your husband had another computer that he used for trades. Well, duh. Of course he had another computer. But they can't find it and if all they have are 'bits of plastic that are consistent with a computer', they've still got nothing. Because bits of plastic could have been put in the garbage by your husband."

"What about the recording?" I asked.

"They presumably had your friend Patsy under full surveillance, including directional mikes, plus probably bugs in the house. That conversation sounded like it was outside."

"We were in her garden," I said.

Lew pulled a sleek phone out of his shirt pocket. "Wonderful things, these. And a lot cheaper than one of those stenographers."

He played back the recording from the garden.

"There was more," I said. "She asked me if I knew George was taking money from her husband's firm, and I said not only that I didn't know, but that I didn't think George would do anything like that."

Lew nodded. "A bit of evidence that will conveniently disappear. The government does not always play by its own rules. But listen to what was said:

"Patsy, listen carefully: you don't know anything. Peter never told you anything. You never suspected anything."

Lew turned off the recorder. "I'm going to make an educated guess that, somewhere else in that conversation, Patsy told you she had figured out what was going on rather than that her husband had provided her some running description of events as they unfolded."

I nodded. "She said specifically that she had figured it out. She didn't say when."

"And so what you are doing is distilling the essence of the truth: 'Peter never told you anything. You don't know anything for certain.'"

I had to admit that, put that way, it was a summary, not advice from a co-conspirator. He turned back on the recorder.

"The innocent spouse rule?"

He turned off the recorder again. "She brought that up. Not you. She had been doing her homework. You weren't doing it for her. The recorder resumed playing.

"Six billion dollars. Peter and his buddies lost six billion dollars in about four hours. And they've been doing illegal stuff for years, most of which made billions. When you lose that much that quickly, nobody's innocent."

Again, the recorder was turned off. "That's your friend's pronouncement, and you're not responsible for the words that come out of her mouth," Lew said. Then, Patsy's and my voice were heard one last time.

"Does Peter have a computer at home?"

"You mean, like the ones I'm not supposed to know about?"

"Would it help Peter or hurt him if they disappeared?"

"I don't know."

"Pretty soon, people are going to come here with a search warrant. Before they get here, you need to know whether you're helping Peter or hurting him by people finding those computers and what's on them."

"This is both your finest hour and your one crumb for the prosecution," Lew said, putting the recorder back into his pocket. "You bring up the subject of a computer. Clearly, it was on your mind. Whitburn, or whoever tries this thing, is going to hammer you on that.

'Ladies and gentlemen of the jury, this woman had to know about her husband's secret computer because she asked her friend if *her* husband had one in the house.'"

I flinched. Yes, right in one.

"But listen to what you say next: 'would it help or hurt if they disappeared?' And, 'you need to know whether you're helping or hurting him by people finding those computers.'" Lew grinned. "Kat, you took the moral high ground. If you had said, 'my advice is to go destroy those computers,' we'd be talking settlement right now. But you said, in effect, 'there's a right choice and a wrong choice, and you need to decide which path you're going to walk down.' If I were Witburn, I'd lose that part of the recording, too, except that it's on the record." He tapped his pocket, "Because it's in here."

"If this is the best stuff they've got – and Whitburn would have shown you his most damning evidence in order to scare you into cooperating – they're nowhere right now. Unless they find your husband's computer or trace his trades – which isn't as easy as he makes it sound – they're going to have to fold their hand."

And then his tone turned serious. "We need to talk about my role in all this, Kat." He folded his hands together and looked somber. "On the one hand, I'm your lawyer and my role is to get you a fair trial if it comes to that. I'm going to offer you the best legal advice I can and see to it that nobody violates your rights in the process."

"On the other hand, I'm an officer of the court. If I find that my client has done something illegal, I have the obligation to report it to the court and I take that responsibility seriously. I'm not required to and I would not report suspicions or innuendo. As a result, there are conversations we will never have and there is advice I will never give. But I will say this: my ability to defend you is a direct result of how candid you are with me. If I get blindsided, you're the one who gets hurt. Do we understand one another?"

I said we did.

*****

They weren't going to find the computer. That much was for certain. During the past week I had either a police or an SEC person tailing me at all times, and often it was both. I assumed I was recorded and photographed and that my calls were monitored.

I had left the house only a few times but I had made them count. I went to Bloomingdale's to buy a black dress for the funeral. When I went to the ladies room, a few pieces of the computer went in with me and did not come back out. Nancy invited me out to lunch and more of the computer stayed behind. In a week's time, the waste bins in eight or nine ladies rooms each gained a handful of components. The hard drive, or at least what I assume was the hard drive, went in three separate pieces. Let the dippy Goth lady on *NCIS* try to put that one back together.

To their credit, my friends rallied around me. Stacks of platters from various food stores piled up in the refrigerator – my friends were not into baking. My parents flew in from Minnesota to console me. Fortunately, they flew back out after the funeral before they drove me crazy and I had to ask them to leave.

There was one giant 'to-do' item left unchecked on my now-mental list. George's accounts had been drained of their assets. If and when the SEC found them, unfortunately, they would lead to 'Benito Morales's' accounts, now flush with uninvested cash. The action item was to move the money in those accounts safely offshore, out of the reach of the IRS or the SEC. I never imagined it would be as easy as hopping a flight to the Cayman Islands and opening a numbered account, but while I was under observation, I could do nothing. I no longer even had a computer in my house.

*****

The SEC had originally been interested in my love life as a means of coercing me to help them put George away. When he died, they shifted their attention away from sex and toward computers and bank accounts.

Now, it was the Boston PD and the Suffolk DA's office that was hot on the trail of anyone I had slept with since prom night. They were running a very thorough murder investigation, even though George had dropped dead of a heart attack.

I spent a few hours each day with Lew's wife, Phoebe. Unlike Lew, she was not an officer of the court so there was no conflict of interest. Her responsibility was to elicit the warts in my life story. "Don't worry, sweetie, it's like Las Vegas. It all stays here," she said. "And you wouldn't believe what stays here. Believe me, it's all been told."

I started with the story of Edward DeVries and the weekend in Watch Hill. She was sympathetic. "You've found out your husband was cheating on you right from the start," Phoebe said. "You're beginning to think you married the wrong man and the right one is sitting across from you at a meeting. I would certainly have been tempted, too. It's too bad you didn't meet him first."

There were other things to tell. You may recall that a few pages into this narrative I said, for several years after the market tanked in 2001, we all laid low and I played housewife.

Well, that's not exactly true. As George's on-the-road affairs began to add up, I had a few boyfriends of my own along the way. They weren't serious and I never thought about leaving George. But I felt angry, betrayed and increasingly bitter. Besides, George was gone all day and I was stuck with nothing to do but housework. With just the two of us and no pets, the house pretty well kept itself clean. And George didn't give a damn what he had for dinner so long as it was on the table, with a drink, at 7 p.m.

One of my boyfriends was George's boss, the one who had listened to that first pitch about the football players' restaurant that got George's career jump-started. He, too, lived in Wellesley Hills and, in the afternoon, would frequently take an earlier train home on some pretext or another. Instead of heading south to his home on Livermore Street, he would head north to come see me. Bill and I had a three-year-long interlude of extramarital bump-and-tickle that ended only when he jumped from PJ&B to another investment banking firm with a stricter code of ethical conduct. Bill was good for my soul. He was tender and never took me for granted. He brought me wonderful gifts, something George never did.

"Didn't the neighbors notice the strange car in the driveway?" Phoebe asked.

"I didn't ask them about the strange cars in their driveways," I said. "At least I never asked in the UPS man for a quickie like my next-door neighbor."

But I did jump the guy who installed my new dishwasher. He was incredibly cute and, to be fair, he made the first move. He came back several times to make certain the system was functioning properly. Some of the repairs took an hour or more.

And there was Cliff, a guy in my book circle. Cliff was a professor at BC who made time on Thursday afternoons to earnestly read and discuss contemporary fiction, the lone man among a group of twenty Wellesley housewives. Cliff was fifty and divorced, sharing custody of two kids. Over the course of two years, he slept his way through the circle. I think I was second.

It was languid, casual sex; easygoing and guilt-free. Boston College would have bounced him for succumbing to any of the dozens of co-eds who threw themselves at him in any given semester. There was nothing in the BC ethics pamphlet, however, about dallying with bored, upper-middle-class housewives. I still get a big smile on my face anytime Margaret Atwood comes out with a new book.

To each one of these admissions, Phoebe made a "hmmm, hmmm" sound, asked for names and dates to the extent I remembered, and put yellow stickies on certain pages of her notebook.

"You think I'm a slut," I said after describing my liaisons with

Cliff, the professor from the book club.

"I think you're a woman with a healthy sexual appetite and an unfaithful, uncaring, and dull husband," she said. "I don't think Sean O'Connell's office is going to find out about the Maytag repairman unless he comes forward for the publicity, but this BC guy sounds like he gets around, and we'll hear about that one."

Translation: I was a slut and was going to be portrayed as one for Channel 4 news.

"Now, Kat, is there anyone in your life right now?" She smiled and picked up her pad.

"Real or fictional?" I asked.

"You'd better explain," she said.

So I told her about my make-believe affair with George's co-worker that I had concocted to explain away to Trish my days and nights of stalking George and his serial string of twenty-six-year-old mistresses.

"I predict some uncomfortable depositions for Phil," Phoebe said. "Unless you told your friends about any of your other liaisons, he's the one they're going to want to put on the stand because he's current and gives you motive."

"They're going to be sorely disappointed," I said.

"So are there any actual boyfriends in, say, the last year?"

There were two answers to that question. The honest one was that on a 'girls weekend' in New York with Trish almost exactly a year earlier, we had allowed ourselves to get picked up in our hotel's bar by a pair of French businessmen. Trish had gone back to the one's guy's room, I to the other's. I was back in our suite in a few hours, Trish didn't turn up until dawn. I know the guy's name was Jean Claude, that he was from Paris, and that one night in July he had a room on the 37th floor of the Palace. Other than that, it was two ships passing in the night and not even Trish could swear that anything had transpired.

"To be on the safe side, I told her about Jean Claude. "But other than that, I've been loyal and true."

She looked at my face as I spoke.

"You remember anything, you let me know immediately," Phoebe said. "I don't want to see some name on a witness list that makes Lew's job harder."

* * * * *

I also spent time with Lew. I had yet to be formally interviewed by the Boston PD. That would wait until they had assembled enough information to make the session worthwhile. In other words, they'd wait until they had enough on me to catch me in a lie.

Lew, though, had excellent sources inside both the police department and the Suffolk DA's office. He received regular updates from his sources on their progress in making me a murderess.

"Means, motive and opportunity," Lew drilled into me. "As far as they're concerned, they've got the motive part nailed: revenge for eight years of adultery and your chance to get your hands on millions of dollars of George's ill-gotten gains."

Which pretty well summed it up, I thought.

"They're thinnest on means," Lew said. "They've got to put Ritvin in your hand that morning and that's not easy. Your computer shows you never researched the drug. You certainly never attempted to get a prescription for it and they can find no evidence you tried to buy it illegally. The SEC warrant made no reference to murder weapons or drugs so anything that was seized would have been tainted fruit. But the SEC came away with nothing. No Ritvin residue on any surface in the house or in the garbage, so there's nothing to argue that something should be allowed under inevitable discovery."

I love that dishwasher, I thought. And the dishwasher repair guy wasn't bad either.

"They're also thin on opportunity," Lew said. "The autopsy showed that the Ritvin was ingested sometime before noon, the Viagra about 5 p.m. Your husband had a stash of Viagra in his office, plus some other bad-boy items like cocaine. You may also want to know that they found a sizable wad of money: nearly ten thousand dollars. You obviously didn't hand him the Viagra tablet so, to prove murder, they've got to show two things: first, that it was you who got him to take Ritvin in the morning and, second, that you knew he would take Viagra later on in the day. That's going to be a stretch unless they come up with evidence that you knew that George was going to an assignation instead of a baseball game."

"What they're going to stress – or at least what I would stress if I were on the other side – is that only half of the Super Viagra cocktail was in his office. There was residue of Viagra, cocaine and a couple of other barbiturates in his office and in his briefcase. But not a hint of the Ritvin. Where did your husband get it, and how did he come to ingest it before noon? It's the first piece of a circumstantial case and it won't hold up on its own, but it's one of the things that keeps the DA's office going."

* * * * *

A few days after the funeral and the first talk with the SEC, Lew interrupted my regular session with Phoebe. He had a 'slightly miffed' look on his face that told me he was seething inside.

"The SEC has inventoried the contents of your computer and shared it with the Suffolk DA," Lew said. "You were one busy lady."

What had I missed? I thought. *Did I forget to erase something?*

He didn't wait for me to defend myself. Instead, he read from a list. "One hundred eighty three photos of your husband and his various mistresses going back seven months. Extensive notes on your husband's activities on seventy-four different dates. And six different downloads of emails and files from the computer Susan Booth kept in her apartment."

Oh… my… god… I thought. *They really can resurrect that stuff from a computer's hard drive.*

Phoebe said, "This is not good."

Lew stared at me. "Start at the beginning."

I swallowed hard.

"Your notes and your photos show you were following your husband as early as last December," Lew said. "Start then." He folded his arms, waiting.

"George started coming home late," I said. "He never did that before. He said he was checking out a restaurant chain that he was thinking about picking up coverage on. One afternoon, I waited outside his office and I followed him. He met this girl..."

Lew consulted his list. "Jenny Fassert," he said.

"Jenny Fassert," I repeated. "Twenty-six, brunette, with big blue eyes and a cute little turned-up nose. What kind of a woman still goes by 'Jenny' after the age of fifteen? She was a graduate student at Berklee, playing the cello and working part time at a Starbucks. George took her to L'Espalier for an early dinner and, believe me, his attention was not on the restaurant. They held hands across the table. She was obviously smitten. George's wedding ring had mysteriously disappeared. After a few weeks of dinners at romantic restaurants, they graduated to her apartment. He'd go up by seven and be down by ten."

"If you were trying to prove he was cheating on you, it sounds like you had all the evidence you needed," Lew said.

I nodded. "I had two dozen photos. I was going to spread them out in front of George and say, 'cut it out.' But I didn't."

"Why not?" Lew asked.

I look at him, and then at Phoebe. "I wasn't sure I wanted to stay married to him. He was boring. He was getting fat. I was on the verge of confronting him when he dumped Jenny. Just like that: took her out for coffee after work and told her it was over. She cried. She really cried over losing him. I have pictures."

"So, I thought, either he's figured out I've been following him, or else he's decided he's strayed long enough and it's time to come home.

But it's neither: two nights later, he's having dinner with another twenty-six-year-old brunette. This one wears her hair exactly like I did when George and I first met."

Another look at his list. "Megan Davis," Lew said.

"Megan," I said. "One of those phony ancestral names parents started giving their kids in the 1980s. She was only a sales girl at Macy's but boy, did she dream big. Meantime, I'm trying to figure out what happened to Jenny, and I find out that George dumped her just before her twenty-seventh birthday. Either he's really cheap and doesn't want to give her a nice present, or else he has this hang-up about twenty-six-year-olds. Which, by the way, was my age when George and I met."

"So, I start following George and Megan, only this time I did my research and found out she was three months away from turning twenty-seven. I figured George recruited his mistresses during his lunch hour and kept them warm until the current model was finished."

"How did you know their birthdays?" Phoebe asked.

"Personal web pages," I said. "These kids have no secrets. Facebook, MySpace, they're loaded with information. So I kept tabs on George, building that perfect divorce case. Sure enough, after a few weeks of footsies at restaurants, Megan takes George up to her place and the lights go out. Except that George must really have liked this one, because all of a sudden, he had to go 'out of town' once a week. 'Out of town' meant he started taking Megan to hotels. Very nice hotels."

"Which started me thinking… how is he paying for all this? It wasn't showing up on our American Express or MasterCard bills. I started trying to figure out where the money was coming from, which is why I didn't confront him."

"He dumped Megan right on schedule and had Susie Perkyboobs on his arm within two days…"

"Who is Susie Perky…" Phoebe asked.

"I'm sorry," I said. "Susan Perkins Booth. Susie Perkyboobs was my nickname for her. She was the cutest yet and, of course, twenty-six years old. At least she had a real first name. She was also a brunette and sparkling blue eyes. Except for the eye color, it was like looking at myself ten years ago. I figured out half-way through Megan that George was re-enacting his courtship of me. There were too many coincidences about appearance and age. But George was 'correcting' some things this time around. For example, he never spent the night in her apartment. He'd always be on one of the late trains home. If he stayed overnight with one of them, it was in a hotel. I figured he was establishing his dominance in the relationship."

"What gave you the idea of following him?" Lew asked.

The honest answer was that I was following George just as I had followed my father. Starting at the age of twelve when it became obvious that 'daddy's poker night' was about women who were not my mother, I had this compelling urge to know who he was with. I started acting on it when I was fifteen, telling my mother I was going to the library but instead going to my father's girlfriend's apartment. There, I would wait outside, knowing full well what was going on inside.

When I was seventeen I graduated to breaking and entering. Daddy's previous secretary had 'quit' and he had recently hired a new one. Gretchen was in her early thirties and not especially attractive. But she had big boobs which she showed to excellent effect with a closet full of Diane Von Furstenberg knock-off wrap dresses. Her blonde hair was courtesy of Clairol and she owned enough Maybelline products to make her slightly scary. She relied on Ortho-Novum for birth control.

When I started these after-school visits, I had thought I might leave a calling card – 'leave my father alone or else', or maybe even a simple 'whore' written in lipstick on her bathroom mirror. But I didn't. My father wasn't going to stop with Gretchen any more than he had stopped when her predecessors departed. He was the problem, not these women.

Knowledge became power. I knew more about Gretchen than my father did because I took the time to analyze her through her closet, dresser and bathroom. Knowing what I did added to my contempt for my father.

All that flashed through my mind when Lew asked the question. What I answered was as simple, "I needed to know."

"How long were you going to let this go on?" Lew asked.

Until I killed him, I thought. *Wrong answer.*

"I don't know," I said, which was also the truth. "I got caught up in it."

"To the point of breaking into Miss Booth's apartment," Lew said.

"I didn't technically break in," I said. "I used George's key. She gave him one. I copied it."

"It's still illegal trespass," Lew said. "So, you were obsessed by your husband's serial infidelities. Why did you download her emails?"

"To be honest, I was curious," I said. "I wanted to know what she said about George and who she told. As it turns out, she told everyone. Friends from coast to coast knew she was having an affair with this big-shot securities analyst with a wife in Wellesley who 'didn't understand him'. She was fairly graphic about describing what they did in bed. That last week, she also told her pen pals George was thinking about a divorce."

Lew nodded. Phoebe made notes. "We have one hurdle to get over," Lew said. "It's a big hurdle. We're going to have to explain why, some time before your husband died, you deleted all those photos and files. While they can't assign a time and date to when you deleted them, they can narrow the window by looking at the last entries. You had emails written by Miss Booth just eleven days before he died and photos of them going into a hotel dated ten days before his death. Sometime between ten days before your husband's death and the day he died, you deliberately erased all that information from your computer. That's powerful circumstantial evidence. 'Circumstantial' is the key, but also powerful."

Note that Lew did not ask me why I deleted the files or when I deleted them. A good lawyer doesn't want his client to lie to him, and he doesn't want to hear words that put him in conflict with that 'officer of the court' business.

"I had decided to have a baby," I said.

Lew did a double-take. "Come again?"

"I had decided to save our marriage by having a baby. I figured it was the one thing that would bring George home."

The lies I tell with a straight face. But it was the same dumb lie I had told Nancy, and it seemed to work with her. And, to buttress my story against the day anyone investigated George's death, I had evidence. Or at least sort-of evidence. I had five books on babies: baby names, conceiving after thirty, stages of pregnancy. I had never cracked the spines much less read them, although I made a mental note to myself to start underlining in them when I got home. But they were in the house and I had carefully saved the dated sales receipts from Wellesley Booksmith. I also had an alibi witness: Nancy.

Eight years earlier, of course, a baby was exactly what I craved. Two of them, in fact. Now, a screaming, diarrhea-producing infant was the last thing I wanted. Of course, having had one of the worst childhoods in modern recorded history, George hated them. And I was left cold by those friends who exulted in motherhood. Children cramped your style. Children were expensive. Children made Caneel Bay a place you might go when they were grown – if you could still afford it – instead of the resort you booked for Christmas.

Also in my favor was the fact that I had gone off the pill six months earlier. George was busy shagging his way through Generation Y and, once I had decided on divorce – and, later, murder – I figured I had better not give him any grounds for a counter complaint. I was also reading things in the newspapers that questioned the long-term impact of the pill. Since I wasn't getting any, I stopped. So, it was his word against mine about the decision to have a perfect baby, and he was in no position to contradict me.

"A baby," Lew repeated, testing out the hypothesis. It was clear he liked the idea.

"Did you tell anyone?" he ventured cautiously.

"I confided in my friend, Nancy," I said.

"A baby," he said again. "A baby is very good. We can work with a baby. You had a neurotic compulsion with regard to your husband's infidelities and so you documented them thoroughly. But you wanted to save the marriage by having a baby."

I wasn't wild about the 'neurotic compulsion' bit, but at least we had gotten over that 'hurdle' Lew had thrown up.

"I like that very much," he said. And this time, he was smiling.

12.

A day later, Lew told me the Boston PD were ready to interview me and asked me to come in at 3 p.m. 'to talk'.

"This is what sets the tone for everything else that comes," Lew said as we drove in. "They've interviewed everyone and they've settled on their theory of what happened. I've got some intelligence but it's far from complete."

"Why won't they just accept that George took two drugs he shouldn't have?" I asked.

Lew laughed. "Because you're the perfect defendant. Rich suburban lady gets revenge on her cheating, thieving husband. Tries to get away with murder. It's the case that will put Sean O'Connell in the Attorney General's chair."

I must have given Lew a blank stare.

"Kat, ninety-nine percent of the crimes committed in the world are done by morons," he explained. "A man shoots his live-in girlfriend and tells the police an intruder did it. The police find the gun in the washing machine with his prints on it. Why did the guy put the murder weapon there? Because it was the last place *he* would ever think to look. Another guy robs a liquor store, shoots the cashier, and grabs a couple of bottles of Remy Martin on the way out. He gets to his car and opens one of the bottles to celebrate. The police arrive ten minutes later and the guy is still in his car, getting snockered."

"Criminals are stupid, Kat. *CSI* isn't real. *Law and Order* isn't real or they skim that one case in a hundred in which the criminal actually thought ahead. Police work is mostly a matter of sweeping up after the mistakes of the flotsam and jetsam of society, and it's boring as hell for them. Most cases end in pleas and the vast majority of those that don't are slam-dunks where the evidence is overwhelming but the defendant insists on his right to a trial for whatever misguided reason."

"Sean O'Connell has been waiting for a case like this for a year," Lew said. "For him, this case is about headlines and television footage. Sean will try this thing himself…"

I interrupted him. "How about guilt and innocence? Shouldn't we be trying to stop this before charges are filed?" I sounded awfully self-righteous for someone who had murdered her husband.

"Kat, you don't understand," Lew said. "Short of eyewitness testimony from someone – and preferably a pharmacology expert - who observed George washing down a couple of Ritvin with a beer at lunch, you're going to be indicted and this is going to trial. Sean O'Connell is the champion of the little guy. You are the stand-in for all the 'haves'. If he can take you down, he can trumpet that victory for the next year and walk away with the Democratic Party nomination."

"What do we do?" I asked.

"Make him look foolish," Lew said. "Tie him up in knots. Get an acquittal on the same afternoon the jury starts deliberating."

The way Lew said that started me wondering if I was just some pawn in a larger game. I asked him the question in just that language.

Lew didn't answer at first. He nodded, as though thinking over what he had said.

"Sean O'Connell is what's wrong with the law," Lew said after a minute. "He tries cases based on the volume of headlines they'll create and the number of minutes he'll be on the news. I'll bet his staff has already approached TruTV about coverage. If I can get you acquitted and take down a prima donna like him at the same time, I consider it a public service."

It wasn't exactly the answer I had been hoping for, but I did like that he had passion.

*****

The interview was held at the Boston PD's headquarters, a fairly new glass building on Tremont Street over by Northeastern University. Of course, there were reporters and television cameras awaiting my arrival. I was still dressed in black. I did not hide my face nor did I acknowledge the dozens of questions thrown at me by reporters. Lew took my arm and we walked into the entrance. There would be no sound bites from The Suspect.

The tone of the questions from reporters, though, was unnerving. I assumed they were all set up by the police and the DA's office. The 'simple' ones just wanted to know if I knew my husband was cheating on me or if I was aware that George was taking payoffs from Quant Four. The more piercing questions asked if I expected to be indicted as a co-conspirator with George by a federal grand jury, or why I had broken into Susan Booth's apartment. One question almost made me turn around and confront the reporter that asked it. "Are you aware Susan Booth claims your husband told her you were going to kill him?"

Detective Tucci met us at the door.

"Sorry for the reporters," she said, shaking her head. "It must be a really slow news day."

Neither Lew nor I bothered to question the absurdity of the statement and ask who had tipped off the media.

"I hope this doesn't take too long," she said, still being Miss Friendly. "We've got a couple of things to cover." Translation:' this could take all night.'

The interview room was a windowless space perhaps ten feet on a side. One wall was a mirror, presumably one-way glass. I could only guess who was behind the glass.

One other person was in the room when we entered. He was somewhere in his mid-thirties with short, brown curly hair, thick eyebrows and green eyes. He was lean and dressed in a well-tailored suit and a Hermes tie that would have done credit to Wall Street. His face was nearly rectangular with a strong chin. He was gorgeous.

"This is my partner, Detective Roy Halliday," Tucci said offhandedly.

He smiled and grasped my hand. It was warm, his grip was firm.

"Ma'am," he said. "I'm very sorry for your loss." His voice was soft and low, like a late night dee-jay on a jazz station.

Now, at this point you're telling yourself, 'Oh, my god, that stupid woman is going to fall for a cop. The cop is going to use his good looks to get the truth out of her, and she's going to jail for the rest of her life.'

No. I'm not stupid.

But when Detective Roy Halliday took my hand in his and smiled, it dawned on me that, for the first time in a decade, I was a single, unattached woman.

On advice of counsel I still wore my wedding ring. I wore black in public. But I was single. I was available. I could jump into bed with anyone, any time and there were no marital considerations. No need to hide what I was doing and certainly no sneaking around.

I had never put guilt-free sex into the mix as a reason to kill my husband. Maybe it was because my other reasons were so strong or maybe it was because my extramarital sexual encounters had been free of guilt anyway. In a sense, George had been the perfect beard; any fling I had was of necessity clandestine and ultimately doomed, and so therefore 'not serious'. I was protected by my wedding ring.

Nor was there somebody standing behind 'Door Number Two' – a fact that was probably exasperating to the two detectives now in front of me. George's death had left me free to remarry, but I had no one in mind with whom to share the rest of my life. Cliff from the book circle? It was fun, but I did not envision myself as a faculty wife and stepmother. Joey the repair guy? Get serious. Even Edward DeVries, that long-ago first adulterous *pas de deux*, was more of a hazy memory, and Phoebe's background check showed he had married, moved to Chicago, and was now the father of three. And to think that could have been me.

My reverie meant I held Detective Halliday's hand a moment too long, and I missed the entry of a third person into the room. But the hand was quickly withdrawn and Detective Halliday virtually stood at attention. I turned around to see Sean O'Connell.

Sean O'Connell. Suffolk County District Attorney. Age, probably forty give or take a year. The man who would be Attorney General, which would be a stepping stone to Congress, which would take him… where? Did he want to be president? He exuded charisma, with perfect, dazzling white teeth and a little cleft in his prominent chin. He was attired in a three-piece suit in July, with gold cufflinks showing. There was a tiny Massachusetts flag on his lapel. This man was a politician.

When he gave interviews to the television news reporters – which he did incessantly – he looked like he was flirting with the camera. Smiling and turning just so to ensure that a three-quarter profile was captured, the better to show off that chin.

I looked closely at O'Connell. The man was wearing makeup. Face powder to blot up perspiration. A little something to highlight the sincerity of the eyes.

"I happened to be in the building on… another matter and thought I'd drop in," O'Connell said.

Like hell.

In the interview room, O'Connell shook hands all the way around. His grip was firm but quick. He lingered only over Lew. The two eyed one another, adversaries from many previous bouts, all but one of which, Lew was quick to tell me, had ended in acquittals or hung juries.

I worried about that one he had lost.

"Well, I won't hold you up," O'Connell said, smiled, and executed a ballroom-worthy about face. Two minutes after he appeared, he was gone.

Three hours later, the six o'clock news would inform the Boston viewing public that I had been asked in for questioning. And because Sean O'Connell just happened to be walking out of the building five minutes after I walked in and paused in his very busy schedule to answer a few questions, he was able to tell reporters that I was there, "only because we want to clear up some inconsistencies in the police department's investigation." I was "not a suspect at this time," he said.

Translation: I *would* be a suspect any minute.

When he left, I was asked if I wanted anything to drink. It was a perfunctory question. I surprised them, I guess, by asking for sparkling water, "San Pellegrino, if you have it, but any will do."

Detectives Tucci and Halliday exchanged a surprised look. I wasn't supposed to have given that sort of an answer.

"We don't keep bottled water around here," Halliday said.

"Do you have a glass and some ice?"

"Yes," Halliday answered slowly.

"Then I'll drink my own," I said and reached into my purse, extracting a green bottle.

Lew grinned behind his hand. The water had been my idea. He had gone along.

Detective Halliday fetched the glass and ice.

"Keep it friendly," Lew had stressed, *"but never give them the upper hand. They have two purposes: to catch you in a lie and to frighten you. You have two purposes as well: to show them you won't be frightened by them, and to give them nothing that helps them build a case."*

I poured my San Pellegrino.

"First of all, there was no excuse for the feds to have executed that search warrant when they did." The speaker was Detective Tucci. She was apparently still trying to be my friend. She was wearing another Macy's pant suit, this one in Kelly green. "I put their actions into my report and I've made certain that it will get read by the right people. If you haven't gotten an apology already, you'll get one soon."

First they'd apologize. Then, they'd freeze my bank account.

Tucci turned some pages in a notebook. "Your husband died of a heart attack brought on from ingesting two drugs, Viagra and Ritvin. His autopsy showed he had taken the Viagra around 5 p.m., two and a half hours before his death. The Ritvin had been ingested some time earlier. Based on his liver and stomach, the ME suggests noon or earlier."

So far, I knew all this. This is what Lew had gotten from his sources inside the police department.

"Can you take me through your husband's last morning?" Tucci asked.

I looked at Lew. I was supposed to look at Lew and wait for him to nod before answering any question regardless of how innocuous. He nodded.

"I remember we overslept. We had watched some movies the night before. I awakened him about 7 a.m. and got him into the shower. I made breakfast. He had pretty much the same breakfast every weekday morning – coffee, orange juice and cereal."

"You made his breakfast?" Tucci asked.

"I said I did."

"You made his breakfast every morning?"

I nodded. "George was helpless in the kitchen."

"You poured the orange juice and made the coffee?" Tucci asked. "You poured the Cheerios from the box and added the milk and sugar?"

"He ate Frosted Flakes," I said. "He ate Frosted Flakes every morning that I knew him. Except Sundays. On Sunday, he wanted pancakes."

"Did he add sugar?"

"No, he said they were sweet enough."

"Banana?"

"He disliked bananas. He said they were tasteless."

"How about his coffee?"

"What about it?" I asked.

"The same coffee every morning?"

"I've been getting the Whole Foods fresh-ground Columbian for the past year or so. Before that it was a French Roast. He apparently tried the Columbian at some food conference and came back raving about it."

"What about cream and sugar?"

"He used both."

"You added them ahead of time?"

I shook my head. "He added them himself. Sugar from a sugar bowl, cream from a pint container. The people from the SEC took them that night. If you have any influence, I would appreciate your asking them to return the sugar bowl. It was my grandmother's."

Neither detective made a note to that effect.

"The orange juice was fresh squeezed? You squeezed it yourself?"

"No," I smiled. "Whole Foods again. George says he can taste the difference." And then I stopped myself. "…Said he could taste the difference." I let my voice trail off.

The switch from present to past tense. Also Lew's idea.

"After breakfast, you washed the dishes."

"I did so every morning after breakfast."

"Just the breakfast dishes? That was all that was in the load?"

"I ran the dishwasher once a day. Lunch if I was home, dinner, and breakfast. I always ran the dishwasher after breakfast."

Lew interjected a comment. "I believe the home was under some sort of electronic surveillance for several days prior to his death. It shouldn't be difficult to establish whether running a dishwasher after breakfast was the usual pattern."

Again, no notes were made to that effect.

"Your husband went to the train station after breakfast?"

"I drove him. He was running late."

"Did he brush his teeth?"

"He said he'd do that at the office. Like I said, he was running late."

"Did he make his train?"

"With about two minutes to spare."

"Did your husband take any pills?"

I nodded. "Lipitor, a baby aspirin and a vitamin. He took them all at night, as he was getting ready for bed."

"He took no pills that morning?"

"No."

"Did you give him any pills to take that morning?"

"No."

"Did you grind any pills into a powder and add them to any of the food he ate that morning."

"No." I wondered what a polygraph would have made of that answer.

"Did you administer Ritvin in any form to your husband that morning?"

"No."

Detective Tucci put a check mark next to a question on her page.

Detective Halliday picked up the questioning. "What did you do after you dropped your husband off for work?"

"I went home, did some housework, went shopping, had lunch with a friend, then got a call from another friend who needed a shoulder to cry on."

"You went shopping on the day your husband died?"

"I didn't know my husband was going to have a heart attack, detective."

"Come on, detective," Lew said. "She told you what she did."

"You have a maid," Halliday said.

"Twice a week."

"She does the cleaning."

"She does the heavy cleaning. I take care of the everyday stuff, the dishes, the laundry, things like that."

"You said you went shopping?"

"Yes. To Chestnut Hill."

"What did you buy?"

"Makeup. And a blouse and a sweater."

"Where?"

"Bloomingdale's."

"Did you go anywhere else in the mall?"

"I looked around in stores. I didn't buy anything else."

"Did you stop for something to eat or drink?"

"I was going out to lunch at noon. No."

"So you didn't stop for coffee or a pastry?"

"She answered your question, detective," Lew said.

"I'd like to hear her say it," Halliday said.

"No," I said. "I didn't stop for coffee or pastries."

"Then you had lunch with your girlfriend?"

"Yes. Trish. Patricia Williams."

"And then you went to see another friend?"

"Patsy Brandt. Her husband is one of the principals of Quant Four."

"And she told you her husband's firm had 'blown up'."

"Yes."

"And she told you she believed your husband was on the take from Quant Four."

"Yes."

"And afterwards, you went home."

"Yes."

"What did you do?"

"Tried on my clothes. Watched television, read. Made myself dinner. Waited for my husband to come home."

Halliday circled nothing on his page of notes.

Detective Tucci took over the questioning. "Were you aware that your husband took Viagra?"

"No."

"You never found Viagra in his briefcase or a suitcase?"

"No." In reality, I had found a baggie containing six Viagra in his briefcase one morning three months earlier. Another question I wouldn't care to answer with a polygraph sensor attached to my fingers.

"You never found a prescription for Viagra or an insurance reimbursement?"

"No, and I handled all medical insurance paperwork for us."

"Do you have any idea of how your husband could have obtained Viagra?"

"Could have or did? I can think of many ways he *could have* obtained the drug. I don't know how he *did* obtain it, any more than I know how he obtained Ritvin." A tour de force of verbal jiu jitsu on my part.

Another check on the page.

"Were you aware your husband was having an affair?"

"Yes."

Detective Tucci drew a circle on her page.

"Did you know with whom?"

"At the time of his death or previously?"

The detectives looked at one another and Halliday whispered into Tucci's ear.

"For the moment, let's confine ourselves to the date of your husband's death."

"I was aware of at least one woman."

"And who was that?"

"Susan Perkins Booth."

"Did your husband tell you about the affair?"

"No."

"How did you discover the affair?"

"My husband began coming home late and began taking more out of town trips than in the past. One day, I followed him. He met a woman."

"Susan Booth?"

"No, this was an earlier affair."

"When did you begin following your husband?"

"December of last year."

"And you followed him for seven months?"

"Yes, off and on."

"And you collected evidence of his affairs?"

"Yes."

"Did you ever confront him with that evidence?"

"No."

"Why not?"

This was an important inflection point in the interrogation and, despite the civil tones, it was definitely an interrogation. Until now, I had answered each question fully but, whenever possible, using 'yes' or 'no.' No elaborations, just an answer. Now, we came to the point where I started being coy.

"I had my reasons."

The two detectives looked at one another again, this time in surprise.

"Could you share those reasons with us?" Tucci asked, leaning her elbows farther across the table.

"No," I replied. "They're personal and I'd rather not 'share' them."

"You could help us close this case if you did." Halliday said this.

"My husband died of a heart attack, Detective Halliday. As your autopsy showed, he took Viagra and Ritvin. That should allow you to close your case."

"We wish it were that easy, ma'am," he said, lowering his eyes almost as though he meant it. "But the volume of Ritvin in your husband's body was disproportionate to what was needed to… enhance the effect of the Viagra. The autopsy suggested he had ingested between two and four Ritvin tablets. Half a tablet is what he should have taken for… his purposes."

"You see our problem," Tucci said.

"That my husband did something very stupid," I said. I took a handkerchief out of my purse and pressed it to my eyes.

"Either that or, sometime that morning, someone gave him those tablets," Tucci said.

I let the silence hang in the air. *"Don't rise to the bait,"* Lew had said. *"No matter how tempting."*

"You said you were aware that your husband was having an affair with Susan Booth," Tucci asked.

"Yes," I said.

"Yet, on the evening of your husband's death, you told me that you didn't recognize that name. Can you explain the discrepancy?"

I shook my head. "I don't remember your asking me that. I guess I don't remember much about that conversation but I guess I was on an emotional roller-coaster. And if I had said I didn't recognize the name, it was because a wife doesn't care to acknowledge to anyone that her husband has a mistress."

Word for word perfect. Phoebe rehearsed me, including getting the tone right. I ceded nothing. I did not confirm that I had said anything in the hospital, but I offered a plausible explanation for the discrepancy anyway.

"Did you know your husband was meeting Miss Booth that evening?"

"No."

"How did he explain his absence?"

"He said he was taking clients to a Red Sox game."

"Did that cause you to believe your husband might be planning to meet Miss Booth?"

"Until that night, he had never said he was taking clients to a baseball game. He said it was a company his firm might take public. It sounded legitimate to me."

"His other evenings out didn't sound legitimate?"

"He was always vague – he was checking out restaurants for a research report."

"Why didn't you follow him that night?"

"I believed he was taking clients to a Red Sox game."

"You could have made certain by following him."

Don't rise to the bait.

"I believed he was taking clients to a Red Sox game."

Tucci turned a page in her notebook. "In our conversation in the hospital, you told me you only suspected that your husband was having an affair. You wondered why he suddenly had so many out-of-town trips. 'He started getting mysterious' on you. Do you recall saying that?"

"No, I do not."

"I wrote it down," she said. "Would you like to see my notes?"

Lew interjected. "She said she does not recall such a conversation with you, detective."

Tucci glared at Lew, then turned a page of her notebook.

"Did you take photos of your husband with his mistresses?"

"Yes."

"Did you document his infidelities? Make computer notes?"

"Yes."

"Did you erase those notes and those photos from your computer?"

"Yes."

"When did you erase those photos and notes?"

"Sometime in the week before my husband died of his heart attack." Note that I didn't say *'before his death'*. Phoebe said the distinction was subtle but extremely important.

"Why did you erase those photos and notes?"

"I had my reasons." Identical answer.

Halliday leaned across the table. "Ma'am, this may be the most important question we ask all day. Please: why did you erase those photos and notes?"

"The reasons are personal and I'd rather not share them."

"Someone could conclude that you were trying to destroy evidence," Halliday said. He sounded so sincere when he said it.

"Someone could say you declined to answer on the grounds of self-incrimination," Tucci added tartly. I guess she no longer wanted to be my friend.

"You have the only answer you're going to get today," Lew said.

Tucci turned another page.

"On the weekend before your husband died, you and he went to his father's birthday party in Ipswich. Is that correct?"

"Yes."

At some point that afternoon, you had a conversation with your brother in law."

"I spoke with all members of the family."

"You had a private conversation with Paul?"

"It was just the two of us but I wouldn't characterize it as 'private'. Anyone could have joined us. We were on the porch. It just so happened that the rest of the family was elsewhere."

"And he discussed protease inhibitors with you?"

"Among many other things."

"And you knew what a protease inhibitor was."

"I said I knew it was an AIDS drug. It was the only thing I knew."

"And your brother-in-law told you that Ritvin and Viagra were a deadly combination."

"He said something like, 'a man who is HIV positive takes Viagra at his peril'."

"Did he also tell you that Ritvin increased the potency of Viagra ten-fold?"

"If he did, it didn't register because my husband isn't… wasn't HIV positive and didn't take Viagra."

"Do you remember your brother-in-law saying that?"

"He may or may not have said it. If he did, it didn't register."

"But you acknowledge that he may have said it?"

"Detectives," Lew interjected, "acknowledging that someone may have said something is also acknowledging that they may not have said something. Find a more productive line of questioning."

Tucci circled something on her page.

"After your brother-in-law told you he had formed a new company and was working on a new class of protease inhibitors, did you ask to visit the company?"

"Paul told me about the new company three months ago. At the party, I invited him and his partner, Jerry, to dinner. He invited me to Cambridge to see the company."

"You didn't ask to see the company's R&D lab?"

"There is nothing to the company but an R&D lab and no, I did not ask to see it. I asked him to dinner, he reciprocated by asking me to see, I think he called it, 'his new digs'."

Tucci put a check mark on her page.

"Why would you accept an invitation like that?"

"To be polite. Also, Paul has an extraordinary eye for architecture. Each of his companies had been in a very distinctive setting. It's a pleasure to see them."

"When you were at the R&D facility, your brother-in-law showed you its pharmaceutical supply room, did he not?"

"Yes."

"Was the room locked?"

"No, it was open as I recall. In fact, I don't remember any doors anywhere in the offices being locked."

"Was there a lock on the door?"

"We spent a few seconds in front of an open door. He gestured at it and said, 'this is the pharmaceutical room' just as he had gestured at a dozen other rooms. As I recall, he was in the middle of explaining that the big pharmaceutical companies viewed his work as off-the-books R&D. If it worked, they'd be at the door looking to buy the company. If not, all it cost those companies was some pills."

"Were you aware there was a supply of Ritvin in that room?"

"In a few seconds, I didn't have time to become aware of anything."

"Did your brother-in-law leave you alone at any time after he showed you the pharmaceutical room?"

"He took a phone call for a few minutes."

"Can you be more specific?"

"Someone interrupted us while we were walking around and said Paul needed to take a call. Paul asked if I would be all right and I believe I said that if he wasn't back in an hour, I'd find my way out and go home. I had noticed a ladies room during the tour. I found it, made use of it, and then went back to a large open area where a drug design computer was being installed. Paul came back perhaps five or six minutes after that."

"Did you see anyone while your brother-in-law was gone?"

"Someone may have walked by. I don't remember. I didn't speak to anyone if that's what you're asking."

"You didn't enter the pharmaceutical room?"

"No."

"You didn't take Ritvin tablets out of a bottle?"

"No."

"And if we told you several of the bottles were only partly filled, what would you say?"

"Detectives," Lew stood up. "My client has told you she didn't go into the room and didn't take tablets out of a bottle. Move onto something more productive."

Tucci looked at Halliday. "Anything else, Roy?"

Halliday shook his head.

Tucci said, "I guess we're finished."

Halliday snapped his fingers. "I forgot one thing."

Yeah, right, I thought.

Halliday reached under his yellow legal pad and brought out an 8x10 photo. It showed me at the valet entrance at the Mall of Chestnut Hill.

"This is you?" he asked.

I was in slacks and a very smart Juicy Couture blouse. I was wearing sunglasses and carrying two Bloomingdale's bags, one large and one small, and I was carrying my big tote with the computer inside. It was taken the day George died, probably by the surveillance van and was time stamped 11:36. I thought I looked rather carefree.

"Yes."

He pulled out a second 8x10 sheet. This one contained four black and white photos; probably enlargements of a security camera tape. The first three were extremely grainy, the last quite clear. The first showed a woman carrying two shopping bags going into the coffee shop in the mall, which was by the rear exit to the parking garage. The second photo, darker than the first, showed the woman with her back to the security camera. She appeared to be taking a laptop out of her tote bag. The third, still with her back to the camera, had the computer, its screen bright, open and in front of her. The fourth, much clearer that the first three but taken from overhead, was of me, inside the mall, with my bags and my tote.

The first three photos appeared to have been taken by a security camera in a store opposite the coffee shop, and its capture of people inside the café was coincidental. The fourth was apparently taken by the mall's security cameras. The time stamps on the first three were 11:13, 11:15, and 11:26. The fourth photo bore a time stamp of 11:29.

"Are these also photos of you?"

Well, the fourth one definitely was and I knew the first three were also of me, because I remembered where I was sitting in the café. But, while the woman entering the café held two shopping bags and carried a large tote, they were not identifiable as Bloomies' bags. The woman entering the café had on light-colored slacks and had dark hair cut roughly the length of mine, but there were no facial features. As for the two photos inside, they could have been of anyone.

"The photo on the lower right is of me. I don't know who the first three photos are of."

"You didn't go into a coffee shop in the Chestnut Hill Mall on the morning of June 27th?" Halliday asked.

"Not that I recall."

"And you weren't carrying a computer with you in an oversize purse?"

Lew jumped to his feet. "The interview's over," he said. "My client will answer no more questions today."

Lew picked up the sheet with the four photos on it and looked at it carefully. "What kind of horse manure is this?"

"This, counselor, is proof that your client went to a mall the morning she killed her husband," Halliday said. "She bought a couple of baubles as a smokescreen, but her real purpose was to find a place with a wireless internet connection where she could transfer the money her husband had stolen. She did that two hours after she laced his cereal with the Ritvin she had stolen from her brother-in-law's R&D lab and eight hours before he suffered a massive coronary as a result of the Ritvin in his system mixed with Viagra. That, counselor, shows premeditated murder. She poisons him, empties out his accounts, and them waits for him to die."

I had to admit it. Halliday had nailed both the timing and the *modus operandi* perfectly.

"And these three photos are your proof?" Lew fumed.

"These photos, plus the missing Ritvin from the pharmaceutical room your client visited just days before he ingested it, plus the proof the SEC will bring when they prove she emptied out his accounts just before he died," Halliday said. "And we're just beginning on the photo evidence. By the time we're finished, we'll have tracked her exact movements all over that mall and put her at that table, fattening up her own bank account even as her husband is a walking time bomb."

"Are you charging my client at this time?" Lew asked.

"She can save us all a lot of time by confessing," Halliday countered.

"Unless you're charging her, we're done." Lew opened his briefcase and began picking up his note pads and pens.

As for me, I sat at the table, staring at the four photos and wondering what else the miracle of modern security cameras might have captured. When I had bought the makeup and clothes I had opened the tote. Could a Bloomingdale's security camera have caught a glimpse of the computer inside? Were there other cameras at other stores that could show me walking by, headed for the café?

More words – fairly heated words – were being exchanged between Lew and the two detectives, but I just kept looking at the photos.

And wondering how I could have been so stupid.

13.

Lew was silent as we left. The reporters had gone back to write their stories so there was no one to accost us.

He continued his silence as we made our way out of Boston and I could see he was thinking. My attempts at light-hearted conversation fell flat and so I, too, fell into silence. And, all the way out the Mass Pike, I silently kicked myself for not having thought through that public places have security cameras, and that cameras record images and save them for a long time.

I wondered if logging onto a café's wireless network left a record, and if the Boston PD or the SEC could now find a record of George's laptop having been used on that network. I wondered if the entire transactions – the emptying of George's various brokerage and secret bank accounts – were now recorded on some file server somewhere, awaiting only the right keystrokes being typed in by some bright kid in a forensic data lab.

And I wondered if I were screwed.

We made it all the way back to Weston without talking.

When we arrived, he said, "I think Phoebe put together something to eat. Come on in."

I followed him.

Phoebe met us at the door. As soon as she saw her husband's face her usual cheerful demeanor was replaced by a worried one. She gave me a look that could have been one of pity or contempt.

We walked to Lew's office. He sat down in his chair – a big, red leather affair that swiveled with a noticeable squeak - and drummed his fingers. Phoebe put a drink in front of him – something clear-colored with ice and a lime slice, and he took a long drink. I could have used one of those myself.

"We've got some catch-up to play," he said after what seemed like a very long time. He looked up at Phoebe. "Get hold of Joe. Pull every damned security tape in that mall so we know what they're seeing. And have him do a count from whatever main court camera they use – what percentage of the women in that mall that day were dressed in white or tan slacks, a light-colored short-sleeve blouse and have dark hair. If the number is what I suspect it is, we may catch a break. Have him also do a population sort by the kinds of shopping bags women are carrying – one bag, two bags."

"Get that computer guy set up for a conference call tomorrow morning." He snapped his fingers. "You know who I'm talking about – the Indian kid with the obnoxious accent."

"Sanjay," Phoebe said.

"Right, Sanjay. I'll need an hour. Also, get Joe to have someone he trusts go over to Kat's brother-in-law's place in Cambridge and start counting pills in bottles – the ones on the shelves and the ones still in packing boxes. See how many bottles are off and by how many pills. Get it independently documented."

"And get an inventory of what the SEC took out of Kat's house that night. I can't imagine that their warrant could have covered her grandmother's sugar dish. See what else they took that it didn't cover. I think Lamont could help us there."

Phoebe wrote everything down.

"What can I do?" I asked.

Lew looked at me intently. "Tomorrow morning, you start converting everything to cash, and I don't mean in a checking account. Start by drawing out the cash. Then liquidate stocks, bonds, whatever. Sell them, get a check, and then cash the check. My guess is that the SEC is going to try to freeze your assets. The one thing they can't freeze is cash. If your husband had an insurance policy, now is the time to file the claim."

"How does it look?" I asked.

Lew shook his head. "Boston PD is depending on the SEC to

provide them the missing link that makes their case come together. They may have a very long time to wait. In the meantime, Sean O'Connell is going to do everything he can to fast-track this case." He looked at his watch. "Speaking of which, maybe we ought to see how the local stations are playing this."

Phoebe turned on the television in the corner of the office. We didn't have long to wait. A late-breaking fire in Revere led the news, but I was right up there. The second story started with Lew and me walking up the steps of the police department building. It was no perp walk. I looked dignified and properly grieving.

The gist of the story was that police were not ready to rule George's death 'suspicious' but nevertheless wondered why a man would ingest six or eight times the amount of a Viagra-enhancing AIDS drug. Was it carelessness, or potentially foul play? Meanwhile, the SEC continued its investigation into George's involvement in the collapse of Quant Four Capital, and investigators were looking for a laptop computer that could tell them the whereabouts of missing millions of dollars. And then came the money shot: the third photo from the four-photo array shown me a few hours earlier.

"…And they wonder whether this security camera photo – taken on the morning of his death at the posh Mall of Chestnut Hill – may be the key to unlocking that puzzle..."

Cut to Sean O'Connell and his smug explanation that this whole interrogation was to "clear up some inconsistencies in the police department's investigation."

Translation: "We're going to nail the lying bitch."

The news moved on to a drive-by shooting of a teen in Dorchester; one of those cases that wouldn't put Sean O'Connell in state government. My mind was still on that grainy image from the café.

Lew took off his glasses and rubbed his eyes. He then looked at both of us. "Like I said, we've got some catch-up to play."

Lost in all of this planning on Lew's and Phoebe's part was a conversation that wasn't taking place: the one in which Lew said he wholeheartedly believed in my innocence and that he would not allow some travesty of justice to take place because of a prosecutor's political ambition. Instead, the discussion between the two of them was all about watering down the state's case and creating 'reasonable doubt' in the mind of a jury.

That silence also had a translation: Lew believed me guilty, and he was now simply giving me the best defense my money could buy.

Of course, I was guilty. Nonetheless, I couldn't help feeling depressed. My friends professed their belief in my innocence. My parents certainly did. It would have been nice if my attorney shared their view.

I guess you can't have everything.

14.

The next morning, I set out to generate cash. George's and my accounts had all been set up as ones 'with right of survivorship'. Well, I was the survivor. I ordered the stocks and bonds sold, and checks sent to my home. I cleaned out the money market accounts and the IRAs. I did it all by phone and so dealt only with people in call centers, most of which were in Kentucky or Mumbai and so had never heard of me.

It was a lot of money. I hoped I would actually see it.

There was also the question of George's insurance. George had been too cheap to take out a 'real' policy but, as part of his benefits package, PJ&B gave him one for five times his annual salary. Five times salary and bonus would have been a much sweeter deal but, even so, the policy was worth nearly a million tax-free dollars.

I tried to collect it over the phone. I was told I'd have to file the claim in person.

In his office in Back Bay, the man from Pilgrim State Casualty contorted himself six different ways trying to get around the two words he couldn't bring himself to use – 'suspect' and 'criminal'.

"There is considerable question as to whether your late husband was abiding by the terms of his employment agreement," the man said, shifting around in his chair and frequently mopping his brow with a handkerchief.

"I see nothing in the language of the policy that would allow you to deny a claim even if my husband shot and killed your company's president," I countered, keeping my tone cool but persistent. "PJ&B gave him life insurance as a part of his benefits package. He died. Therefore, his heirs and assigns get to collect that insurance."

The man – Quentin, I think his name was – went even paler. Out came the handkerchief again. "There's also a question as to whether you would be entitled to collect his insurance given that you are… that the circumstances of his death are clouded."

This is a man who watched the six o'clock news.

I held my temper. "Please point out the place in the policy where it says that unless there's incontrovertible evidence that a beneficiary *didn't* kill the insured, that said beneficiary cannot collect." I handed Quentin a copy of George's policy.

"You'll need to talk to the home office," he gurgled, not bothering to read the policy.

I called Lew. Lew made some phone calls. The insurance company dug in its heels. Pilgrim State Casualty said it was acting on advice of its internal counsel. Lew said the insurance company's president could look forward to reading about its denial of claim in the Boston *Globe*. That threat earned Lew an immediate call from the chairman of PJ&B.

The back-and-forth revealed one important fact hidden until that moment from everyone's view: Peavy, Jensen & Beck was on the brink of dissolution.

It seemed there was a new story in the *Wall Street Journal* every other day. Quant Four had its tendrils deeply into the firm. In addition to George, Peter Brandt and his buddies had at least two other PJ&B analysts and an investment banker on its secret payroll. The analysts had in common with George that they covered many small, relatively obscure companies that the firm had once taken public but that were now largely 'orphaned' by Wall Street. If PJ&B analysts were the only ones who provided coverage of a company, then changes in the analysts' opinions could greatly influence the price of those companies' stock. With the analysts signaling pending opinion changes to Quant Four, Peter's hedge fund buddies could bid the prices of the stocks up and down like a yo-yo.

The PJ&B investment banker was offering tidbits on transactions. For example, let's say Amalgamated Cookie had received an unsolicited takeover bid from a buyout firm at thirty dollars a share. Or, Sneaky Sam's Restaurants was planning a private placement of shares. Inside information like that allowed Quant Four to load up on Amalgamated Cookie and go short on Sneaky Sam, then dump the shares and cover the short as soon as the news became public. They might own the stock for only a few days, yet see a twenty or thirty percent return on their money.

George had been the first analyst identified because he had the misfortune to die the night of the SEC raid. But word got out about the others, either through newspaper articles or through the financial community's well-developed grapevine. On a scorecard of tainted personnel, PJ&B led the list with four. Five other firms had one analyst each.

The analysts and the banker had all been suspended but the damage was done. No one wanted PJ&B to handle their IPO, municipalities went elsewhere to issue bonds, there were no more corporate mergers to broker. PJ&B's executives put out reassuring statements, but the destruction was apparent. A few more news stories about the firm's internal financial crisis would be all it would take to provide the final nails in the PJ&B's coffin.

The explanation to Lew from PJ&B's chairman was straightforward. To keep down its insurance premiums, PJ&B had agreed to pay four-fifths of any claim from its own pocket. Thus, George's near-million-dollar life insurance policy was really for only one time George's base salary, with PJ&B liable for the bulk of the payment. PJ&B had rolled the dice that its employees were a healthy bunch. They hadn't counted on my stoking George up on Viagra and Ritvin.

PJ&B's chairman told Lew that because the brokerage firm was responsible for roughly $800,000 of the insurance proceeds payments, it would take a few days to free up the cash. Lew gave him until 5 p.m., after which his next call was to the Boston bureaus of the *Wall*

Street Journal and the New York *Times.*

"When it comes in, cash it fast," Lew told me after the call. "These guys are on the edge."

I never got the check. Instead, at 4 p.m., PJ&B issued a statement that they were putting themselves up for sale and would not be paying any bills until such time as their future 'had greater clarity.'

And to think my George did all that.

* * * * *

The next morning, I had a call from an attorney or, rather, from an attorney's aide, who said her boss sought a 'face-to-face meeting as soon as possible' at an unfamiliar Atlantic Avenue address in the center of Boston. I said I'd get right back to her.

I immediately called Phoebe. As soon as I said, "weird call from an attorney" she said, "You should go see what they want." She then changed the subject to discuss Lew's busy schedule.

Because Phoebe was not in the habit of interrupting me, and because she didn't offer to put me through to Lew, I drew two conclusions: first, that my phone was being tapped, and second, that Lew had set up this meeting with a second attorney.

Still having no computer to call my own, I drove to the library and Googled C. Warren Marshall. He turned out to be a tax attorney in private practice.

OK. Lew wanted me to see a tax lawyer. At least he wasn't referring me to another criminal defense lawyer, which would have been crushing.

I called back the aide and said I was available any time.

She asked if I could be in Boston at 1:30.

"Today?" I asked.

"Mr. Marshall will make time to see you." Her reply carried just a whisper of expectation that if C. Warren Marshall, Esquire, could bend his busy schedule to accommodate such a quick meeting, I ought to show some flexibility, too.

"I'll be there."

*****

Back in the heyday of Boston's building boom of the 1990s, a wonderful structure went up on Atlantic Avenue. It had a huge, six- or seven-story arch through which passersby could see the harbor, a benefit that became apparent as soon as the old Central Artery was torn down. I knew the Boston Harbor Hotel was in this complex because I had been there several times. I also knew, vaguely, that there were condominiums in one building. I was not aware that a third finger of the structure contained offices.

C. Warren Marshall's office was on the sixth floor of that finger, out at the very end, with nothing to look out on through the floor-to-ceiling windows except Boston Harbor. Puffy white clouds dotted the sky and seagulls circled. Attorney Marshall's desk was in one corner of the vast office, which was paneled in light oak where it wasn't glass. A sofa and comfortable chairs were arranged to take advantage of the view.

I had a sense this was going to be a very expensive meeting.

The aide, who was a few years older than I and had an impeccable air of discretion as well as a good eye for clothes, had greeted me warmly and ushered me directly into the office. Sodas and bottles of water were arrayed on a coffee table.

"Attorney Marshall will be right in," she smiled brightly.

On cue, that man I assumed to be C. Warren Marshall entered through a discreet side door, possibly from an oak-paneled private washroom.

A meter started running in my head.

He was somewhere between forty and fifty, tanned and lean. A man who played tennis or racquetball every morning and probably took fifty-mile bike rides on weekends. He wasn't especially handsome but I suspected he didn't care what people thought of his looks as long as they paid attention to what he said. He was dressed in khakis and a blue shirt – no tie, no jacket. The uniform of the Boston investment banking community, except that he was a lawyer.

He offered his hand, smiled, and then indicated the sofa.

"My apology for the short notice and the cryptic nature of the call," he said, "but Lew suggested you and I ought to talk as quickly as possible." He opened a bottle of water and used tongs to lift ice from a silver bucket into a glass.

The meter in my head sped up.

"Lew suggested you need some assistance in creating an off-shore account," he said, sipping his water. His legs were crossed and one arm was thrown across the back of the chair in which he was seated. "I want to walk you through the mechanics of what we'll need to do."

All kinds of things slid into place, like tumblers on a combination lock. First, Lew now firmly believed that it was me in those grainy photos at the Café Au Lait. He also firmly believed that I had emptied George's accounts on the day he died. He had concluded, correctly, that I had not been able to take the final step of getting the money out of the country or otherwise beyond the reach of the IRS and the SEC.

And he had tapped into his circle of acquaintances to help me out.

Which left me with two options. I could deny that there was any money to transfer and walk out in a huff. That way was certain to end in George's ill-gotten gains eventually being found by some pimply-faced government employee, who would no doubt get a three hundred dollar bonus for nabbing me. Of course, if I placed my affairs in the hands of this total stranger, I could wake up one morning and find that my account numbers were bogus and I was penniless.

"How do I know you're really going to help me?" I asked. "How do I know this isn't some scam to wipe out a widow's last dollar?"

I had never thought of myself as a widow. Such an emotionally charged word.

"You are not the first person Lew has referred to me," he said, grinning. "Would you like to speak to him?" His voice was a very pleasant baritone – almost like an anchor on a 'serious' news program. It was a comforting voice.

I nodded, and he took a phone out of his shirt pocket. He tapped the screen a few times, waited while until the number was answered and said, "Hey, Phoebe, it's Warren. Can someone speak to Lew for just a second?" He handed the phone to me.

Lew was on the line as soon as Warren handed me the phone. "You can trust him," Lew said. "He's the acknowledged expert in this kind of thing."

"What do you need to know?" I asked Warren Marshall.

He smiled, exposing a mouth full of white, straight teeth. The client was sold, the fish reeled in.

"A foreign account isn't as easy as just walking into a bank in the Cayman Islands and telling them you want to buy a certificate of deposit," he said. "We're going to set up a corporation, the corporation is going to have an international affiliate…" He went through a lengthy checklist of things that were going to have to be done to thwart the long arm of Uncle Sam.

The meter whirred at an ever higher speed.

"We'll need to have an unaffiliated legal entity domiciled in the Cayman Islands…"

"What's this going to cost?" I asked.

He stopped and looked at me in surprise. "I'm sorry, I thought you and Lew had already covered that."

"His wife told me I should see you. I never talked about it with Lew until a few minutes ago."

He nodded. "Of course. It's a criminal case."

I mentally winced at the word, 'criminal'.

He must have seen my reaction. "I mean, most of my work is with simple, civil stuff. Your family has a liquidity event and you want to keep part of the proceeds off the table. Or a spouse contemplating a divorce wants to keep certain financial assets out of the community property pool. In those cases, you and your principal attorney would have gone over all the options, including expenses. Lew pretty much had to hand you over to me cold." As he spoke, he used his hands, animating his conversation with gestures to show assets being kept off the table. Warren Marshall was a fascinating man to watch at work.

"So, what's this going to cost?" I repeated.

"Round numbers, three hundred thousand."

I winced again.

"The amount is the same whether you're transferring fifty dollars or fifty million," he said. "There's also an annual administration fee of about fifty thousand, with the first year payable in advance."

I started doing math in my head. The proceeds were just under five million. I'd still have four and half million available afterward. OK, so I lost seven or eight percent.

"How long does all this take?"

He shrugged. "I'd start this afternoon. The first thing is to get the money out of whatever accounts they're in now. From what I understand, there is some urgency."

I love lawyers. This guy had very carefully never asked me why I had this money that I wanted to get out of the country. He made no reference to the fact that there was maybe a moral obligation on my part to turn the proceeds over to the SEC. He only understood that there might be 'some urgency'.

Maybe it was one of these cases of him wanting 'plausible deniability'. "Gee, your honor, I had no idea that this was money her husband had stolen. I just assumed it was a liquidity event."

"What do you need to get started?" I asked.

"An account number, a routing number and a password." He picked up a little notebook from a tea table next to his chair and clicked a pen, ready to write.

I gulped. Honest to God, I gulped.

"How long does it take?" I asked, trying to think of intelligent questions that would stall the inevitable.

"Four weeks, give or take," he said. "The money will be out of your account by wire transfer this afternoon and will be effectively untraceable after that. The process of setting up your accounts is what takes a few weeks. I assume these aren't funds you need for your immediate expenses."

"What about references?" I asked. "Can I talk with someone else you've done this for?"

He laughed. I had apparently managed to ask an unexpected question that caught him off-guard. "If I gave you the names of people who have offshore accounts and you called them, how do you think they'd react? How would *you* react if next month or next year I used you as a reference? I don't think you'd be very happy."

All right, so I wasn't going to get any references.

"Guarantees?" I asked. "What can go wrong?"

He nodded. "There are risks. There are always risks. I can say that I've been doing this for the better part of ten years and in all that time, not one account has ever been compromised – and that covers many, many accounts."

"How do I know my money is there? Do I get account statements?"

"How about a debit card?" he countered. "Or a toaster for opening the account? You will have access to statements, but they'll come through here and they'll be computer-generated. You'll know the money is there because you can access it through wire transfers – which will originate with my office. The goal is that your money is secure. It's in a safe haven. It's free from taxes and not subject to seizure by any government. From there, it can be invested – you can even buy U.S. stocks and bonds. I'll walk you through all that when the time comes."

I swallowed hard. I thought about some pimply-faced kid in a cubicle in some government office calling up brokerage account records, looking for shares traded in certain stocks on certain days. Some day in the not-too-distant future, that kid was going to find one of George's accounts. When he did, he'd see the transfer to the second account and that would link back to all the other accounts George had set up.

That first account found would set off the chain of dominos that would end in my going to prison.

I took a deep breath. "Are you ready to write down the numbers?"

15.

There was good news and not-so-good news over the next week. The good news was that a statistically significant percentage of the bottles of various pills that had been delivered to Paul's company were off by one or more tablets from the count listed on the bottle. Also on the good news front, my fingerprints were nowhere to be found on any bottle of Ritvin. Equally heartening was the determination that nearly one out of five women at the Mall of Chestnut Hill the morning of George's death were wearing light-colored slacks and a short-sleeved, light colored blouse. Many of them carried two shopping bags. Thus, the grainy images on the video could have been any of several dozen women, so the Commonwealth of Massachusetts had a long way to go to prove that I had used a computer in the Café Au Lait, or pilfered Ritvin from Paul's makeshift pharmaceutical supply room.

The additional good news was that I received checks totaling nearly a million dollars from various brokerage firms. I was going to incur a hell of a capital gains penalty for converting everything to cash. Given that my more immediate goal was staying out of prison, writing out a large check nine months hence seemed a petty concern. I endorsed the checks over to Lew, who would keep my money out of the hands of the SEC until my issues with that organization were resolved.

The bad news was that just about everything else in my fragile universe came apart.

It started with my using an ATM at my local Bank of America branch. "Cannot complete transaction – please see teller" the machine said.

I went in to see a teller. And found that my account was frozen. Within half an hour, I found the same was true for my credit cards. Most importantly, liquidating transactions representing more than a million dollars at our Fidelity brokerage accounts – the 'honest' money George and I had accumulated during our marriage - had been 'placed in abeyance'. The money was frozen solid. That particular bit of disturbing news would take a few days to arrive. There would be no more checks.

That was just the SEC's opening salvo. I was called in for a 'formal statement.' My new nemesis, Jason Whitburn, was now flanked by two other attorneys, neither of them over the age of twenty-five, which meant the three of them must have had a combined legal experience of maybe ten years. One of them was a lady lawyer with a serious case of incipient shelf butt. They all had sneers on their faces.

They also had a computer expert with them. In Lew's and my presence, some guy who looked like he wasn't allowed to drive without an adult in the car with him read a lengthy report into the record. It was completely over my head, but the gist of it was that between their review of Comcast's records and their scrutinizing of my and George's office computer's 'event log', they had determined that on no fewer than eighty-three occasions dating back a year, a third computer had been logged onto our Comcast account. This third computer had accessed some fifty websites, including eight financial institutions where secure transactions had taken place.

The fifteen-year-old nerd could not help throwing in the additional information that seven other web sites among the eighty-three were pornographic in nature. This drew a leer in my direction from the male junior attorney. Shelf-butt just rolled her eyes.

"We will ask you again, for the record, if you were aware of the third computer in your home," Whitburn intoned.

"No, I wasn't," I said.

"You never used this computer at any time?"

I said I did not.

"You were unaware of your husband's transactions with these financial institutions?"

Completely unaware, I said.

Whitburn slapped down a handful of sheets of paper on the table. "We have focused on coincident stock transactions at the eight financial institutions, and identified eight accounts that appear to have been opened by you or your husband. These accounts were opened in various names that do not tie to the social security numbers provided when opening the accounts."

Whitburn squatted down to look me in the eye. "Do you still maintain you had no knowledge of these accounts?"

I said I had no knowledge.

Whitburn nodded at the kid, who continued his recitation. "Seventy-five of the eighty three transactions carried time stamps before 7:30 a.m. east coast time. Eight of the transactions bore time stamps of between 8:00 a.m. and 11 a.m. east coast time," the kid read.

"What time did your husband leave for work?"

"Around 8 a.m.," I said, and began feeling a noose tightening.

"And what time did you leave for work?"

"I haven't worked outside the home for seven years," I said.

"You were home most of the day?"

"Most of the day."

"And was anyone else in the house with you?"

"I had a maid twice a week. And friends. I frequently had friends over." What in the hell did I say that for?

Whitburn thumbed through his papers. "The eight transactions in question – those made after 8 a.m., each authorized a second signatory to the accounts with a link to a single account at an internet bank." He squatted again. "Are you still saying you knew nothing of these accounts?"

"I knew nothing of them."

Whitburn turned up one more sheet of paper. "On June 27 – the day your husband died – between 11:15 a.m. and 11:30 a.m., someone logged onto these accounts and transferred every last dime to that internet account. The total was nearly five million dollars." From an envelope, he took copies of the photos I had been shown at the police station: the woman with the glowing computer screen at the café. "These photos are time stamped 11:15 and 11:26. Do you still maintain you had no knowledge of these accounts?"

It was at the point that Lew, who until now had done nothing but take notes and let me hang myself, jumped in.

"Excuse me, Mr. Whitburn, but you said those last internet banking transactions were at what time?"

Whitburn read times from his notebook. The earliest was 11:15, the latest was 11:29.

"Is that what it says on the transaction slip? 11:15 Eastern Daylight Time?"

"No, it's 8:15 Pacific Daylight Time. The bank's computers are in California."

"So that transaction could have been made at 8:15 a.m. from across the street in San Francisco, or at 4:15 p.m. in London, or 5:15 p.m. in Paris?"

"Yes, but she was at the café at 11:15 in Boston," Whitburn said.

"So you're just supposing that the transaction was initiated in Boston. You have no proof," Lew said. "It could also just as likely have been 12:15 in Buenos Aires for all you know. There's no proof."

"Here's the proof," Whitburn said, with a triumphant look in his eye. He whipped another photo from out of the envelope. "Last week, your client went to meet with a tax attorney who specializes in creating offshore tax havens." Sure enough, there was a photo of me walking through that arch into the fancy Rowe's Wharf office building containing C. Warren Marshall's offices. "Half an hour after your client left his office, the money in the internet bank account was transferred out."

"And I assume you traced the money to its next stopping point," Lew said.

Whitburn's face fell slightly. "We completed the trace of these transactions just yesterday evening, we're still…"

"Well, what was the money's next step?" Lew asked, the way you'd speak to a sixth grader. "What account got it next? Let's see the next photo."

"The money has disappeared. For right now," Whitburn added.

"Are you aware of anything else that happened in the world that afternoon, other than my client going into an office building? Did anybody else in this or any other country go see a tax advisor? Did anyone anywhere else in the world log onto a computer?"

"We're not talking about anybody else," Whitburn said sarcastically. "We're talking about your client and the money she and her husband stole, and then moved around the internet until she could get it into an offshore account."

I had indeed gotten it out of the country, I thought. About one day ahead of the SEC. Thank God I didn't postpone that meeting.

"So, let me see if I have this straight," Lew said. "A computer in my client's house that no one can find is used to salt away roughly five million dollars in various brokerage accounts. Somewhere along the line, transfer instructions and joint signatory rights got added to those accounts. On the day that my client's husband died – but while he was still very much alive, raising the distinct possibility that it was him who made that final transaction – someone liquidated those accounts from somewhere in the world and moved them to that joint signatory's account. A couple of days ago, the money got moved yet again and you've lost track of it."

"No, Whitburn snapped. "Your client's husband, probably with your client's full knowledge, put nearly five million dollars into anonymous accounts over a ten-month period. The money came from bribes from one or more hedge funds. It also came from trading on inside information, and probably from other illegal activities as well – we're still investigating that. Your client – behind her husband's back –

created those transfer accounts. On the day she poisoned her husband, your client liquidated the accounts and transferred them to accounts over which only she had control. Then, knowing we were closing in, she had the money moved offshore into someone else's account while she set up her own."

"Your problem," Lew said, a grin on his face, "is that my version of events makes just as much sense as yours."

Whitburn was silent.

We left the SEC office a few minutes later. Outside the building, I remarked that we had countered every argument quite well and that it had been a good session overall.

Lew shook his head. "No, Kat. Don't confuse posturing in front of another attorney with reality. Our problem is that they're getting very, very close. They've been blindly bumping around in the dark for the past few weeks, but now, they've figured it out and they're getting their proof in place. All they need is one lucky break."

He stopped and looked at me. "If they get that break, it's all over and all I can do for you is negotiate."

I went to bed that night wondering what might constitute 'a break'. The barista at the Café Au Lait had glared at me because I had taken up a table for half an hour while sipping a single, small iced coffee. Perhaps she could identify me. Those security cameras at Bloomingdale's might show me opening my purse with the distinctive profile of a personal computer inside it. Computer enhancements might show what was clearly me walking into that café. C. Warren Marshall might get pressured into giving up a client.

The possibilities were endless.

*****

The next morning, I awakened to hear that Peter Brandt had been indicted by a federal grand jury for insider trading, along with the three other managers who made up Quant Four Capital.

Patsy Brandt – his wife and my friend – was also indicted as a co-

conspirator.

They did the perp walk into the federal courthouse down on the waterfront, both in sunglasses, flanked by four attorneys. The breathless intonations by reporters shed little light on the specifics. Phoebe provided the facts: Quant Four's collapse had triggered a massive investigation into cash-for-information from analysts and investment bankers. Before Peter Brandt stopped talking, he named half a dozen names, including George's. All those individuals – or at least the ones still breathing - were now facing indictment or arrest.

Peter Brandt kept two computers in his home, all keeping track of the data being purchased by the firm – advanced copies of recommendation changes and analyst reports, M&A reports, and whatever else the firm could get its hands on. Peter was also the 'bag man', doling out payments to those on the firm's private payroll. Financial guy that he was, everything was there, in the computer, in spreadsheets. But he had been sufficiently secretive that it has all been coded and encrypted.

Patsy's downfall lay in her knowledge of the computers. She not only knew of them, she used them for on-line shopping at Nieman Marcus and Nordstrom's. For her, nothing was encrypted. Her digital fingerprints were everywhere.

Peter and Patsy were released, though their passports were confiscated. Their accounts were frozen and they were rumored to be moving out of the house on Abbott Road. Either they hadn't gotten the same advice as Lew gave me or else the feds had moved more quickly.

And, with that news came the renewed speculation that police were 'close to a possible arrest' in George's 'strange death'.

Oh, and Susie Perkyboobs announced she was pregnant. With George's child.

She had been out of the news for almost three weeks, so I guess it was time for some new headlines. She appeared at a press conference, beaming and already in a maternity smock, to announce that she was preggers with George's love child.

The same day, an attorney served me with papers indicating Susie would be seeking child support and a share of George's estate for the sake of Susie's little bastard.

The next day, Lew and I went back to Boston PD headquarters. I thought it was for another Q&A with Detectives Tucci and Halliday, and I was fully prepped on what not to say.

Instead, I was formally charged with the murder of my husband.

16.

On *Law and Order*, a bailiff calls a docket number and all those rich defendants represented by well-groomed attorneys in three piece suits stand up in a straight line and make their appearance before a judge. The judge asks the most expensive looking of the attorneys, usually a Tony Roberts look-alike, how his client pleads. The client, a smug look on his or her face and perfect, fresh done hair, pleads 'not guilty'. The judge makes a great quip, sets some obscenely high bail, bangs his gavel, and says, 'next case'.

That's not how it works in real life.

In real life, Lew and I showed up at the Boston PD headquarters on Tremont Street at 11 a.m. As soon as I got in the door, Detective Halliday was there with an enigmatic smile on his face. "We've got a surprise for you."

"Neither I nor my client like surprises," Lew said.

The surprise was a lineup. I was handed a card with the number '2' on it and told to go sit in a waiting room with some beat-up, government-issue metal chairs. Lew, of course, was going ballistic at the no-warning escapade. After about five minutes, four women joined me. All had dark hair that had been brushed into a vague approximation of my style, but two looked to be barely thirty and one was definitely pushing forty. One had enough foundation makeup on to be Michael Jackson in drag. Two of them were plug ugly and they all looked like they had taken advantage of the final markdowns at Filene's Basement. I didn't know who was supposed to be identifying me, but this looked like a setup of the worst kind.

They all spent the next several minutes looking at me out of the corners of their eyes. They all worked for the police department, of course, and were in on whatever joke was unfolding. They all knew one another and kept making low murmuring remarks in a shorthand I couldn't understand. The comments, I was certain, were about me and were unflattering. Cheap laughs for the hired help.

Detective Halliday stepped into the waiting room. "It's going to be a few more minutes." He had a weary look on his face. In the background, I could hear Lew talking steadily, though I couldn't tell to whom.

The four of them went back to peeking at me while pretending to be looking elsewhere. Finally, one of them – the one pushing forty and who also needed super-duper-control-top panty hose to keep a bulging tummy from popping open her blouse – nodded at me and said, "So what have they got you in for?"

As if she didn't know.

"Jaywalking," I said. "I tell you, this town is tough on crime."

One of the others sniggered. They went back to muttering among themselves.

Ms. Tummy Bulge, though, wouldn't let up. "I mean, what happened? Everybody around here thinks it was justified. And with that whore saying she's pregnant… I mean, hell, I'd poison my husband, too."

I rolled my eyes. This was supposed to be where I made an 'excited utterance' that was not protected by any confidentiality.

The conference room door flew open. Detective Halliday stalked in, his face purple. He waved at the four women. "Out," he said. The four women obediently got out of their chairs and filed out of the room.

He pointed at me. "You, come with me."

We walked down a short hallway, Halliday muttering a string of obscenities aimed at no one in particular but, I suspected, caused by my attorney.

He pulled open another door. Lew and Detective Tucci were inside, seated on opposite sides of the table. It was a smaller room than where I had briefly met Sean O'Connell, but it had the same one-way mirror taking up one wall.

I threw Lew a questioning look and he shook his head to mean, 'later'.

"We're here for one more chance to get your story – the real story - before this escalates," Halliday said, biting off his words. Whatever had transpired, my side had won. He took out a notebook from his back pocket. "Tell us in your own words, what happened on the morning of June 27th…"

Lew jumped in. "No," he said. "There will be no free-form narratives today. If you have some specific questions, we'll try to help you. But no soliloquies."

Halliday bit his lip. "This is ridiculous."

Detective Tucci stepped up to the plate. "Let's go back to early April when you discovered your husband had started dating Susan Booth. When, to the best of your recollection…"

And so it went for three hours. My story was written down and every detail was explored. The closest thing to 'new territory' was an interest in why I had come to rent three James Bond movies the night before George died. I said my husband had seemed depressed and I wanted something to take his mind off of work.

At the end of the three hours, Tucci and Halliday looked at one another. Tucci got up and left the room. Halliday played with his pencil.

Five minutes later, she was back. With her was a uniformed policewoman who stood inside the door but said nothing. As soon as Lew saw the second woman, he said angrily, "Oh, come on. This is ridiculous…"

"…placing you under arrest for the murder of your husband," Tucci said, ignoring Lew. "You have the right to remain silent. If you give up that right, anything you say can be taken down and used against you in a court of law. You have the right to an attorney. If you cannot afford an attorney, one will appointed for you. Do you understand these rights?"

As I said that I did, she placed a pair of handcuffs on me.

Through all this, Lew was chewing out the two detectives, calling it a 'grandstanding act' and 'the kind of stunt that ends careers'.

"Take her across to booking," Tucci said to the uniformed policewoman.

As I was led away, I heard Halliday say to Lew, "You play rough, we play rougher."

Booking was a relatively simple matter. A desk sergeant took down my name and the charge against me, which the policewoman provided. I was asked for two forms of identification. I wondered what would have happened if I had only one? Would they let me go home? Then, the desk sergeant said, "Molly, please hold on to the accused's purse. Also her belt and shoes. Take her down to holding. We're a little backed up at fingerprinting and it may be a while."

"What?" I said.

I was roundly ignored.

One floor down from booking were four holding cells. Three were for men, one for women. I was still in handcuffs. As I was led past the men's holding cells, each of which contained four to five occupants, I got wolf whistles and, 'Hey, mama' calls. Because it was supposed to be a police interview, I had worn a longish black skirt and a grey silk blouse – my modified grieving widow outfit. There was nothing even remotely sexy about the way I was dressed, which made the taunts all the more insulting.

There were three women already in the holding cell. Two were African-American girls in their teens who looked like the most serious crime they could have committed was shoplifting. The third was a Latina, very heavy-set in her early twenties, who followed me with her eyes as I was led in.

"Why are chew here?" she asked in an accusing voice. "Chew here to keep watch on me? Chew tell them I say no-sing. An go fauk yourself."

I went off to the farthest corner from her. Unfortunately, the cell was only ten feet square.

A bench ran around three sides of the cell. One of the two girls came over and sat beside me. She fingered my silk blouse.

"Where'd you get that?" she asked.

All right, I was nervous. I had just been charged with murder. My attorney was nowhere to be seen. I was in a cell with bars across one side of it where a dozen men undressed me with their eyes and loudly told me how good they could make me feel. The whole place smelled of urine and disinfectant and the air conditioning was one step away from being completely non-functional. There was a crazy woman on one side of the cell who, but for lack of a good sharp knife, would gladly remove my liver to show 'them' she was not to be toyed with. And now one of the cell's other occupants was eyeing my blouse.

"Bloomingdale's, probably," I said.

"Where's that?" the girl asked.

"Chestnut Hill."

"Where's that?"

This conversation was going nowhere.

Half an hour later, the policewoman came back for me. Wordlessly, she took me back upstairs, where I was to be fingerprinted and photographed. I asked for an opportunity to at least comb my hair, and I drew a smirk. So, because I was sitting in a hot cell in an anxiety-inducing environment, I had raccoon eyes from smeared eye liner, a puffy red face from being overheated and, because I had sweated profusely, hair that looked like someone had poured a bucket of warm water over me. Naturally, I would see that mug shot five hundred times in newspapers and on television.

Also, because I still had no shoes, my height in the mug shot was shown as 5'6". I consider the three extra inches from my heels to be part of who I am, and it's right there on my driver's license. This was sheer pettiness.

I also asked to use the bathroom and was told I'd need to wait until I got to the courthouse. More pettiness.

Next came the arraignment. For this, I had to be transported over to Pemberton Square to the Suffolk County Courthouse. I was put in a van for the two mile trip. I was the lone passenger.

The van went nowhere. No driver, no attendant. Just me, locked in the back in a vehicle that was sweltering. Half an hour went by and still I sat. I was drenched in sweat, my blouse clinging to my body and my skirt wet to the touch.

Finally, there was a noise of a car door being unlocked. The driver's door opened and a man got in, grinning. "Gosh, I guess we forgot about you. Sorry about that."

The attendant got in the back with me. She looked cool and refreshed. The engine started and we pulled away.

Forgot, my ass.

The van went to a basement loading dock at the courthouse and I was led in, still in those damned handcuffs, wet from head to foot, and taken to yet another holding cell.

I asked to use the bathroom. I was told I should have done that back at the police station.

This time there were five women in the cell. Two were African-American and one of them looked as though she pumped iron, or maybe lifted cars for a hobby. One was a thin Caucasian woman who looked to be high on something. She sat in the corner and whimpered the whole time I was there. The last two were Latinas with matching cold eyes. I could see either of them carving their boyfriend's initials into the forehead of any woman who crossed them.

So, there I was, looking like I had been thrown into a swimming pool and needing very badly to pee. One of the Latinas walked up to me and looked me over head to toe. She curled her lip.

"You're the bitch who poisoned her husband," she said. "My

boyfriend say I ever pull that kind of shit on him, he going to pump me so full of holes I look like some kind of cheese."

Where the hell was my lawyer?

The other Latina came over and did the once-over. "Your man cheat on you? You couldn't keep him happy?" I felt like I was being measured for a noose made from my own pantyhose.

"You bitches leave her alone," said the woman who bench-pressed buses. "That's one brave lady. Yeah, he cheated on her with some conniving little whore who says she carrying his baby. Except I don't believe that for one second. You get that little baby one of those DMV tests. I'll bet it's some other man was sticking it in her. Girl like that ain't happy with just one woman's man. She be wanting two or three. So this lady give him those pills and his heart blew up. I say she did the right thing. If I had give my man them pills, I'd be better off than I am now. So you leave her alone, or you answer to me."

This was a jury of my peers. No question but they all figured I did it. It was just a matter of whether the homicide was justified. Somehow, I had a feeling that the judge's instruction to the jury would include a warning to disregard whether a 'DMV test' showed that Susie Perkyboobs' bastard was the result of some other guy sticking it in her.

The two Latinas looked dubiously at the weightlifter and backed off. The African-American woman smiled at me. I wondered what crime she was accused of that poisoning her 'man' was the lesser crime of what she was being arraigned for.

I returned the smile, grateful that I had a defender in this cell, even if her personal verdict was Murder with an Explanation. Her smile back at me widened into a toothy grin. I hoped whatever prison was in her future had decent dental care.

And then my name was called. I was taken to an elevator and the matron pressed a button for the tenth floor. When the door opened again, Lew was there. I had last seen him when I was led away to be booked – just about 2 p.m. It was now 4:45. My first words were something like, 'Thank God, where were you?'

"We've got about five minutes," he said, pulling me to a corner of the foyer outside the courtroom. "I've spent most of the time trying to put the brakes on this thing but this is Sean O'Connell's turf. Kat, in a few minutes they're going to take you in and ask how you plead. All you say is 'not guilty'. I know you'd like to scream at the judge and everyone else, but don't do it."

"They were going to do a lineup for the barista at the café," he said. "Can you believe it? Six weeks after the event, and after your face has been on everything but a box of Wheaties, those two clowns wanted to put you in front of the barista and see if she remembered you. I told them I'd have their badges if they did. It took three calls to put a stop to that. I've spent the rest of the time arranging your bond."

"Remember, your arrest is all part of getting Sean O'Connell elected to statewide office. This is all part of a script he's written and timetable he's devised for his own expediency. You're his high-profile case going into the primary. He puts you away and it's proof that rich people aren't above the law, and he's the champion of the little guy. You're three weeks of headlines and evening news commentary right before the primary. You're what's going to get him the nomination for attorney general."

It was all sinking in. Sort of.

"So just walk in, say those two words, and let me do everything else."

A bailiff came over and tapped Lew on the shoulder.

"Show time," Lew said.

"I look awful," I said.

He started to pull my hair back from my face but then stopped. "You look like the judicial system just put some poor, innocent woman through the wringer. You look like the poster child for police brutality and official misconduct. You look… sympathetic."

And so we filed into the courtroom and, after the judged banged his gavel and said, 'Next case', we approached the bench. But instead of that impeccably attired smartly coiffed defendant standing next to her attorneys, there I was, looking like a brunette Raggedy Ann dressed in wrinkled grey. Lew, at least, looked the part.

My docket number was read. The people of the Commonwealth of Massachusetts versus me. Premeditated murder.

"How do you plead in this matter?"

"Not guilty," I said in the clearest, strongest voice I could muster.

"Do the people ask for bail?" The judge looked over at the other desk.

Sean O'Connell, the DA from Central Casting, rose from his desk and buttoned his coat.

"Your honor, the People ask that the defendant be remanded without bail. This is a capital murder case. She is a flight risk and is believed by the Securities and Exchange Commission to have aided her late husband in a series of illegal market dealings that netted them many millions of dollars. The People cannot sleep as long as she has control…"

"Would two million dollars make the People sleep better?" the judge asked.

"The defendant has assets…"

"Two million dollars, cash or bond." The judge banged his gavel. "Next case."

At 4:55 p.m., timed perfectly for the evening local newscasts and the morning papers, Sean O'Connell stood in front the Suffolk County Courthouse and spoke of the 'overwhelming body of evidence' that had been gathered both by the Boston police and the SEC.

"Though she is a woman of means from a wealthy suburb, she is not above the law," O'Connell said. "We intend to prove she murdered her husband – poisoned him in a way to ensure a gruesome death – with malice aforethought. Her conviction will demonstrate that justice is blind."

It just might have been the worst day of my life… or at least my life so far.

17.

American jurisprudence is a wonderful thing. 'Innocent until proven guilty' and 'reasonable doubt' really are the way it works. Better yet, the deck is stacked against the prosecution. Through this wonderful thing called 'discovery', the police and the district attorney are required to turn over everything they have to the defense. They have to lay out their case in its entirety – though not necessarily in the right order - and the defense gets to weave that evidence into anything that might establish uncertainty in the mind of a jury. The defense, on the other hand, needs only turn over little more than a list of potential witnesses.

On the other hand, there is also trial by press.

Sean O'Connell excelled at selectively leaking material. Over the course of a few days – a tidbit or two each day to keep the story fresh, and rotating those tips among various favored media outlets – all of New England knew that Paul and I had discussed the effect of Ritvin and Viagra, that I had appeared at Paul's offices a few days later, and that Ritvin was missing from the company's unlocked pharmacy. The press also knew that I was a round-heeled trollop who had been cheating on her husband since our first anniversary and whose taste in reading ran to acting out 'Madame Bovary' with the lone male member of my book circle.

Other leaks filled in my motives. George, obviously, was no saint, and my intention was to get rid of him to in order to get my paws on his ill-gotten millions. I had stalked him and his various girlfriends for months, waiting for the right opportunity. George also wanted to get rid of me, though in the conventional, non-deadly way, in order to marry the Other Woman, or at least that was what Susie Perkyboobs said in her affidavit. It was all a question of my getting rid of George before my husband gave me the boot.

In response to this onslaught, our side said… nothing.

"Let Sean try his case in the press," Lew said. "If he taints the jury pool, he hurts himself. Be patient. Time is our friend."

So was having a lot of home equity. My bail had been set at two million dollars because I was considered a 'flight risk'. My house was pledged as collateral, but the bond carried an effective interest rate of ten percent. I was getting poorer by the week waiting for trial.

Sean O'Connell's calculated leaks provided us the opportunity to see bombshells coming. It didn't always mean we could readily defuse them, though. Take, for example, the Boston *Herald* headline:

SUSPECT TOLD LOVER, 'MURDER AN ALTERNATIVE TO DIVORCE'

All right, so Cliff – the professor from my reading circle – and I had some pillow talk between bouts of lovemaking. And, sometimes that talk centered on what a lout George was. I will acknowledge that I said things that I shouldn't have. My affair with Cliff was winding down right about the time that George started prowling around for twenty-six-year-olds who didn't mind pudgy, thin-haired, married boyfriends.

One languid afternoon as we lay in bed, waiting for Cliff to recover, I remember getting on the subject of the astronomical cost of divorce. I think the genesis of the conversation was Donald Trump separating from his fourth or fifth wife. Cliff asked if divorce was always the only alternative for unhappily married couples, and I said something like, "well, there's always murder," and then added with a Nixonian twist, "But that would be wrong."

Honest to God, when I had that conversation, I wasn't thinking about killing George. I wasn't even thinking about divorcing him. I was just a Wellesley Hills housewife who was getting even with her philandering husband by engaging in some tit-for-tat afternoon delight. I was having a roll in the hay with a good looking guy who paid me lots of compliments and was still fascinated by the sight of me prancing around naked.

That's not the way it came out in the *Herald.*

The way the newspaper played it (and of course, the way it was picked up by the rest of the media), I had wondered aloud if I might be better off with George dead with a lot of help from me, rather than the two of us squabbling over the value of Great Aunt Agatha's Tiffany vase in a lawyer's office. Moreover, my openly discussing such an alternative had sent Cliff fleeing from my bed, never to return.

"I concluded she was one very strange lady," Cliff was quoted as saying. When he said it, he was probably puffing a professorial pipe, wearing a tweed jacket with elbow patches, and resting his hand lightly on the knee of the female reporter interviewing him.

After the article appeared, I gave Phoebe all the pertinent unpublished details, including the information that, after Cliff worked his way through two more members of the book circle, he decided he wanted to come back for seconds with me. By then, however, I knew what George was up to and had taken my vow of temporary chastity. Cliff was persistent, though. He plied me with flowers and copies of erotic Victorian novels. Whatever his reason for fleeing my bed, it was only a temporary adjustment.

My permanent adjustment was to take Cliff's name off of the list of men I wanted to look up after all of this was over. If it ever was over.

It was also heartwarming to see how George's family lined up in the matter of my innocence or guilt. The two 'original equipment' children, Carl and Celeste, branded me a harlot and an adventuress who had attempted to gain entry to the family fortune by marrying their slightly dim and easily swayed half-brother. Their lone regret was that they had not more forcefully intervened to prevent George from marrying me in the first place, but I had railroaded through the engagement in such record time that they had never been able to pull George off to the side for a heart-to-heart about the true nature of his scheming beloved.

Carl, true to the roots of the Republican Party, also wondered aloud if this might not be an opportune time to re-open the issue of capital punishment in the Commonwealth. After that remark, I took Carl off of my Christmas card list.

Their intimation that George was a few silver spoons short of a tea service also helped buttress the family's contention that my late husband's foray into securities fraud was not part of a larger family tradition. Carl hinted broadly that I 'must have played a major role' in leading George off of the straight and narrow, and the family vowed to expend 'whatever resources were necessary' to prove that I was leading George by his weenie. It was another reason to leave him out of my future holiday plans.

Rachael fell squarely into my camp, not that anyone listened to her. Her opinion, preached to every reporter who made the mistake of getting remotely near her or calling her for comment, was that George was a poster boy for male predators everywhere, seeking out impressionable, misguided needy women searching for a father figure with Daddy Warbucks-size bank accounts. It didn't make much sense, but it got her tenure in 'Womyn's Studies' at her doinky college. I wrote her a congratulatory note.

Paul said… nothing. He apparently responded truthfully to the questions put to him by Boston PD investigators. Working alongside Phoebe, I read the transcript of his affidavit line by line and could find nothing that strayed from the truth either in my favor or in condemnation of me. He accurately recounted the conversation with me at his father's home – it was Detectives Halliday and Tucci who tried to twist that one into my inviting myself over to prowl around. The detectives repeatedly attempted to get Paul to say he might have told me there was Ritvin on the premises. They went away empty-handed.

My problem, of course, was that the conversation took place just as Paul described, and a prosecutor could argue – as was exactly the case – that our discussion planted the seed in my head that Ritvin plus Viagra was the way to get George out of my life.

The heartrending part of the transcript was Paul's description of the family dynamics. George, Paul, and Rachael were stateless refugees within the house, cut off emotionally from their father and consigned to seldom-visited suite of rooms in the care of a string of nannies and housekeepers, most of whom considered their primary responsibility to be keeping the children out of sight at all times. Paul made these points to theorize why George had ventured into solicitation of bribes and the sale of advance information to hedge funds.

The police, of course, were looking for a link back to me. They didn't get it. Instead, they got, on the record, a sad tale of a dysfunctional family that had produced a brilliant biochemist/entrepreneur, a ne'er-do-well miscreant, and a tight-assed Republican. And those were just the menfolk.

Lew read the transcript and said Paul's description of George's early family life would help our case. I told Lew that unless we absolutely needed such testimony to win my freedom, we should leave the family's troubles back in Ipswich. I guess I had no desire to drag Paul through his family's muck. I figured I owed him that much.

While the Boston PD was turning over rocks looking for nasty things to say about me, Lew's band of investigators was off looking for, if not exculpatory evidence, then things that would point a jury in a different direction.

They found quite a collection of fun facts. To start with, George was already reeling in his next twenty-six-year-old playmate. He would troll for them over lunch, looking in restaurants, hotels, and shops. When he found a possible candidate, he would get a name and then start researching using all the tools available to a securities analyst. If George was able to impress women of a certain age with his hipness and knowledge of things that interested these post-collegiate cuties, it was because he had steeped himself in exactly what they professed to love about life. If Debbie dug INXS, George downloaded a dozen tunes and could sing the lyrics. If Bonnie went ga-ga over some obscure Mexican beer, George could be seen swigging a bottle and declaiming its virtues.

In the days before he died, George had narrowed his next conquest down to a field of three, all of whom had been wined and dined over lunches and, in one case, a long walk along the Charles that ended in a tentative kiss. My husband, ever the romantic.

Susie Perkyboobs, who if not the prosecution's star witness, was certainly their link to my motive, was turning out to be considerably more complex than anyone ever imagined. For one thing, she had a child.

Yes, at the ripe old age of twenty, Susan Perkins Booth had given birth to a girl, now six and living with her maternal grandparents. The father, her sophomore-year boyfriend at Hofstra, where she had done her undergraduate work, had protested that he was not the father until DNA evidence sealed the deal.

Neither an engagement nor marriage was ever contemplated, as a full-cut wedding gown with an Empire waist was not what Susie had in mind when she walked down the aisle. However, the father's family had been induced to pony up a very large settlement in lieu of a lifetime of child support.

On the one hand, Susie could be portrayed as a brave, single mom, looking for the love of her life after being seduced and abandoned on that leafy campus. On the other hand, she had dismissed her pregnancy to her friends as a delayed case of the 'freshman fifteen' and handed over her newborn to grandma and grandpa between semester breaks. Thereafter, she made no mention of any kiddies to any of her friends, male or female. She had also not been to visit her daughter, now in first grade, since Christmas. Susie was definitely not Mommy Track material.

Lew predicted Ms. Booth would not hold up well on the witness stand.

There was also a matter of some computer fraud in her background. In her senior year, Susie and some friends had bought and sold term papers with abandon. She had netted a few thousand dollars but had stopped promptly when it was apparent the college had caught on. The transgression was apparently considered minor by the college, as it had neither kept Susie from graduating from Hofstra nor from being accepted at Cornell's School of Hotel Management. The rampant plague of term papers being sold over the internet was still a few years in the future.

To a nimble lawyer, however, it was a fairly simple leap of *modus operandi* to go from peddling cut-and-paste term papers on Ibsen and the Modern Drama to pushing George into seeking a few hundred thousand for an advanced peek at his treatise on concept restaurants.

Lew predicted a field day, and the best part was that he didn't have to tell Sean O'Connell anything about what he had in mind, whereas Sean had to turn over every transcript and scrap of paper he was using to build his case. Oddly, Susie's youthful transgressions did not turn up in any of the discovery material that arrived by the box load each week. If the prosecution hadn't investigated their own witness, tough luck.

* * * * *

And then one day in late August, the SEC called. They wanted, they said, to offer a deal.

Jason Whitburn, of course, had something else in mind. The sneaky little bastard would say anything to get you into a meeting and then he would start throwing papers on the table. It was August, he ought to be on vacation. Instead, he was spending his summer bound and determined to put me in jail.

We were in the same drab conference room as we had been in seven weeks earlier, though this time there was no one transcribing the conversation, which I thought ominous. Whitburn and one deputy, Miss Shelf Butt, handled the meeting.

It took only about six minutes to get to his real purpose. Whitburn threw down three transcripts. All were from executives of small restaurant chains that George had taken pity on and initiated coverage. All three company CEOs spoke of George requiring a 'side deal' to kick-start coverage: $175,000 wired through a series of accounts, with continuing payments after the first year.

Two of the companies had also paid $50,000 to secure an upgrade to a 'buy' recommendation after George initiated coverage with a 'neutral' rating. George had said the rating would not change until the additional payment was made.

"The train's leaving the station," Whitburn said, flexing that obnoxious rubber band between his fingers. "We've got the Quant Four payments, we've got the insider trades, and now we've got the solicitation and acceptance of bribes for research coverage. Out of the $4.9 million you and your husband stole, we've now accounted for $4.4 million."

Note how he kept saying, 'you and your husband stole.'

"Half a million to go," Whitburn said. "We believe those half million in payments were from other hedge funds for the same information you and your husband provided to Quant Four. If you help us nail the other hedge funds, there's a deal to be made. The minute we get the names on our own, we're going to hang you out to dry so long you'll get stretch marks."

I loved the guy's mixed metaphors.

"Turn over the computer or the copies of the hard drive I'm sure you made, and maybe we can work on a plea deal that keeps you out of prison," Whitburn said, twiddling his rubber band. "Keep playing coy and you and Mrs. Brandt are going to have adjoining cells, and it isn't going to be someplace where you can polish your tennis game."

Now, the truth of the matter is that I never broke the code on the names on George's entries. They were Alicia, Patricia, Joanie, and Queenie. 'Queenie' had the largest number of entries and was for the greatest aggregate amount. With twenty-twenty hindsight, 'Queenie' was Quant Four. It would follow that the names of the other three hedge funds began with the letters 'A', 'P', and 'J'. Unfortunately, that narrowed the field to about three hundred funds.

As to back-up disks, I shredded them between the time I fed George his Ritvin and when he took the second part of his lethal cocktail. So, even if I had been of a mind to assist the SEC in bringing evil hedge funds to their knees, I couldn't.

I smoothed my skirt. "I'm sorry, Mr. Whitburn," I said softly. "I never knew my husband had some other computer, and he never shared any information about anything illegal he might be doing."

Whitburn glared at me, his face a few inches from mine, his pointed teeth clacking away. He had acne scars that a little day surgery could have erased. "You're going down, you know. You're going down hard. And it's going to be my pleasure to put you away for a very long time."

While I was composing a tearful retort, Lew jumped in.

"Jason, did you ever follow up on my suggestion to search Miss Booth's apartment?"

Whitburn looked up from me, where his scowl was giving me the creeps, to Lew. "What suggestion?" Whitburn asked.

"The suggestion I made right after our first interview," Lew said. He snapped open his briefcase and withdrew a six-page letter. Lew put on a pair of glasses and flipped to the second page of the letter. "'I suggest you treat Susan Perkins Booth with the same suspicion that you have for my client,'" he quoted. "'Miss Booth had at least as much to gain as did my client. I would expect, at a minimum, a thorough search of her home and workplace.'"

Lew took off his glasses and handed Whitburn the copy of the letter. "Well, did you?"

Whitburn took the letter and glanced at the paragraph. "That's none of your business," he said. There was a hint of defensiveness in his voice.

"I'll take that as a 'no'," Lew said. "You've got a young, impressionable paramour who will do anything for her lover. Hell, he's convinced her he's going to leave his wife and marry her, according to her statement to Sean O'Connell. Let's say he asks her to hide the computer for a few days because he suspects the SEC is on his tail. Do you think she'd hesitate for even a moment? I believe your records show that the computer wasn't used from my client's house either the day before or morning of his death."

"That's bullshit," Whitburn said. "We've got your client on video…"

"You've got diddly-squat, counselor," Lew said. "You've got a couple of grainy photographs that could be of any of fifty women. The computer wasn't in my client's house when you searched it just hours after her husband's death, and I can't imagine that poor Kat was contemplating a visit from the storm troopers the same evening her husband succumbs to a heart attack. Did it ever occur to you that the computer might be at his lover's apartment, stashed away from prying eyes?"

"No, and I'm not going on any wild goose chases to help you keep your client out of prison on her husband's murder charge," Whitburn snapped. But there was an undercurrent of concern. Whitburn's eyes went to the letter. He quickly skimmed its contents. "Defense lawyer bullshit, pure and simple. Go peddle it somewhere else."

"Oh, I intend to," Lew said, and there was a twinkle in his voice. "'SEC single-mindedly pursues just one suspect, ignoring anything and anyone else that doesn't conform to its theory of the crime.' God, I love my job."

"You forgot about her using that computer all those days after her husband left for work," Whitburn said, smirking.

"And you can prove old George didn't take the day off? Or just go in late? Do securities analysts punch time clocks these days? Come on, Jason. You've got a case that was already full of holes, and now it turns out you didn't even check out the girlfriend's apartment. I sure as hell hope you're not contemplating an indictment. Prosecutorial misconduct can make getting a job in the private sector a real bear."

Whitburn tugged on his rubber band so hard it snapped, which must have really hurt.

"I can get an indictment an hour after I walk into that grand jury," Whitburn said. "Your client is dirty. You know she's dirty. Sean O'Connell knows she's dirty. Hell, everyone in Boston knows she killed her husband, and you'll probably see a raft of copy-cat murders by every housewife who ever suspected her other half was getting some on the side."

A pause, and then Whitburn said, "Get her out of here, counselor. We'll find the funds on our own. We've got the list of suspicious trades. Someone else will take the deal and name the names. Then, your client is going on trial for securities fraud and solicitation of bribes. She'll get twenty years and, when she gets out, she won't be young and cute any more. She'll be one more old, wrinkled, gray-haired broad coming out of prison, living in a half-way house and dressing from Goodwill. Just get her out of here. Get her out of my sight."

If his intent was to hurt me, he succeeded. If he was trying to scare me, he also did a fairly reasonable job. I had never contemplated prison. I intended to age very gracefully and take full advantage of cosmetics and anti-wrinkle drugs. I had no intention of allowing my hair to go gray before I was sixty-five and I had not worn second-hand clothes since I was eleven, and even then, I had told my mother I would rather go naked than wear someone's hand-me-downs.

Jason Whitburn laid out an alternative future, one that was unpleasant to think about.

As we walked back to Lew's car, I asked him how he thought it had gone.

"He's probing, I'm probing," Lew said. "I stuck him hard with that letter, and now he's going to have to go back and cover his behind on every one of those points, which is going to cost him time. But you have to understand that it used up an arrow in my quiver, and we don't have that many arrows."

"What I'm trying to do is avoid a securities trial," Lew continued. "I'm trying to avoid an indictment. I'm trying to get Jason to concentrate on going after the big fish and leave you alone. His problem – which means it's also your problem – is that George was his one, dead-to-rights conviction and it was only through Jason's sheer stupidity that George hadn't already been brought in and charged."

"Jason could have offered George a deal: two to five years, disgorgement of gains and the loss of his license in return for naming the names of the funds what were paying him and agreeing to testify. All the circumstantial evidence was already in place. Jason wasn't going to learn anything else with those vans parked outside. It was just him using his perks as a prosecutor – 'get me 24/7 surveillance on that guy and turn his life inside out'. Had he pulled George in one day earlier, he'd be king of that sad little hill of humanity that is the SEC. He'd have a bunch of hedge funds on the record as bribing analysts. He'd have multiple analysts on the take. George would be his star witness and George would have single-handedly made Jason Whitburn's career."

"Instead, two things happened: Quant Four blew up over copper, and your husband died. For Jason, the frustrating thing is that Quant Four's coming undone over copper never involved anything illegal. Peter Brandt and his buddies figured out an angle: take a basic commodity and control the futures market in it. There's nothing illegal about trying to manipulate the law of supply and demand because, over the long term, you can't. By bidding up futures sky-high, they brought in a whole new supply of copper for sale right now. At any point in time, Quant Four could have sold those futures and pocketed those billions. But they got so enamored of their genius that they forgot about their exit strategy."

"So far as Jason is concerned, the one good thing to come out of that debacle was Peter Brandt and his attack of conscience. For about eight hours, he told them everything they wanted to know. Then Peter got smart and clammed up. His attorneys will claim duress and they might have a shot at getting the entire interview quashed. But there are the computers, and if they manage to break the encryption codes and get them introduced into evidence, Peter Brandt and your friend are pretty well cooked. We'll see, though. I once said I wouldn't want to be your friend's lawyer. She may yet find a way."

"The second thing that happened that day was that your husband had his heart attack. When George died, there went Jason Whitburn's career-making move. No deputy attorney general offer. No promotion to head of enforcement. He's just another schmo with a caseload of investigations who missed his big opportunity because he made the rookie mistake of waiting too long to haul in the fish."

Lew had been carrying on this monologue for two blocks as we walked. Now, he stopped, turned to me and took me by my arms. "He's transferred that blame to you, Kat. You're the reason for everything rotten that's ever going to happen to him for the rest of his sorry life. In his mind, you're the reason he doesn't have his star witness in front of that grand jury. And so, even though it's probably going to cost him his career, he's going to do everything in his prosecutorial power to prove that you were the power behind the throne."

"Kat, you've got a problem of being in the wrong place at the wrong time. Sean O'Connell wants to get you so that he can be the next attorney general of Massachusetts. Jason Whitburn wants to get you because it's preferable to admitting to himself that he did a major screw-up."

"And Kat, when it's personal, people start playing games with the truth. I want you to be prepared: it's going to get ugly."

If I was scared before, now I was terrified.

18.

When George died, my family and friends formed a tight cocoon around me. They believed me to be a bereaved widow whose husband had died tragically. George's dying in the arms of his mistress brought me substantial additional sympathy.

As knowledge of George's illegal activities became widely known, though, the cocoon loosened a bit. Surely, people thought, I must have had *some* inkling. The invitations dropped off, although I could still have dined out on any given day.

Then, I was charged with George's murder and, overnight, everything changed. Apart from Trish and Nancy, my friends abandoned me. Like most law-abiding citizens, my former friends believed that police departments do not maliciously arrest innocent parties and that first-degree murder is a charge pursued with utmost care and attention to civil liberties. If I had been arrested, there must have been a great deal of evidence and certainty on the part of that nice, sincere Suffolk County District Attorney. Because DAs would never, ever do anything just for political gain.

The phone still rang, but the callers were increasingly creepy. Magazines wanted me to tell them my story. 'Independent journalists' wanted to help me write a book about my ordeal. The *National Enquirer* and *Weekly World News* wanted me to confess to them exclusively, in return for which I would be paid handsomely. And *Penthouse* wanted me for a photo shoot; no doubt for something that would bear the title, 'The Girls of Maximum Security'.

Also, there were the pictures of me. Without nude snapshots, the internet would collapse from the collective boredom of its users. A fifteen-year-old photo of me, taken back at Syracuse at a fraternity party when I was blind drunk and wearing nothing but a grass hula skirt, made its way into the top ten list of requested links. Another, more intimate, photo, one that could only have been taken by Mark, my one-time fiancé, also attracted widespread viewing. Seeing that one hurt a lot. I learned to live with it, and to let all calls go to the answering machine.

One hot afternoon, just before Labor Day, I was in the den, watching some dumb, tearjerker made-for-TV movie on Lifetime, when the phone rang. As usual, I ignored it.

"Kat, this is Warren Marshall. I suspect that along about now, you're a lady who could use an uncomplicated day on the water. If so…"

I picked up the phone.

"Hello, Warren," I said, breathlessly. Yes, I had entrusted nearly five million dollars to this man, but I also longed for a non-judgmental voice.

"I'm going sailing Saturday morning," he said. "I thought you might want to come along."

"I'd love to," I said. So call me easy. He gave me an address in Manchester-by-the-Sea, a very, very expensive swatch of real estate on the north shore. He suggested nine o'clock.

It had been a very long time since I had looked forward to anything. George had been dead now for a little over two months. For most of that time, my world had revolved around defending myself. Lew and Phoebe were my family, occasionally interspersed with a quiet lunch or dinner with Nancy or Trish.

I spent an hour trying on clothes that Friday evening before settling on white capris and a simple tank top.

It's not a date, I kept telling myself. He wants to tell you about your account and he wants to do it out of earshot of investigators.

Then, why was I spending so much time looking at myself in the mirror, trying to decide if I had put on weight? Why did I take half an hour to do my makeup, then wash it off and apply just the basics before leaving the house?

Manchester-by-the-Sea is a remnant of the gilded age. Lots of old mansions, especially on the Atlantic Ocean strip. The mansions are situated on bluffs high above the water and there's frequently a beach down below. There's also a picturesque, sheltered harbor with lots of sailboat anchorages, and I imagined Warren's boat would be one of the big ones bobbing in the water as I drove up Route 1A.

The address I was given was on Gales Point Road, which turned out to be a short, poorly marked road. At the end of it was a driveway marked, 'Marshall'. It had a gate, the gate was open.

Warren Marshall had the best of both worlds. The house was on the protected side of the property and behind it was a dock. A short stroll across the grounds was the pounding Atlantic. This was a man with a lot of money.

Warren greeted me in the driveway – he had apparently been monitoring the camera that kept watch on the gate. He was in blue jeans and a very worn Harvard sweatshirt. He grinned and shook my hand.

"Come on in for a minute," he said, smiling broadly and showing a lot of dazzling white teeth.

When I had met him at his office, I had put Warren at somewhere between forty and fifty. Either the morning light was very flattering or else wind-tousled hair has a youth-inducing effect because I now put his age at the low end of that range. He wore round, wire-rimmed glasses, another youthful touch. His face, like his build, was long and lean. If I were looking for faults, I would say his ears protruded a bit too much and his nose was crooked, as though broken long ago.

When I saw him that first time, I hadn't thought of him as handsome. Maybe I had just been having a bad day. This morning, he looked… good looking. He also looked confident.

I stood in the foyer of a gorgeous, beautifully decorated house that clearly had a full-time housekeeper to keep it sparkling.

"Can I help?" I asked. Warren was quickly moving from room to room, gathering objects. One of them was a very large wicker picnic basket.

"I think I'm ready," he said. "I'm on my own this morning so I'm a little disorganized."

In front of me was now a picnic hamper, an insulated cooler, and freshly laundered towels. If this was disorganized, I couldn't wait to see the rest of it.

I had hoped for a tour of the house – I could see a large kitchen and a great room with a vast expanse of window overlooking the harbor – but instead, Warren handed me the towels and hefted the two containers as though they were five-pound weights.

"It's a 43-foot Northwind," he said without prompting as we walked down the dock. "It's about as big a boat as I care to handle by myself."

The boat – it was too small to be called a yacht – was all polished teak and mahogany. Everything gleamed, everything was tied down.

"Who does the bright work?" I asked, running my hand over a polished brass rail. I had heard that line in *The Philadelphia Story*. It exhausted my knowledge of nautical-speak.

"Not me," he said, and grinned again. "I go out, I come back. I call a guy up in Gloucester. The next day, while I'm at work, he and his crew do the scut work and it looks good as new by the time I come home. I also didn't cook the food. I don't claim credit for things I didn't do."

He started the boat's engines, which made a muted, purring sound. He untied some ropes and we pulled away from the dock.

"The first part is the roughest," he said. There was a chair behind him in the cockpit of the boat. I took my seat and held onto the railing.

We went out of the harbor and into the ocean. In a matter of seconds, the gentle bobbing was replaced by ocean swells. Warren gunned the engines and we turned into the waves. He gave his full attention to getting the boat clear of the rocks that jutted out of the water at the tip of the peninsula. For ten minutes, he said little but, 'hang on, we're about to get slapped.'

Fifteen minutes later, the shoreline was an interruption of the line between water and sky. Warren hoisted two sails.

"Are you sure I can't help?" I asked.

"The hard part's done," he said. "Now, we get to do some sailing."

We sailed for more than two hours. Warren pointed out landmarks back on shore and identified other boats out with us on the open water. He could even name boat owners based on a glimpse of a particular craft or its sail at a distance of a thousand feet.

We were sailing generally northward and Warren apparently had a destination in mind, though he didn't share that information with me. He trimmed sails and continually checked monitors, showing me how to read the depth meter and occasionally asking me to give him soundings. I wandered the boat but mostly stayed topside, enjoying the cool sprays of water on a morning that had been warm and humid on the mainland.

I had expected that my fascination with sailing would taper off after half an hour. Instead, I got into its rhythm. I began to sense small changes in the wind direction and speed, and would follow Warren's adjustments to settings and sails. He would explain why a sail had to be let out or pulled in. After an hour, I could predict what he would do. When I said, 'the wind is shifting about five points, you may want to trim the jib,' he replied, 'Instead of me doing it, why don't you?'

I felt like I had just passed my first test in sailing school.

Then, just about noon, he lowered the sail and I saw a small cluster of rocky outcroppings in the distance and, in their midst, a lighthouse. Warren took us to the sheltered side of one of the crags and dropped anchor.

"Where are we?" I asked.

"Safe from prying eyes, safe from eavesdroppers," he said. He pointed to the coast six or eight miles distant. "That's Portsmouth and Kittery. This is the Isles of Shoals. Star Island is a few miles up thataway. Just beyond it is Appledore Island, where Childe Hassam painted and Celia Thaxter wrote." He pointed generally north. "Star Island has an old hotel and gets some tour boats. But I don't think we'll be disturbed here."

I went with him below deck to a small galley and saloon. Warren had been right: everything was tied down, in its place. Books, charts, plates and glassware were all in compartments, some behind glass, others accessible by lifting brass knobs on teak hatches. In a few minutes, he had pulled out dishes and eating implements for two. The contents of the picnic hamper had been stowed in a refrigerator. Now, he began lifting out containers of food.

"This part I can help with," I said.

"Then be my guest."

While I took out food to feed a dinner party of eight, he turned his attention to the cooler. He extracted two bottles of white wine and held them out for my inspection. "Do you have a preference?" I shook my head and he weighed them in his hands before choosing one.

Then, the food was unpacked and on platters. The centerpiece was a lobster salad the way I had learned to enjoy them: all lobster meat with just enough dressing to hold the meat together. But just in case I was allergic to lobster, there were three different salads – chicken, beef and Greek. And if I wasn't a salad person there was a fruit platter heaped with cherries, peaches and grapes. And, if I happened to be a hedonist, there was a box of wonderful looking pastries. I was definitely a hedonist. And Warren was an exceptionally thoughtful host.

We filled plates and carried them up to the sailboat cockpit, where we ate with trays balanced on our knees.

He opened the wine, poured two glasses, and raised his in a toast. "To the start of journeys," he said.

Which made me wonder what kind of journey I was beginning. Was today the start of a fresh one? I hoped so, because the last two months had been fairly rotten as journeys went. On the morning I gave George that Ritvin, I had all manner of wonderful dreams in my head. I imagined I would be wealthy, well-dressed and single, surrounded by good looking men, all of them trying to catch my eye. I would be in Paris or Rome, or some luxurious spa where the weather was perfect.

Instead, I had no passport and was on an allowance from Lew, who had control of those funds I had been able to liquidate before Jason Whitburn froze everything in place. I couldn't go to some on-line dating service because I would attract every creep in the universe. Blind dates were out of the question because, while I might not know the person taking me to dinner, my face and biography had been dissected in lurid detail by every newspaper and local TV station. I was 'That Woman'.

I was ready for a new journey. I raised my glass and smiled.

Over the course of lunch, I learned a lot about C. Warren Marshall, tax attorney. He spoke freely of himself though not once did he ever say anything that even remotely sounded like a boast. I needed only prompt with a brief question to get a torrent of information. I learned he was forty-two and, true to his sweatshirt, had graduated from the University of Chicago and Harvard Law. His father had been the third-generation president of a bank in a small town in northern New Hampshire and had expressed some dismay when his son professed a preference to the law over the hallowed halls of finance. But tax law intrigued him more than the rote calculation of yield spreads.

He had married at twenty-seven, two years out law school and an associate at Hunter and Frederick. His wife, too, was a lawyer, and from a well-to-do Boston family. She practiced law on behalf of philanthropic organizations. It was a perfect life for a perfect young couple, he said. At thirty-two and with their first child on the way, they took the plunge, sold their one-bedroom Back Bay condo and bought a house in Manchester-by-the-Sea. Not the one I had been in that morning; a different one, a short distance away. In three years, there would be two children, a boy and a girl.

About the time they bought the house, Warren had discovered a wrinkle in the tax code. It was a loophole smaller than the eye of a needle, but through it could pass enormous amounts of money, untaxed and uncounted by the Internal Revenue Service. Warren had applied it on behalf of a Hunter and Frederick client being hounded by the IRS, and it had worked. This tiny hole allowed wealthy people to channel assets into offshore trusts, principally in the Cayman Islands, which had banking laws that placed an exceptionally high value on secrecy.

Other Hunter and Frederick clients learned of this loophole and demanded Warren's services. Hunter and Frederick's ethics partners scrutinized Warren's work and found that it skated right up against the edge of the law without ever quite crossing into illegality. Still, for a respected, conservative firm, it was just a shade too close to the edge. Warren was asked to refrain from using Cayman Islands trust accounts in the future.

The shade of the cockpit canopy shielded us from the late summer sun and a light breeze made the day seem endless. Warren poured a glass of iced tea from a pitcher. It was real, brewed tea; not something from a can or a bottle.

"That's when I quit," Warren said. "I had made partner. I had a future, or so I was told, as the head of the firm's tax practice. But I had a group of people in mind that could use my counsel, and most of them weren't the kinds of clients that Hunter and Frederick wanted to attract. So, I set up my own practice, and it blossomed."

"It sounds like the perfect ending," I said.

"Except that Cheryl hated the whole thing. I had a thriving practice and a secure future, but my wife said it was illegal and I was consorting with crooks. She said she couldn't live with someone who helped people evade taxes. She gave me the choice of going back to practice 'real' law or she would leave me."

"I explained that tax law was all about minimizing the payment of taxes. She had lived in this rarefied world of legal work for groups that had never paid taxes in their existence, even though some of them had massive endowments and paid their executives high six-figure salaries. I asked Cheryl if she thought some of her charitable trusts ought to be forking over some of their portfolio gains, and all she could say was, 'that's different.'"

"In the end, we divorced, although I suspect that the reason was less to do with my practice and more to do with basic personality issues. She and the kids still live in the house we bought. The place I'm in now came on the market two years ago. It let me be close to my children. It also had a dock. Those were the two things I had on my check list."

"Has she remarried?" *'Is there any chance of the two of you getting back together again?'* was the question I really wanted to ask.

He shook his head. "After the divorce, Cheryl jumped head-first into the 'mommy' thing. What work she still does is from home, and she is first and foremost a mother. If she's had a date in three years, I haven't heard about it."

To me, Cheryl sounded exactly like an alimony drone. But I held my tongue.

All through this long conversation, I had been braced for two things. The first was an invitation to retire to the huge cabin at the aft section of the boat where there was a very nicely made up queen-size bed. I had made up my mind just about the time I took out the three kinds of salads that I would say 'yes' to such an invitation. He was a thoughtful man, and I had a sense that the sex would be about me and what I wanted, instead of some macho display of athletics. I was also eight months into an unintended celibacy and was, frankly, ready and maybe even eager to get back to an activity I had always enjoyed.

But he never asked. He never even hinted obliquely.

The second thing I was braced for was The Question. I was expecting it from any direction – 'why did you kill your husband', 'when did you decide to kill him' or 'why did you choose Ritvin and Viagra over, say, electrocution in the shower'.

The question never came.

Instead, he asked me all about myself – especially about growing up in Minnesota. He reached into his pocket and pulled out a quarter. "I bet you were a cheerleader."

"Varsity or junior varsity?" I responded.

He looked me in the eye. "Varsity."

He kept his quarter.

He asked about hobbies, interests, films I had enjoyed, and all the other things that someone asks when they're interested in you. But there was not a question about George, how we had met, or what had gone wrong. And there were no questions about why, when I walked into his office that afternoon a month earlier, I happened to have the account number and routing information for a checking account in the name of Benito Morales containing $4,877,252.39, and have all the proper passwords to tap every last penny of that account electronically.

In fact, business reared its head only once, but it was a lulu. We were sailing back, the water was smooth and we sliced through it, throwing up a light spray that was cool and refreshing. We were sitting at the front of the boat, side by side, feet over side. I had one hand solidly on the deck rail. Warren, who expertly rose and fell with the boat and thus needed nothing to hold onto, sat beside me.

"Your accounts are all in place," he said softly. "It's all done and accessible at any time from anywhere in the world. It's in short-term

T-bills while you decide what you'd like to do over the longer term."

I gulped a 'thank you.'

"You know, you have another option in all this," he said, gazing out to the east, where Europe was the next landfall. "You could go someplace where they don't extradite Americans. Where, with the money you have, you could live very comfortably. I know a special kind of travel agent who could help you." Then he was silent, his piece said.

"Thanks," I said. "I guess I need to have that in mind as a backup plan. But I'd rather walk away from this a free woman who doesn't have to look over her shoulder every day for the rest of her life."

"You're on a relatively long leash right now," Warren said. "As you get closer to your trial date, it will get a lot harder. Eventually, it won't be an option."

I nodded.

We docked in Manchester in the late afternoon. I had not had a day like that in years. A blissful day with no worries or concerns. A day where it seemed nothing hung over my head. Eight hours after we pulled away from his dock, we eased back in.

Warren walked me to my car.

"Thank you," I said. "I didn't know how much I needed a day like this."

He said nothing, but he put his arms around me and kissed me. It wasn't one of those 'woman, now you belong to me' kind of kisses. It was a 'this is the start of something' kind of kiss, or at least that's the way it felt to me. I went weak in my knees.

"If you needed a day like this, then you'll need another one soon," he said.

"Oh, yeah," I said. "The sooner the better."

19.

When you are accused of first-degree murder, and when the SEC calls you an 'as-yet-un-indicted co-conspirator', you have one thing to think about when you get up in the morning: preparing your defense.

Lew handled one case at a time. Had I called him even a day later, someone else would almost certainly have called before me and I would have received a polite, 'he's not taking on any new clients at this time,' turndown from Phoebe.

I came to understand just how lucky I had been to get Lew as an attorney. He had spent thirty-five years as one of the 'name-on-the-door' partners at a Boston law firm specializing in criminal law. He had walked away from the practice five years earlier after losing a case he had thought he was going to win. Lew told me it was because he had spread his case load too thin, representing three clients while wooing a fourth. Phoebe told me it was because Lew had come to rely too much on associates whose sole aim was to gain as much experience as possible before hanging out their own shingle.

Whatever the reason, Lew had resigned his partnership and its probable million-dollar-a-year gross billings, and moved his office into a room of their Weston home. Phoebe, who had been a paralegal before marrying Lew and raising two children now in their thirties, became his secretary, legal assistant, and sounding board. Lew relied on a tight-knit team of free-lance specialists such as investigators, but he kept to the vow he made when he walked away from Griffith, Faircloth and Tate: one client at a time, no exceptions. Mine had been the first call after the Winstead jury returned its 'not guilty' verdict. My case sounded interesting. Lew took it.

Because much of my time was spent with Phoebe, I got to listen to many of the pleading calls from people who needed a top-notch defense lawyer. Phoebe was always polite and sympathetic. She was also firm. "I'm sorry, dear," she would say, and would mean it. "it's unlikely he'll be able to take on a new case until April at the earliest."

Oh, yes. I had a trial date. March 18. The day after St. Patrick's Day which, in Boston, is a legal holiday, except that it's called Evacuation Day. On the morning of March 18, with much of Boston hung over from drinking green beer, the grand Irish-descended Suffolk County District Attorney would begin jury selection. He would be looking for working class men and women who viewed the wealthy with suspicion and who believed there were inherently two justice systems in the country. One was for the rich, the other was for everyone else. He would seek out Catholic women who inwardly believed that murder was a mortal sin and that wives should be subservient to their husbands. He would seek out men who bore a grudge against women in general and uppity women in particular, regardless of how they answered qualifying questions on court.

Lew opined it would take a week to seat a jury, and then three weeks to try the case. That would put closing arguments right about April 15, the day everyone paid their income taxes and the day everyone was reminded that the rich avoided their fair share through financial shenanigans like offshore accounts. The case would go to the jury on April 17, Lew figured, and it would take the jury a few days to make their decision. They'd come back on April 19 or 20.

Which meant that for a solid month, Sean O'Connell would be a regular fixture on the front page and – barring another interesting murder or a three-alarm fire – the lead story on the evening news nearly every day. He would speak confidently about the state's case and the tenacious work of the men and women in law enforcement.

Very conveniently, the statewide primary would be held three weeks later. With the current Attorney General running for an open congressional seat, there was no incumbent to unseat. A conviction would make Sean O'Connell a shoo-in.

But that was months in the future.

Right now, we had to sort through the state's case, which arrived as un-numbered pieces of a jigsaw puzzle, and we had to build our own defense.

There's an old saw in the legal profession that says, when you've got a strong case, try the evidence. When you've got a weak case, put the other side's witnesses on trial. When you've got a really weak case, put society on trial.

Lew felt confident about the case inasmuch as it was all circumstantial. No one could prove I knew George had banked nearly five million dollars and there was no proof that I knew George had a stash of Viagra that he used to keep up with his hot young things. No one saw me take Ritvin from anywhere and the autopsy only indicated he ingested the drug sometime before noon.

But Lew was also a cautious man. Anyone who spoke in support of the state's case had to be called into question – 'put the other side's witnesses on trial'. Investigators developed dossiers on everyone on the state's list, from the investigating detectives to their expert witnesses. It was frightening how much of a person's life could be uncovered by a good investigator.

As the state's list grew, there were a few surprises. Jean Claude Martin, for example. Yes, in their third interview with Trish, she had acknowledged to Detective Tucci that the previous summer, she was reasonably certain I had a one-night stand with someone from Paris during our girls' weekend in New York. Detective Tucci had diligently contacted everyone from France who was in the hotel that night and found Jean Claude. He would be flown over for the trial to provide further proof that I was a shameless slut.

Trish also volunteered that I had spoken of having an affair with Phil Forster, George's co-worker at PJ&B – the one I had invented in order to deflect attention from my plan to murder George. This led to four increasingly heated interrogations of Phil by Detective Halliday. Phil truthfully swore that, while he may have made a pass at me at an office party and generally lusted after my body, we had never been involved. It was only when Phil could produce more-or-less ironclad evidence that he was in meetings or out of town when we were supposedly in our love nest at the Four Seasons that Halliday gave up and accepted that I had been lying to one of my best friends.

Ultimately, this led to a nasty call from Phil saying that my overactive imagination was going to cost him his marriage because, while he had finally been able to convince the police there was no affair, his wife remained unmoved. Like most calls, I did not pick up the phone. Instead, I listened to him alternately rant and cry for five minutes until my machine ran out of storage. I played the recording for Lew, who sympathized but said I was not to respond under any circumstances.

The way Lew saw it, I should plan on my reputation taking a beating at trial.

"But it's a long, long way from being an unfaithful wife with an even more adulterous husband to being a murderess," he said. "And, we have our secret weapon."

Our secret weapon: my decision that it was time to start a family – with George as the male parental unit.

Because we didn't have to disclose our strategy to the DA's office, we assembled our 'pregnancy defense' in complete secrecy: prescriptions, books, receipts, OB/GYN visits and conversations with Nancy on the subject.

Nancy had been interviewed twice by Detectives Tucci and Halliday. In the first interview, she had mentioned that I spoke of wanting a child. Because of their experience with Phil Forster, they ignored it as just more of my habitual lies. Instead, they pumped her for names of possible liaisons. Nancy, of course, had none to offer.

It must have been frustrating for the detectives. Their easiest path to a conviction would have lay in the discovery of an affair with someone – anyone – that would explain to a jury why I wanted to be free of George. For the first time since I was in high school, keeping my knees clamped firmly together had proven to be the right decision.

Through all of this, Lew pored over transcripts with me, asking me questions about why people said certain things and whether their recollection might be faulty in some regard. He also warned me that this was 'BIB' phase of the trial preparation process.

"O'Connell is going to bury us in bullshit," Lew said. "He's sending over some useful stuff, but he's also sending over garbage, knowing that we have to read it all, looking for that buried nugget that could hurt us. He's got two investigators and a staff of six taking depositions and evaluating evidence. While we're reading this stuff, he's also developing his 'real' case, which he's going to spring on us at the last possible moment. He'll argue to the judge that it's all material that came to his attention in the last weeks before the trial. It's called the 'Opening Argument Surprise', because it will come right as the trial opens, or even a few days into it."

"That's the stuff I'm bracing myself for," he said, looking me in the eye, "and it's why you've got to be absolutely honest with me whenever I ask you a question."

Lew also said that, unless the jury had a very plausible alternate theory of the crime, there was a very good chance that a civic-minded jury would insist on making someone responsible, and so would vote to convict the defendant. And so he worked to develop multiple theories, looking for the one that the jury could most easily follow.

In Lew's mind, there were two options. One was that George was experimenting with Super Viagra and accidentally over-medicated himself. It had the benefit of simplicity. No conspiracy was needed and the jury could just say, 'stupid bastard' and go home, feeling they had done their civic duty.

The problem with the first option was that there was no evidence George had ever spoken of Super Viagra or Ritvin. He had never researched it on his office computer, nor had he acquired any through the same sources that got him the cocaine and other drugs found in his office. It would take a leap of faith that George had done all of this in secret and that, further, he had over-medicated himself six-fold in his first experiment with the drug.

The second option was that someone else gave George that Ritvin. Someone else knew about George's stock market chicanery. Someone else had gained his complete confidence and knew the secret codes where his bribes and payoffs were kept. And, once that other person knew these things, George had become expendable. That other person might have even feared that she, too, was not part of George's long-term plans. That person had with cold calculation drugged him, wiped clean his accounts, and then watched him die that excruciating death.

That person, of course, was Miss Susan Perkins Booth. Our very own Susie Perkyboobs.

20.

Warren called about an hour after I got home that Saturday evening, just to make certain that I had found my way back to Wellesley. He thanked me for a beautiful day and for my sportsmanship at being willing to try something different.

Oh, was I hooked.

The following Wednesday, he called again and asked if I might be free for dinner Friday night. We went to one of those of-the-moment South End restaurants. As the parking valet opened the car door for me, I asked how he had gotten an 8 p.m. reservation on a Friday night on two days notice. He shrugged and said, 'investors get special treatment.'

I had been worried that people would recognize me. I needn't have bothered. From the moment I stepped out of the car to the time we were seated at a secluded table was under a minute.

The meal was perfect, the wine was just right and the service solicitous. This had been the kind of place where George squired his chippies except that I bet he never got a table this good or the waiter who did not hover but could be summoned with little more than a nod of the head. All George had was money to throw around and a good-looking brazen hussy on his arm. Warren had influence.

Dinner went on for a leisurely two hours. I remembered reading a review of the place when it opened a few months earlier, and the reviewer's complaint was that the check arrived with the coffee, unprompted, so great was the demand for tables. I guess no one rushed an investor.

Part of the dinner conversation had been about the business of running restaurants. Oddly enough – or perhaps it was symptomatic of the man I had married – George had followed the restaurant industry for eight years and had never spoken to me about the nuts and bolts of what it took for a restaurant to break even. It wasn't that I had showed no interest, it was just that George's work, like his womanizing or soliciting bribes, was something he kept compartmentalized.

Warren, by contrast, asked if I was interested, and then dissected the restaurant, table by table. Table 6, the one closest to us, had started with martinis and then ordered two bottles of a fairly expensive California cabernet for the party of four. "That's going to be a thousand dollar check before the evening is out," he predicted. "Four hundred dollars of wine and spirits, four hundred dollars of food, and two hundred for tax and tip. If the waiter is good, he'll bring out the liqueurs on a trolley and move up the bill – and his tip – by another hundred."

By the time the evening was over, I understood restaurant economics as well as if I owned one.

But we also talked about places we had seen, and he was especially interested in where I had traveled and what I had enjoyed. I was embarrassed at the shallowness of my experience – various islands in the Caribbean and resorts in Mexico, mostly. One of my two trips to Europe had been in high school, but Warren said that it all counted. "You see the world through others' eyes, and that's the important part. His travel had included 'a couple of dozen countries', some on walking tours. "I like to see it slowly."

Then Warren handed his keys to the waiter. As quickly as we had entered the restaurant, we were back in his car.

I was thinking about the inverse of 'seeing it slowly' as he drove me home. Speeding things up was what I had in mind. He had touched my hand across the table a few times and it sent one of those shivers down my spine. He put his arm around me as we made our way out of the restaurant, and the touch was cool and dry.

So, when he walked me to my door, I invited him inside, where I fully intended to rip off his clothes and mine, make love on the first level surface I encountered, and be damned if I got a rug burn on my back.

"Come on inside," I said. "I'll put on some coffee."

He kissed me very tenderly on the lips.

"Kat, you're still in a tough spot. The last thing you need is to turn on your television tomorrow morning and see one of those empty-headed reporters breathlessly telling everyone there was a strange sports car parked in front of your house overnight."

Note that he had seen right through the offer of coffee.

"But I'm going sailing next Saturday morning. And I'd be delighted if you'd join me."

I thought about that lovely, queen-sized bed in the aft cabin.

"I'd love to," I said.

* * * * *

The following Saturday morning at approximately 10:14 a.m., my eight-month celibacy ended.

If you want lurid details, make them up. Or read Tami Hoag. It was beautiful, it was wonderful, it was private. And everything I suspected about Warren was correct. He made it all about me.

Afterwards, there was Champagne. It was a celebration, after all.

In my experience, there are two kinds of women. One treats sex as recreation, the other as some kind of sacrament. I've always been solidly in the recreation camp. But, when you've gone without sex for a prolonged period, you pay attention to all the little details, which pushes it slightly over to the sacrament side.

I noticed the details. Like the smell of his soap and the feel of his tender hands. But, damn it, I said no lurid details. So I'm going to stop.

Also in my experience there is sex that just blends into the general background noise and there is sex that lingers in memory. Sex that you can instantly recall and get an involuntary shudder weeks later. Sex that makes you gasp.

No, damn it. No more.

Afterward, we sailed. Warren opened the sails full and we raced faster than I thought any boat could travel, the hull slicing though the dark blue-gray water of Cape Cod Bay. We sailed in the direction of the wind, wherever that was taking us.

It was a metaphor, I imagine. Two people, running at top speed without really knowing where they were headed. The thrill was in putting the past behind us, putting distance between the point we had started and the present.

At three o'clock, Warren checked his watch. "We'll need to get back," he said. "I have the kids for the rest of the weekend and I'm supposed to pick them up by six."

He smiled as he said this and his eyes told me that this was the truth. There was no irony in his voice and no regret. I was his from nine in the morning until six at night. Then, he shifted gears, closed one door and walked into another world.

But he held me for those remaining hours. We stood in the cockpit, hands around one another's waist. Eventually, the shoreline came into view.

C. Warren Marshall had two mistresses. I was the second. For many Saturdays afterwards, we would sail and make love on the ocean, the swells becoming part of our rhythm. When the weather turned foul, I still arrived Friday night or Saturday morning but we stayed in his grand house and lost ourselves under eider down comforters and antique quilts. We raced through the house in thick terrycloth robes, swam in an indoor pool, and fed grapes and cherries to one another in front of a crackling fire.

Shortly after five each Saturday, I would collect my things. There would be long, lingering kisses in the driveway and expressions of joy for a wonderful day.

At six o'clock, he would leave to collect his first mistress: the legacy of that earlier life and marriage and commitments he chose to keep. I did not ask to become part of that other life. It is not something that a mistress asks if she wants to keep her place in her lover's life. I could long for him to invite me to stay, to be there when he returned with those two children. But I could not expect it.

We lived in the moment, getting to know one another intimately and – at least on my part – finding that familiarity bred fascination. Warren possessed none of the traits that had caused me to grow bored with George. He was the man of my dreams.

Was it reciprocal? He once asked me if I minded what he did for a living. "I hide money for people," he said. "I abuse the tax code, distort the law to benefit the already wealthy."

"Are you ashamed of what you do?" I asked in return.

"No."

"Then how can I mind? Why should I mind?"

It was the end of the discussion.

But not the end of my thoughts on the subject. What if George had confessed to me at the outset that he was taking money from hedge funds? What if he had shown me the accounts and admitted that he was being paid under the table by companies that needed research coverage?

I know what I *wouldn't* have done. I wouldn't have asked him if he was ashamed of what he did. Instead, I would have screamed that he was an idiot and demanded that he stop. I would have told him that he probably needed to hire a really good lawyer and go to the SEC and make a voluntary statement. And I would have started preparing for my life to come apart.

So, why was it different with Warren? Was it because what he did was legal, at least for the moment? Hadn't Jason Whitburn of the SEC said that Warren was also under suspicion?

I knew it was different. I just wasn't certain I knew why.

I did know one thing, though. I was achingly in love with Warren.

21.

Massachusetts is one of a handful of states with what is called a 'reciprocal discovery' law. In theory, it requires that the defense turn over to the prosecution any information that the defense intends to use to impeach a prosecution witness. The idea is that if the defense knows that expert witness Joe Smith has lied about having a PhD in computer science, then the prosecution won't waste its time putting Joe on the stand, only to have the witness's testimony blown to smithereens when it is revealed that the 'doctorate' is really two years at a junior college plus a stint as a computer programmer. Also in theory, reciprocal discovery ought to allow the defense to demonstrate that a key prosecution claim isn't supported, thus winning a dismissal of charges and avoiding an expensive court trial.

Lew, however, said that in practice, reciprocal discovery is used to help prosecution witnesses lie better. His view is that professional witnesses such as police detectives and medical examiners are very adept at 'modifying' their testimony to accommodate expected cross-examination questions. When defenses turn over damning statements made in previous trials or in interviews, the prosecution merely helps the testifying detective to 'refine' those statements. And, don't bother trying to depose a police officer. They'll have three lawyers in the room objecting to every question.

Also in Lew's view, an aggressive prosecutor like Sean O'Connell sees pre-trial preparation as a game rather than as a truth-seeking function. Accordingly, Lew took reciprocal discovery with a grain of salt, treating 'statements' in its narrowest sense. We knew all about Susie Perkyboobs' tainted brush with motherhood, but we didn't know about it from her because we never deposed her. As such, there were no 'statements' to turn over to the prosecution. Susie was going to get her comeuppance without any advanced warning, and if O'Connell didn't bother to check her out, well, tough luck.

All through the winter months we prepared our case. Discovery documents from the district attorney's office slowed to a trickle and then stopped. We lobbed over a handful of documents intended more to consume investigators' time than to offer up any clue as to our defense.

Slowly, the jigsaw puzzle that was O'Connell's case came together. A handful of facts tied together what was otherwise a largely circumstantial case. I knew all about George's affairs. This was a fact because they had recovered hundreds of photos I had taken and notes I had made from my old Gateway computer. They *assumed* that if I knew about his cheating on me, I had also figured out about his peddling information to Quant Four and other nefarious deeds. The physical evidence was slim: that missing third computer had been used multiple times after George had supposedly left for work.

So, I had a cheating husband who had also secretly banked a couple of million dollars. Add to that the incontrovertible evidence that I was a Woman of Extremely Loose Morals. Their witness list included everyone who had ever gotten to second base with me, and the trial judge had been given a thirty-page brief explaining why allowing instances of my sluttiness was worth sharing with the jury. Lew read the brief and concluded that he could spend a couple of weeks fighting it, but even if it were excluded, O'Connell would just leak out the information in the days before the trial.

Kat was easy. So move on.

From there, O'Connell's case required a leap of faith on the part of the jury. George was rotten, but instead of just divorcing him, I decided I was going to kill him. The lone evidence was Cliff's recollection of my 'well, there's always murder' musing.

"This is the part he's holding back," Lew said. "If O'Connell is going to convict, he needs stronger evidence that you contemplated murdering your husband in the weeks before June. That's going to be the surprise evidence."

And, in Lew's view, manufacturing such evidence was not beyond Sean O'Connell.

From there, the DA's case picked up steam. With murder firmly in mind, I began looking for the opportunity. I followed my husband as he changed girlfriends yet again. I had a mountain of evidence for a divorce, so it must be murder I was contemplating.

Then came the fateful birthday party and the conversation with Paul. I learned all about Ritvin and how it could turn Viagra into a lethal weapon – and I had to know about the Viagra George was taking because pill dust was found in his briefcase. A few days later, I was at Paul's company, left alone near an unlocked pharmacy where bottles of the stuff were on opened racks – bottles from which pills were missing.

Now, the prosecution's case was sailing along. I waited for a day when I knew my husband would be meeting his latest mistress, I spiked his coffee or his cereal and sent him off to the office with one-half of a time bomb in his system. Knowing George would take the Viagra before leaving work to meet his mistress and that death would follow soon after – and suspecting that George was under investigation – I carried off the secret computer to the mall, where I emptied out five million dollars and transferred the money to accounts where only I had the passwords and routing codes. Out would come the mall photos.

Then, I went home, erased the damning computer files, and waited for George's heart to explode.

When I was rushed to the hospital that evening, I had my alibi straight, except that I hadn't counted on anyone suspecting foul play. I told the sympathetic detective that I had no idea my husband was fooling around on me when it was demonstrably obvious that I did. I said I had never heard of Susan Booth when I had copiously documented their affair. I said I hadn't emptied the accounts but I hadn't counted on there being security cameras in the mall.

Lies upon lies.

And, of course, O'Connell had gotten it all exactly right. The man was one extremely smart prosecutor.

Our defense was built around skepticism. 'This is evidence? She had a rotten marriage. Her husband cheated on her almost from the first. So she cheated. You don't put people in prison for twenty years for adultery. She said murder was an alternative to divorce? Well, let me tell you about this Cliff guy. Ms. Booth said he never used anything except Viagra to enhance his virility? Let me set you straight about this vixen. The detective said Kat lied to her? First, prove it, but even if she did, people don't like to admit to strangers that their husbands are philandering cheats. Missing pills? Lots of other bottles had missing pills, too. And grainy photos of someone in a coffee shop? Let me show you the Virgin Mary in a loaf of rye bread.'

"Reasonable doubt," Lew said. "Plus a plausible alternate theory of the crime."

The plausible alternate theory was that Miss Susan Perkins Booth, twenty-six-year-old adventuress and consort of married men, had deliberately killed her lover because he was no longer of use to her. It was a wonderful tale, albeit not backed by any proof. In fact, it was backed by a kind of anti-proof: the police had failed to treat Susie as a suspect. But you didn't need proof; all you needed was that alternate scenario.

* * * * *

There were two other pieces of news of note over the course of the winter. The first was that, on December 31, Peavy, Jensen & Beck passed out of existence. The firm had failed to find a buyer. Institutions no longer made trades through them and there was no investment banking business to speak of. An insignificant, regional brokerage firm evaporated.

The chairman of PJ&B issued a statement mourning the passing of a Boston institution and marveled that the 'malicious acts of a few rogue employees – and one deceased employee in particular – had been able to bring down a proud name that had such a long and illustrious history.'

It goes without saying that I never saw PJ&B's slice of George's life insurance payout.

The second piece of news was that in early January on an otherwise slow news day, standing on the steps of the state capitol building, Sean Michael O'Connell announced that he was humbly offering himself as a candidate for Attorney General of the Commonwealth of Massachusetts.

He said his decision was based on the pressing need for court reforms and to upgrade legal training and a lot of other things that sailed over the heads of every prospective primary voter.

But then he also spoke darkly of a system in which 'giant corporations and wealthy individuals' receive one brand of justice, while 'the hard-working men and women of the Commonwealth' make do with a lesser version of the system that is supposed to be blind.

"When I am Attorney General, corporations will not rape the land, secure in the knowledge that their deeds will go unpunished," O'Connell thundered. "Any more than today, as District Attorney, the rich think they can murder their spouses and get away with it."

I think he was talking about me.

I was the campaign issue. The poster girl for everything wrong with the system of justice. If he could get a conviction in my case, he could bring down General Electric or the power company or whoever was a sitting duck target.

I watched the announcement at Lew and Phoebe's home. O'Connell was in full moral high dudgeon.

"He's got something up his sleeve," Lew said.

*****

It wasn't that Jason Whitburn and his crew of merry men at the SEC had forgotten about me. To the contrary, Jason couldn't wait to put me in jail, take my money, and generally make the rest of my life a living hell. He was a man with a mission.

Lew told me that higher-ups in the SEC organization had already called him on the carpet for blowing it with George. Whitburn's protestations that he couldn't have foreseen his big catch being murdered by his wife was met with stony silence. The simple facts of the case were that the evidence against George had been in good shape for weeks. A search warrant had been approved days earlier and the decision to put a monitoring van outside the house was just plain stupid.

In the meantime, several million dollars worth of very high-priced legal talent was going like a buzz saw through the evidence against Quant Four. Piece by piece, it was being found to be tainted by something or other. Some rule had not been followed or some piece of evidence properly tagged. Peter Brandt's day-long singing session was being characterized as coerced from a man full of remorse for having lost so much of his clients' money and there appeared to be a real possibility that it would all be ruled inadmissible. If Peter's confession went, the case collapsed.

Except for George. With George, the evidence was air-tight. There was money in secret accounts and corporations that acknowledged he had solicited bribes for coverage. The insider trading on pending deals in the PJ&B mergers and acquisitions universe was fully documented. George was toast.

Of course, George was dead and you can't try a corpse.

Getting me would be the next best thing. There was the pesky fact that George's secret computer had disappeared and that a search of our home just hours after his death had not turned it up. That had apparently been quite unexpected. But there were the purported photos of me at Café Au Lait and, most damning of all, my visit to Warren's office a few hours before the money trail evaporated into a cloud of untraceable electrons.

Getting me would also make up for the fact that evidence linking

George to the other hedge funds – the ones that had paid him half a million dollars for advanced information – had proved impossible to find. Hedge funds are apparently built around secrecy, run by men who were once boys who played with secret decoder rings. They revel in mystery and concealment. Trades that ought to be straightforward are frequently done in roundabout fashions. As a result, an order to buy or sell a hundred thousand shares of one of George's restaurant chains would be routed through some third firm or even through a European stock exchange, all in the name of hiding the identity of the firm conducting the transaction. Ephemeral holding companies executed trades, then vanished without a trace. The fact that much of what was going on was patently illegal may have had something to do with the secrecy.

So, it wasn't that Jason Whitburn's interest in me was flagging. It was that he was waiting for something. Either I was going to slip up and make a mistake, or I was going to be convicted on the murder charge. With that on my résumé, getting a jury to believe I had aided and abetted George in his skullduggery was a piece of cake.

While Whitburn was waiting for me to screw up, he was also doing a very effective job of keeping on the pressure. There was still more than a million dollars of funds sitting in escrow accounts that I couldn't touch. Lew filed motions asking that it be released so that I could pay for a more effective defense. The SEC filed counter-motions expressing the opinion that the source of those funds may well have been tainted and that, once in my hands, that money would never be seen again.

As a result of this, I never dared touch my Cayman Islands accounts. I visited Warren in his office one afternoon in January and, from the sanctity of a satellite-connected internet link inside a room that was meticulously swept for listening devices, we perused that glorious offshore haven, which was solidly earning a decent rate of return by being invested in good old American T-bills.

Warren cautioned me that, at least for now, it wasn't safe to withdraw funds from the accounts. "After the trial, or maybe a few months after that, you'll drop off the government's radar screen and no one will care where your money comes from," he said. "I'll have an account set up for you at a nice, staid money management firm. You'll be able to write checks and charge things, with the payments coming out of this account. When the time comes, I'll be there to guide you through the process."

The joke was that the Securities and Exchange Commission needed look no further that the Department of the Treasury to find me. But the Financial Crimes Enforcement Network and the SEC did not speak to one another and were forbidden to share files. I learned to love those privacy laws.

*****

From Monday to Friday I worked on my case, reviewing what Lew or Phoebe put in front of me or rehearsing testimony. Nancy and her husband invited me for dinner one night a week but, because I was forbidden to talk about the case, the conversations were often strained. Trish was on the prosecution's witness list, so contact with her was forbidden. Patsy, rumored to be living in California. was also off limits because of her SEC problems.

Oddly, I found that I didn't miss Trish. We had been friends for years, sharing a common love of shopping, restaurant-hopping and gossip. But something had happened to me along the way. I no longer went shopping – a little matter of not knowing whether my remaining money was going to last through the trial – and restaurants didn't interest me. I found I also didn't care about 'things' the way I once had. I didn't need a new purse or coat because I already had several, and if my shoes were last year's models, well, so be it.

I had changed. I had matured. Who knew that murdering my husband and being charged with that crime would cause me to grow up?

The two people I missed most, it turned out, were Patsy and Paul. Patsy had never forgotten her middle-class roots. She had treated the huge house and staff as transitory things, which they turned out to be. My hope was that when this was all over, I could renew that friendship with Patsy. We would certainly have a lot to talk about.

Paul was also on my mind. He was going to be one of the prosecution's key witnesses. His testimony was likely being counted on to put me away. But we had been friends, and not just in-law friends. I genuinely enjoyed being around him, listening to his plans and popping in the occasional intelligent question. Only Lew's warning of the dire consequences of initiating contact with Paul stopped me from calling him.

Through all this, Warren was my anchor. I had been careful to tell Lew that I was involved with Warren and that I saw him weekly. Though he never said so directly, I could tell Lew wasn't wild about the idea, but at least Warren wasn't part of the case. Lew just asked me to be careful and to never talk about trial preparations.

Each Friday afternoon when our trial prep work was done, I made my way north up Route 128. My heart would beat faster when I entered Manchester. The harbor was empty of boats in the winter and the summer-only shops were shuttered, but it was the contours of the land and the shape of the inlets that resonated in me, not the man-made features. I would skirt the harbor and make my way to the point of land that held his house. I carefully never arrived before I was expected – I didn't want to force my way more deeply into his life than I already was – but neither did I ever arrive more than a few minutes after the time we had agreed upon.

He would meet me in the driveway and we would fall into one another's arms. From then until late Saturday afternoon would be the tonic that kept me sane the rest of the week. There was no schedule and no routine. One weekend we watched old movies. Another one we played Monopoly. The best days were the ones with hours spent in bed or on a thick rug in front of a fire.

Gradually, though I was not supposed to, I came to talk about the case. Warren asked few questions. Rather, he would wait for me to expound on something I said earlier. He said that, because he was a lawyer and represented me in the establishment of the offshore trusts, we had attorney-client privilege and that anything I said would go no further.

We missed only two weeks. He was flying back from Japan one Saturday. The other was Christmas. He explained that Cheryl and the children were joining her parents in the Caribbean and that 'his day' with his children would be Saturday rather than Sunday. I wondered why he didn't invite me for Sunday instead, but did not ask. He gave me a beautiful necklace with a silver sailboat as its pendant for Christmas and I cried all the way home.

*****

There was one other blessed event before the trial. On March 10, just a week before jury selection was to begin, Susan Perkins Booth gave birth to a baby girl, Georgina Perkins Booth, weight seven pounds, six ounces. With the birth came renewed demands for payment of maternity expenses and for the exhumation of George's body to establish paternity beyond any reasonable doubt. All members of George's family had roundly refused to submit DNA samples – even a simple swab of the gums – to aid Susie in her quest. George might be ignominiously dead and un-mourned, but the family name would not be besmirched by the acknowledgment of an out-of-wedlock child.

Lew ignored the demands. "Let's get through the trial, then we'll deal with it."

That was easy for him to say. Susie Perkyboobs wasn't after half of his net worth. His fee was already safely in the bank.

22.

And then it was March 18.

Boston is full of wonderful old government buildings, classically-inspired structures that echo the foundations of civilization and aspirations of the rule of law. The Suffolk County Courthouse is not one of them. It is a decades-old high-rise slab of impersonal stone and glass that gives no hint that there is justice lurking inside.

To get into the courtrooms requires running a gauntlet of metal detectors and guards with beeping wands. Cell phones are forbidden as is anything capable of capturing an image. It is, in effect, a little prison.

On that morning in March, I sat with Lew as jurors were interviewed. My purpose in being there was so that either bench could ask if the potential juror recognized me or I, them. I had a costume for these sessions: a full, black skirt that fell below my knees and a dark gray blouse; attire suitable for a woman still in mourning for her husband. My jewelry was restricted to a wedding and engagement ring and a pair of simple gold earrings. No bracelets, no necklaces. My makeup was minimal and my hair was kept simple. I was a widow, falsely accused of murdering her husband. Sex should never cross the mind of any juror.

Lew explained that there is a science to picking a jury. We did not have the money to use a jury 'consultant' – that would have been an extra hundred thousand – but Lew had successfully gained acquittals without their use and he knew what to look for.

Lew's ideal juror: a young woman, non-church-going, professional in occupation and college-educated. He didn't care if she was single, divorced or happily married; each one worked to our advantage. He didn't care about race.

Sean O'Connell would challenge any juror that met such a

description. He wanted men and older women. He wanted Catholics who went to confession. He wanted people who thought sex was for procreation and adultery was the steppingstone to perdition. He would settle for an African-American Baptist woman provided she had a low-paying job and a grudge against rich white people.

My problem was that Boston was full of the kind of people Sean O'Connell wanted and who were ready to buy into his circumstantial case. Moreover, they were civic-minded and had lots of time on their hands because they were retired or had union jobs that required they be paid full wages while on jury duty. Conversely, the people who were pre-disposed to side with me avoided jury duty by every means possible. I had done the same when I was working – pleading the flu or an immutable doctor's appointment. Jury duty meant you sat in a large room filled with unpleasant people and I wanted no part of it.

The first panel of twenty-five was two-thirds men. Half of them had surnames that indicated Irish ancestry. Many of the men had bloodshot eyes from getting drunk the day before. One older woman glared at me, hatred in her eyes. Of those twenty-five, exactly two were who Lew was looking for. Both looked at me with interest. I made eye contact with them and smiled.

Each prospective juror had filled out a questionnaire. It asked age and occupation and whether the person had read or seen news on the case. Sean O'Connell paged through the questionnaires until he found the two sympathetic women. He asked the first one if she knew of any reason why she could not serve on the jury.

The woman immediately launched into a tale of how she was the sole support of her aged mother who exhibited early signs of dementia and could not be left alone for more than six hours or else she would have to be sent to a nursing home. If there is book called *Jury Duty Avoidance for Dummies*, this woman had read and memorized it.

"Your honor, I ask that this woman be allowed to be excused," O'Connell said.

"I agree," the judge said, not even asking Lew if he concurred.

The second woman pleaded a pending deadline for her company and a boyfriend who was a trial lawyer. She had obviously not read the jury avoidance book as these were not grounds for being excused.

"This juror is acceptable," Lew said.

"I'll use a preemptory challenge," O'Connell said. "The other jurors are acceptable."

Each side got six preemptory challenges – excusing a juror without having to give a reason. Rather than using his challenges, Lew questioned the jurors who were most likely to be disposed to conviction. And, rather than challenge jurors one by one, he allowed them to purge themselves in groups.

"What do you know about this case?" Lew asked Juror #1. Juror #1 promptly volunteered a few facts, such as, 'somebody spiked her big-shot husband's Viagra with something that killed him while he was diddling his girlfriend.'

"Can you add anything to that, Juror #2?" Juror #2 added some lurid details.

Juror #3 had minor children at home and would prefer to serve on a jury when school was not in session. Juror #4, the one who glared at me when she first sat down, allowed that fornication was specifically called out as a sin in the bible and that Lot's wife wasn't spending eternity as a pillar of salt for nothing.

"Your honor," Lew said, "we have a serious problem. Given this panel's knowledge of the case and lack of willingness to start from a neutral base, it may be necessary to ask for a postponement and a change of venue."

"In my chambers," the judge said.

Two hours later, Lew and O'Connell emerged, both angry and red faced. But Lew gave me a conspiratorial wink.

Over lunch, he told me what had happened. Without acknowledging culpability, but under withering questioning, O'Connell acknowledged that, indeed, the panels appeared to be front-weighted with friends of the prosecution; prospective jurors who were of the right ethnic, religious and political persuasion. Lew, of course, would be forced to use all of his preemptory challenges, leaving O'Connell free to hand-pick the jury of his choosing. O'Connell said he had no idea of who had perpetrated this horrible miscarriage of the jury-selection process, but would make any amends in order to avoid a delay – or, worse, a move to Pittsfield or Springfield, where the news coverage would consist of a single newswire account every one or two days.

The solution imposed on both attorneys was that the jurors' names would be pulled at random and the judge – more about her in a moment – would ask the questions. Any challenge would be for specific cause. The quid-pro-quo, however, was that the jury would 'look like Suffolk County'. It was a solution neither side liked, but a damn site better than the one O'Connell had cooked up.

The next panel was seated at 2 p.m. Twelve men and thirteen women. Four Hispanics, five African-Americans, fourteen Caucasians and two Asians.

Massachusetts has a long history of what could be loosely defined as judicial activism. Individual judges and groups of judges have often taken it on themselves to rule on cutting-edge issues where there is no precedent. Massachusetts trial judges have earned sobriquets like 'Turn 'em Loose Bruce'. Others have been censured for improprieties such as falling asleep during trials. Superior Court Judge Karen Richardson was most decidedly not among these loose cannons and avant-garde jurists. She had been on the bench twenty years – one of the first to break the gender barrier – and she took her role very seriously.

Her rules of evidence were strict and she regularly fined attorneys for stepping out of bounds. She was also known for fairness and a willingness to compromise. That lengthy treatise delivered to her by O'Connell asking for the right to parade a dozen witnesses to demonstrate that I was a cheap date resulted in a ruling that the Commonwealth could put a maximum of three witnesses on the stand to make their point and that, if Judge Richardson found the first one or two sufficiently compelling, she would wave off the others.

Lew had tried two cases before her over the years. Surprisingly, because O'Connell tried few cases in person, he also had only two. Lew's previous encounters had earned him some sharp rebukes but he had won both cases. O'Connell had won both of his, so neither attorney had a series advantage.

Judge Richardson conducted the questioning. She asked by show of hands how many had read about the case. Virtually all had. She asked if any of the potential jurors had ever had a close friend or relative accused of a serious crime. A few hands went up and Lew circled those names on a chart in front of him. She asked if any of them had ever lost a large amount of money to a stockbroker. Two hands went up. A half a dozen more questions followed.

At the end of it, Judge Richardson excused eight jurors.

"I need three alternates," Judge Richardson said. "Unless I hear a compelling argument otherwise, you can each challenge one juror, and those that remain are our jurors."

What was supposed to take a week had been accomplished in an afternoon.

The final pool was six women and six men. Not one had bloodshot eyes or a hangover. It wasn't ideal but it was fair.

Sean O'Connell, of course, played it as a victory for the judicial system. "As Attorney General, I will fight to implement the 'Judge Richardson Rule' for serious crimes," he told the press later that afternoon. "We must think beyond a 'jury of our peers' and think in terms of juries that accurately reflect the makeup of the community..." Blah, blah, blah.

Over dinner at his house that evening, Lew told me, "Kat, I've got to let you know that I'm a little worried about that jury. We can't be in this for a hung jury. If that happens, O'Connell will come back fast and with a prosecution tailored to correct any mistakes he may have made the first time around. He'll also get a friendlier judge who either won't notice or won't care that the jury pool is stacked."

"We have one chance to get an acquittal," he said. "It's got to be with this jury. And I'm still waiting for O'Connell's surprise."

23.

With a jury impaneled, the business of putting me on trial for murder got down to cases.

The next morning, O'Connell started his prosecution with an impassioned opening argument about no one being above the law. He also noted that even rotten excuses for humanity like George deserved to see justice done. "A man died a horrible, excruciating death," O'Connell said. "That he was less than perfect does not mean that his death counts for less than if you or someone in your family were the victim."

O'Connell also prepared the jury that there were no smoking guns. "The defendant covered her tracks well," he said. "She does not lack cunning. But sometimes, even when someone has used all the tools of wealth and privilege to hide their crime, there still remains the incontrovertible fact that the preponderance of evidence point to one, and only one, person as the guilty party."

"It isn't going to be an easy case to follow," he warned. "You will be listening to expert testimony about drug interactions and the effect of those drugs on the body. You will hear a lot about financial crimes and trails of money in bank and brokerage accounts."

"But you will also learn about the defendant and, in doing so, you will understand why the trail leads back to her and her alone. You will hear about her sordid affairs and her dark obsession with documenting her husband's infidelities. And you will see a cold-blooded killer at work. Even as her husband goes off to work, the poison acting on his body, she calmly steals his money and transfers it into her own account."

"This is a case of first-degree murder," O'Connell concluded. "The defendant knew exactly what she was doing. She thought she knew the consequences. Now, it's your responsibility to show her exactly what those consequences are."

*****

We were first treated to a gruesome medical seminar. The EMTs who arrived on the scene described George as a man in extreme pain, fighting for his life and not knowing what had hit him.

"Would 'excruciating' be too harsh a word?" O'Connell asked.

"Excruciating would be a very good word," the EMT said.

The head of the emergency room team that treated George described the extent of the injury to his heart muscle.

"A heart can only beat so fast or pump so much blood. The victim's heart was completely out of control," the ER doctor said.

"His heart exploded?" O'Connell asked.

"That's a fair layman's description," the doctor said.

*****

Next up was the pharmacologist, who described what Viagra did and what Ritvin did, and then explained what happened when you mixed the two together.

"It enhances the effect of the Viagra tenfold," the pharmacologist said.

"Meaning you'd get an extremely strong erection?" O'Connell asked.

"If you added half a grain," the pharmacologist said.

"What if you mixed in six grains?"

"As soon as you engaged in any kind of strenuous physical activity, you'd set off a chain reaction," the pharmacologist said. "The Viagra would open blood vessels to allow greater flow, and the excess Ritvin would act as a supercharger."

The pharmacologist was the first witness Lew chose to cross-examine.

"Are there any body changes when you take Ritvin? Do you sweat? Feel more energetic? Have nausea?" Lew asked.

"Not that I'm aware of," the pharmacologist said.

"So, if someone gave the victim that Ritvin surreptitiously, he wouldn't even know it," Lew said.

"Provided it was administered as a powder and not as tablets."

"What's the window of effectiveness for Viagra?" Lew asked.

The pharmacologist thought for a moment. "The Viagra has an efficacy period that starts about an hour after being taken and has a window of four to six hours depending on the individual."

"After which it is just some powder somewhere in the body, waiting to get eliminated?" Lew asked.

"Its effectiveness plummets."

"Have you ever heard of 'Super Viagra'?" Lew asked.

"It's Viagra plus that half-grain of Ritvin," the pharmacologist replied.

"Are you aware that men sometimes deliberately mix the two drugs for enhanced or prolonged sexual pleasure?"

The pharmacologist was aware of such things.

"Are there web sites where someone can learn about this?"

The pharmacologist said he had seen such sites.

"And the web sites are full of warnings that too much Ritvin is dangerous?"

The pharmacologist agreed.

"So, someone who ingested six grains of Ritvin plus Viagra was either extraordinarily stupid, suicidal, or being murdered."

O'Connell objected and Lew withdrew the question. Although, of course, murder was exactly O'Connell wanted to prove. He just didn't want the other two options on the table.

*****

After lunch we got to the medical examiner, who took us through George's autopsy.

"He was moderately overweight and appeared to get insufficient exercise, so his arteries showed early signs of arteriosclerosis," the ME said. "He was a man who, without modification of his diet, could have been looking at heart disease before he was fifty."

The ME had brought along a helpful diagram of the upper cardiovascular system. He pointed to stress points that had sustained serious damage when George's heart went on its rampage. It was like one of those Hurricane Katrina levees that had been breached at a dozen spots.

"Could the victim have survived?" O'Connell asked.

The ME shook his head gravely. "Not for any period of time. Not with that level of damage. There was also a considerable period of time when the brain was deprived of oxygen which would have further complicated his prognosis."

From there, O'Connell moved on to the timing of the ingestion of the drugs.

"Based on absorption in the bloodstream, I estimate the Viagra was taken around five. The Ritvin is more difficult to estimate, but it was definitely before noon," the ME said.

"How long before noon?" O'Connell asked.

"In a twelve hour window before that time. It was fully absorbed in the bloodstream and the liver had more than trace amounts."

"And you could tell how much of each drug?" O'Connell asked.

"The Viagra was fairly easy because it had been ingested just a few hours earlier: one pill. The Ritvin was more difficult but we believe it was six grains – three tablets."

It had sounded to me like fairly straightforward testimony. But all during the direct examination, Lew had sat beside me, his toe tapping excitedly, a sign that this was a witness he had been waiting for. Lew jumped up quickly for his cross-examination.

"Did you find evidence of sexual contact on the victim?" Lew asked.

The ME nodded. "The exterior of the penis contained vaginal secretions."

"So the victim was having sex at the time of the attack," Lew said.

"The victim wore no clothing. I would conclude that the victim was having intercourse during or just prior to the attack."

"And the exertion of the sex triggered the reaction?"

"I believe that's an accurate conclusion," the ME replied.

"You said that Viagra has a window of four to six hours during which it is effective. If the victim had abstained from any physical activity – if he had gone to sleep or just taken the train home and watched television, what would have happened?" Lew asked.

The ME cocked his head. "We have no way of knowing."

Lew nodded. "Just one more question: did you examine the victim's sperm?"

"I did."

"Find anything unusual?"

"The victim was sterile. Seminal fluid was present but no sperm."

"The victim had a vasectomy?" Lew asked.

"No. A blockage in the vas deferens. A cyst."

"So, he wasn't going to father any children." Lew asked.

"The blockage could have been removed surgically," the ME said.

"Was there any indication that the victim knew he was sterile?" Lew asked.

The ME shook his head. "He would only have known if he had consulted a fertility specialist. It had no effect on his ability to maintain an erection or to ejaculate."

That last exchange took a minute to register in my head. I had been focused on the part about sex triggering George's attack.

Sterile. No sperm.

And then the light dawned, a shout of heavenly hosannahs was heard, and a Greek chorus began chanting, *Who's your daddy, little Georgina?*

I saw a look of consternation cross O'Connor's face and he began rummaging his desk for a copy of the autopsy report.

It meant my 'Kat wants to be a mommy' defense was still intact.

And it gave that mercenary skank, Susie Perkyboobs, who was demanding half my money for her illegitimate brat, a bona-fide motive for killing George.

"I think that's enough for one afternoon," Judge Richardson said. "We'll re-convene tomorrow morning."

Yeah, quite enough.

24.

Lew poured drinks all around that evening.

"I saw it in the autopsy report back in August, circled it, and waited for someone on O'Connell's staff to pick up the importance of the information." Lew said. Then, to me, he added, "If I seemed cavalier about her demands for child support from your husband's estate, it was because I didn't want to do anything to tip off O'Connell that one of his witnesses was seriously tainted. As it turns out, though, they don't care about Miss Booth's pregnancy. All they care about is her pillow talk with George: his talking about divorce. She was going to be on the stand for about ten minutes. I guess she's officially off the list now."

Naturally, I was elated for multiple reasons.

But on the whole, that first day had gone the prosecution's way: George had died an excruciatingly painful death because he had taken two drugs hours apart. The chances that he would have self-medicated were about zero. Net conclusion: George had been murdered with malice aforethought, and in a way guaranteed to make his last minutes horrible ones. A horrific crime had been committed and someone ought to be held responsible for it.

*****

Day two of the trial was intended to introduce the jury to George.

First up was the former chairman of PJ&B. He remembered interviewing George just after he had gotten his MBA. Based at least in part on having an old-Boston family name, George had been offered a typical starting position of assistant to a research analyst. For the first three years George had barely registered a ripple in the organization and there was some question of whether he was going to be kept on.

Then had come his out-of-the-blue M&A idea – the one I came up with and gave him full credit for. A new George had emerged, bringing in business, at least during those go-go months of the Nasdaq peak. When it all crashed, George was kept on, largely because he wasn't especially highly paid, but also because the industries he covered – food, beverage and lodging – were holding up better than the market as a whole.

Then, about two years ago, George began to change. His work habits became more erratic. It was also whispered that he was seeing someone on the side. But he continued to churn out reports and bring in M&A deals. The institutions liked him and gave him acceptable ratings, in large part because George followed companies that no one else did. He initiated coverage on a few companies that seemed a little small or outside of PJ&B's geographic universe, but in an era of Reg. FD and Sarbanes-Oxley, one did not question analysts about why they chose to cover certain companies.

* * * * *

Next up was the SEC. Interestingly, Jason did not testify. Instead, it was Rich Cordell, the other man who had been at the hospital the night George died.

Cordell said George had come to their attention from a tip that a hedge fund – Quant Four - was making unusually prescient bets on the movements of certain restaurant stocks. They piled into stocks they had never owned just days before those previously uncovered stocks gained an analyst following. Quant Four then bailed out just before an opinion change.

An SEC check showed that George was the analyst in each case. A file was opened. It wasn't long before the file became thick with examples of George's stocks generating huge trading volumes just before volatile price changes caused by analyst reports. To the SEC, it was a classic case of an analyst leaking information to a favored client.

The closer the SEC looked at PJ&B, the more they saw that they didn't like. When firms are working on projects involving mergers and acquisitions – 'M&A' in the parlance of the industry - the stocks of the companies involved go on 'restricted' lists that make it impossible for anyone in the firm to buy or sell those stocks. Yet, there were certain 'prescient' trades in the shares of PJ&B M&A clients. Not huge trades, but ones that defied the odds.

After the M&A announcements were made, the SEC looked at the luckiest of the trades and found that people with names Juan Dominguez and José Calderón were consistently picking up the stocks of companies that were in secret negotiations to be acquired, then selling them with the announcement. The taxpayer identification number for these accounts was not for anyone named Juan or José.

Was it George who was 'front-running' these stocks? They couldn't be certain, but they started looking closely at George as a person and a consumer. What they found was a man who led a double life. He had a wife at home in the suburbs but a string of young girlfriends in the city. He stayed at posh hotels and paid cash. He squired his girlfriends to expensive restaurants where he flashed wads of hundred-dollar bills.

They concluded George was dirty.

An order was secured to monitor computer use in George's home by noting the unique address each computer gave the network. Over the course of several weeks, a pattern emerged: one computer was apparently shuttled between home and work and was frequently on the internet in the evenings or early mornings. A second computer, apparently permanently positioned in the house, was in use sporadically during the day. There was also a tantalizing third computer. It was used very infrequently, always in the early morning. But on a few occasions, it had logged onto the internet just after 8 a.m.

Cordell said certain staff members at the SEC concluded it was time to bring in George for interrogation. Others, however, felt a stronger case could be built by instituting an intensive watch over his home and workplace, including tapping of his home phone and audio surveillance of the conversations that took place therein. Their particular interest was in determining whether the victim's wife had knowledge of her husband's financial schemes.

Five days after that intensive eavesdropping began, unfortunately, George died.

The SEC's testimony was obviously important to the prosecution's case. I watched the jury as O'Connell led Cordell through their mountain of evidence against George. Some jury members got it; a few even nodded their heads in agreement as points were made. But others fidgeted and one older woman seemed to doze off as Cordell read off trading dates and company stock symbols.

Was it damaging to me that George was a thief? I imagined it would turn on whether, back in the jury room, those who nodded in agreement with O'Connell and Cordell were able to translate the financial jargon for those who were baffled by it.

"I will reserve the right to recall this witness later in the trial to cover that surveillance in the final days of the victim's life," O'Connell said.

* * * * *

A final witness for the day was called; the CEO of a restaurant chain with a depressed stock. He testified that the company pitched its story to a dozen analysts, all of which termed the company too thinly traded and lightly capitalized to be of interest. George, however, said he would be willing to pick up coverage – for a price.

"What was the price?" O'Connell asked.

"He demanded $175,000 in cash, up front," the CEO said.

"And you paid it."

"It was the only way to get our stock moving," the CEO said.

Over dinner, Lew expressed satisfaction with the trial's progress. "Your husband was a nasty guy and he died a horrible death," Lew said. "Some people on the jury might even conclude that he deserved what he got. I suspect that tomorrow, they're going to introduce you to the jury."

*****

And the next day, Sean O'Connell did just that.

His first witness was Marcia Kelly, who described my presence at Hill, Holliday as a distraction to getting serious work done. I had favored tight sweaters and short skirts, and I had a habit of leading with my breasts. I was there to entice potential clients with a promise of sex.

"But all this changed after the defendant got married, didn't it?" O'Connell asked, as though he didn't know the answer.

"No," Marcia said. "Same outfits, same behavior."

A very good hairdresser, wardrobe consultant and makeup technician had helped Marcia, but all they had been able to do was to turn a dog into a well-groomed dog. I hoped the jury could see the jealousy factor at play.

When I had worked with Marcia, she had many annoying habits. The worst one was that, when she became agitated, her voice rose to a screech. O'Connell had apparently noticed it as well and assigned her a voice coach, because this morning her tone was well-modulated. For fifteen minutes, O'Connell led her through a series of Kat stories, all designed to show that I had been hired by the agency with one purpose: to be the resident sex object.

I had encouraged Lew to go after her in cross-examination but he had said all it would do was evoke sympathy for her. "She's not attractive, you are," he said. "The jury can see that. They'll assume her testimony is colored."

*****

Marcia stepped down and the prosecution called Edward DeVries.

I knew Edward was on the list. I had been prepared for this moment for months. But seeing him walk to the front of the courtroom – never turning to look at me – left me with a feeling in my stomach like I was going to throw up.

Edward – I had always called him that – was older and more

mature now. He was strikingly handsome and had a thoughtful look on his face as he listened to questions. The years were being kind to him. I knew he was married now and the father of three. I could only imagine what had happened when he told his wife he was flying back to Boston to testify in a murder trial of a married woman with whom he had once spent a weekend.

O'Connell led Edward through the facts. Eight years earlier, he had been an assistant advertising manager for an area technology company and Hill, Holliday had been the company's agency of record. He had gone to a meeting at the agency one day and I had been there. I had flirted with him in a friendly, casual way. The same thing happened at another meeting, a week later. He had asked me to lunch.

"You knew she was married?" O'Connell asked.

"She said she had been married almost a year," Edward said.

But I did not 'act married'. I made it clear I was interested in him, touching him on the arm and giving him a light kiss at the end. The following week there was another lunch that lasted through much of the afternoon. I took off my shoes and rubbed my stockinged feet against his leg. He said he mentioned my being married several times and that I just waved my hand or shrugged. "Maybe I rushed into it," he accurately quoted me as saying.

When we went out for lunch a third time, he said he would have the use of a friend's beach house in Watch Hill for the following weekend, and would I like to join him? He said he expected me to shrink back or tell him he had misunderstood me. Instead, I said, "I thought you'd never ask."

It was a beautiful weekend in October. Edward was filled with anticipation over this wonderful woman who seemed unperturbed about entering into a relationship with him even though she had marked her first anniversary only a week earlier.

"The weekend included sex?" O'Connell asked.

"The weekend was mostly about sex," Edward replied. "We

almost never had our clothes on."

The jury looked at me and I cringed, staring at the table and the floor. If there were one thing I could take back in my life at that moment, it would be that weekend. I had been so angry with George about the woman he kissed in baggage claim. I had felt deceived. Worse, I had felt as though I had been dumped, against my will, into a re-run of my parents' marriage. If I had confronted George that evening it might have put a stop to his behavior before it soured our marriage. But I had to prove that two could play at that game. Stupid, stupid, stupid.

"Did you talk about her marriage during that weekend?" O'Connell asked.

"Yes," DeVries said. And I silently mouthed along the answer I had given eight years earlier. "She said, 'this isn't about my marriage. This is about me and us and being alive and making the most of every day.'"

On Monday, he had bought the biggest bouquet of roses he could find and sent them to me at the office.

"How did she respond?" O'Connell asked.

"She didn't," Edward said. "I heard later she had gotten into trouble at the agency because of the flowers."

And there had been fallout for him. That same day, Edwards said he was called into the office of one of the company's senior vice presidents and asked point blank if it was true that he had spent the weekend with me. He had said it was true. The executive had told him that he paid ad agencies for creativity and results, not so that his managers could get laid. The following week he was shifted out of advertising and into sales. He never attended another advertising session at Hill, Holliday. He only heard through friends that I had left the agency a few months later.

"And you never heard from the defendant again?" O'Connell asked.

"Never."

The court took a recess and I attempted to recover my nerves. What Edward's account omitted – because he could not have known - was what it was like suddenly finding out you were married to a man who casually cheated on you after a lifetime of watching your father slowly destroy your mother with serial adulteries. My fear was that I had made the biggest mistake of my young life. Edward DeVries had been a blissful interlude that let me know that I could still change my life.

* * * * *

After the break, the prosecution called Bill Browne.

Here it comes again, I thought.

Bill was looking good, with silver hair against a well-tanned face. He had jumped PJ&B at the right time, going to a larger firm as the number two in research and getting promoted into the top spot two years ago. The PJ&B scandal never touched him. He had been divorced and remarried and had a big house down in Hingham.

O'Connell led Bill through the sordid details of our relationship. He had been George's boss and I had flirted with him at an office Christmas party and them again at the firm's summer outing on the Cape. Bill said his own marriage was on the rocks and he had decided to find out if I was just naturally flirtatious or serious. He also lived in Wellesley Hills and, one morning, when he knew George had already caught the train into Boston, he drove to my house.

"I told Kat I was hoping to catch her husband before he left because I wanted to give him some papers to look over. She said he had already left, but would I like some coffee. We ended up in bed."

Bill went on to detail our three-year affair, which was mostly mornings or late afternoons in my house, with George toiling away at his desk while Bill and I smoked marijuana and then screwed. Bill used the more polite 'made love', but given the backdrop – him waiting at the far end of his street, engine idling, waiting for George to leave the house at his punctual 8:00 to catch that 8:15 train. George would be barely out of sight before Bill was in the driveway. There were times when we would be undressed and in bed before George's train left. It wasn't 'making love', it was screwing.

"Did she ever talk about her husband?" O'Connell asked.

"Kat said he was boring. She said George was the least interesting man she had ever known. She said she didn't know why she had married him and she felt trapped."

Every word was accurate. I had told Bill just enough for him to understand that what he and I had was an of-the-moment thing and not a prelude to a bid on my part to become the next Mrs. Browne. I never shared with him George's series of out-of-town affairs, in part because Bill was George's boss and George was using PJ&B's expense account to extend his trips to facilitate his romances. Bill might have felt obliged to act on that information, meaning I would have had not only a philandering husband, but one who was unemployed.

I also, frankly, had no desire to bare my soul to anyone about my father. So, what Bill got from me was the truth, but only that part of the truth I chose to share with my bedmate.

When O'Connell was finished with him, Lew wisely said, "no questions."

O'Connell looked at Judge Richardson. "May I call my next witness?" It was a signal. He had Jean Claude Martin on tap, flown over from France, to demonstrate that my slutty ways were current to at least a year before George died.

But Judge Richardson determined that the jury had heard enough and O'Connell had made his point. "Let's give the jurors some time off for good behavior," she said. "We'll pick it up Monday morning."

* * * * *

We convened back at Lew's home. On the way out to Weston he offered what comfort he could.

"I won't pretend it wasn't a bad day, Kat. We took some heavy punches. The worst part is that O'Connell started chronologically and it was fairly clear to the jury that Judge Richardson limited him to two witnesses. The jurors have the weekend to wonder how many more there would have been and what they would have said."

"I warned you your reputation would take a beating, Kat. But O'Connell gets to tell his side of the story before we tell ours. Just hang in there."

When I got home later that afternoon, there was a message waiting. It was from Warren. He was terribly apologetic. Something had come up and he'd have to cancel Saturday.

I listened to the message again. I wondered what had happened. The time on the call indicated it had come in while court was still in session. Warren would have called about the time Bill Browne was providing graphic details concerning my ravenous sexual needs and my complete disregard for my marriage vows.

Did Warren have a confidante in that packed courtroom calling him with periodic updates? Had Warren concluded that he was just the latest notch in my bedpost?

I played back the message yet again. *'Kat, it's Warren. I'm very sorry for the short notice, but I'm going to have to take a pass on this weekend. Something's come up that I can't get out of. I'm really sorry to be having to leave a message like this. I'll talk to you soon.'*

He's dumping me, I thought. *After what happened in court today, I'm not the right kind of person to be around. I'm a slut who uses men. I'm one step up from a hooker.*

For the first time in my life, I wondered why I had stayed married to George after I caught him in that first tryst. If, less than a year into the marriage, he was cheating on me and I was ready to have a fling with the first handsome guy who walked into my life, why didn't I just call it quits back then? We were living in his ratty condo, he showed absolutely no sign of wanting to make something of his life. Under Massachusetts law, I could have filed for divorce and been back in circulation in three months. Why in hell did I stay?

Because I wanted to prove I wasn't my mother? Because I wanted to show the world that I hadn't married George just because Mark had unceremoniously dumped me?

No. I had stayed married for the money.

George's family was wealthy. Back then, I didn't know he was never going to inherit. When George married me, he automatically assumed my college loans. I stayed married because of the money. Hookers are in it for the money. So was I.

I listened to the message one final time, then erased it.

For the first time in a very long time, I got drunk. I started with a bottle of white wine around 6 p.m. and, when that gave me a pleasant buzz, I switched to vodka tonics. The buzz got more pleasing and I eliminated the tonic water.

Sometime after midnight I passed out. Sometime after that I retched on the bathroom floor. I awakened Saturday morning well past the 8 a.m. time when I would have started toward Manchester-by-the-Sea. I cleaned up the vomit, nauseated by the smell.

Sometime in the early morning hours, I had stopped feeling sorry for myself.

Now, all I felt was the emptiness of being alone. Again.

25.

I looked at the faces of the jurors on Monday morning. I looked for any sympathy or for any understanding that the woman portrayed by Sean O'Connell was not the same woman who sat at the defense table today. I had made mistakes. O'Connell had put those mistakes under a magnifying glass.

Most of them pretended to look elsewhere or to talk with one another before the court session began. A few looked at me with interest. A young woman – maybe thirty, maybe a year or two older – regarded me frankly. But she betrayed no emotion and no sign that she might have had empathy with what I had gone through when I sought comfort in the arms of Edward or Bill or any of the unnamed lovers who followed.

Judge Richardson entered and we rose. She smiled curtly to the jury, wished them a good morning, and then the court was in session.

O'Connell did not go directly for the jugular that morning. He had in mind more of a death by a thousand cuts. A forensic accountant began detailing the booty George had accumulated. Lew objected, saying that what George may have done illegally had no bearing on my guilt or innocence. O'Connell said that George's ill-gotten gains were at the heart of the prosecution's case. Judge Richardson agreed it was relevant.

And so for two hours, the jury came to understand the magnitude of George's illegality. All $4,877,252.39 – except for the still-unknown hedge fund payments – were accounted for and a timeline produced. Once George began stealing, the various deposits in the "Juan Dominguez" accounts – O'Connell's catch-all name for the various phony-named accounts George had used - mushroomed. George did not dip his toe in the water. Sometime in November a year earlier, he had made a determination that he was going to steal everything he could.

O'Connell pointed to a dot on the timeline in early May.

"What's this?" he asked.

The accountant took off his glasses and squinted at the chart, an effective piece of theater for anyone who didn't know it was all rehearsed.

"That's the day 'Benito Morales' became a joint signatory to the various brokerage accounts," the accountant said.

He proceeded to explain that, until that time, the accounts had been in only one name. Now, a second person had full access to the funds, with rights to liquidate and transfer out the assets at any time.

"Is that unusual?" O'Connell asked.

"Not in a joint-tenant account," the account said. "But transfer privileges are usually set up when the account is opened, not months later."

"Would it be hard for someone to do without the account owner knowing about it?"

The accountant pretended to think about the answer for a moment. "These are internet brokerage accounts and their rules are far more lax than, say, an account at Merrill Lynch. It would all be done electronically. If you had the account numbers and the passwords, anyone could do it."

"All you'd need were the account numbers and the passwords," O'Connell repeated. He then pointed to the red dot on June 27th. "What happened here?"

Again, the glasses came off as the accountant looked to see what date O'Connell had in mind.

"On June 27th, between 11:15 a.m. and 11:30 a.m., someone systematically liquidated those accounts and moved every penny into a money market fund bearing the name of Benito Morales."

"Every penny," O'Connell repeated. "On the morning the victim died, someone looted $4,877,252.39 – all the money he had stolen –

from his brokerage accounts." He looked at the jury with satisfaction.

The accountant provoked Lew's first serious cross-examination. The accountant readily admitted that '11:15' was strictly an east coast convention and that the transfer could have come from anywhere in the world. There was no return address on the transfer order and no way to trace it back. 'Benito Morales' could have been in China or South America.

"Could 'Benito Morales' have been George?" Lew asked. "Could he have sensed someone was on to him and it was time to consolidate those accounts and get a new alias?"

This time, the hesitation was real. The answer was a cautious 'yes.'

"So the victim could have made that transfer himself?"

"Yes."

Score the first points for the defense.

*****

After lunch, George's brother, Paul, was placed on the stand.

I had hoped, for Paul's sake, that O'Connell would limit his questions to our conversation of that afternoon in June and our subsequent meeting at 'Rev 3', Paul's company in Cambridge.

But O'Connell had more blood to draw. He led Paul through the family's history, this time asking questions that led the jury to see George as a child of privilege whose turn to crime appeared to have been prodded by some external, malevolent force. Someone like me. George had a prestigious degree from a top-ranked university. The sky was the limit, as Paul himself had proven.

My introduction to the family was explored. Except for Paul, who found me a much-needed breath of fresh air for a clan whose pedigree bordered on in-breeding, the family had disliked me. When the family gathered for Christmas, I was the one whom George's father inexplicably forgot to buy presents for. Having failed to deliver grandchildren to dote on, it was assumed I was selfish.

Left out of this by careful phrasing of questions was the fact that

George was *persona non grata* in his own family, a fate ordained by being the offspring of Wife Number Two. Lew whispered that we could recall Paul when the defense presented its case, if we thought it necessary.

Then O'Connell got to the birthday party and our conversation. Paul dutifully repeated what he had said in his deposition, with O'Connell repeating anything that sounded even faintly damning.

Paul added nothing to his deposition. He was being truthful. He had talked about the interplay of Ritvin and Viagra. If I wasn't already thinking along those lines, Paul had definitely planted the seeds. Regardless, it was impossible that, after the conversation, I didn't know what would happen if the two drugs were mixed.

Then we jumped to my visit to 'Rev 3' and O'Connell put Paul and me in front of that pharmaceutical storeroom.

"No locks," O'Connell said. "Not even a door. Just an open doorway through which anyone could walk and rummage through the pill selection."

A diagram of the 'Rev 3' offices as they existed on that day in June was produced. The pharmaceutical room was only about two inches from where Paul left me when he went to take that phone call from the SEC. The room was barely an inch and a half from where he found me six or seven or eight minutes later. And I was carrying a purse. There could have been anything inside that purse when he came back from taking that call.

When Paul told me about the nature of the call – that George and I were under investigation by the SEC – my face had shown, at minimum, concern, and maybe even fright.

Coming on the heels of Friday's debacle, it was another not-good day for the defense. And we were still waiting for Sean O'Connell's 'surprise'.

* * * * *

That night, Lew called me a little after 9 p.m.

"Come on over and plan to spend the night," he said. "We need to have a serious talk." There was no friendliness in his voice and no option about whether this could wait until morning.

What now? I thought, all the way to Weston.

Lew, Phoebe and I sat in his office. There were no preliminaries. They sat, together, on one side of the large desk, where they could both get a good look at my face as I answered questions. I was on the other side, not knowing what was about to hit me.

"Does the name Joe Pettinari mean anything to you?" Lew asked.

I said it didn't.

"Think very hard," Lew said, studying my face for those subtle, tell-tale signs of lying. "Have you ever met with, spoken with, or even heard the name of Joe Pettinari?"

"No," I said.

Lew look at Phoebe and they exchanged one of those looks that allow long-married couples to communicate silently.

"Do you remember what I said about a 'surprise'?" Lew said. "Do you remember my telling you I was afraid O'Connell was going to hold something back?"

I nodded.

"About two hours ago, he went to Judge Richardson and said a witness had come forward. He claimed he was taken completely by surprise. The witness is Joe Pettinari. Pettinari said that about ten days before your husband died, you approached him and offered him ten thousand dollars to kill George."

Suddenly, I couldn't breathe.

"I'm going to ask you again – and, Kat, you've got to tell me the truth – did you ever contact, or try to contact, anyone to kill your husband?"

"Never," I said, shaking my head for emphasis. "I never did."

Another look passed between Lew and Phoebe.

"Then O'Connell is engaging in the biggest piece of prosecutorial misconduct I've ever seen. If we catch him, he's disbarred. If he gets away with it, you're going to be convicted."

Once again, I couldn't breathe.

"I've only know about this for an hour, Kat," Lew said, trying to calm me down. "Judge Richardson wants to see O'Connell and me in her chambers tomorrow morning – so there's no court session. The judge threatened O'Connell that if he leaks any of this, she won't allow the testimony, but I don't see any way this will stay under wraps for a day and a half. You'll have five TV cameras camped outside your door as soon as the press gets a whiff of Pettinari's testimony. We're going to put you up in our guest room here until I get all the information."

"How can O'Connell get away with putting this Pettinari guy on the stand?" I asked. "Isn't it too late to add witnesses?"

Lew nodded. "Under ordinary circumstances, yes. The trial is underway. But O'Connell claims he never knew about this witness until this evening. As long as he hasn't rested his case, the judge can allow the witness – if she believes the testimony helps advance the 'search for truth'. It would have to be fairly powerful testimony."

"Don't you get to question him ahead of time?"

"O'Connell claims he's spoken to the guy exactly once and just long enough to conclude his testimony may be pivotal. Of course, that's exactly the right answer he has to give to get a witness in at this late date. Yes, I get to question Pettinari. The trial doesn't continue until I've had that opportunity. And I'll use every means at my disposal to find out how O'Connell put him up to it. But you've seen how O'Connell preps a witness. He's very good and covers all the angles. If he's had Pettinari on ice for a while, Pettinari will be very convincing to a jury."

"For now, let's get some sleep," Lew said. "We'll know more tomorrow."

But I didn't sleep. I lay in a strange bed, staring at the ceiling and listening to the noises that an old house makes.

No, I hadn't gone to some hit-man-for-hire web site and pulled up Joe Pettinari's name. Sean O'Connell had decided he wasn't winning the case decisively. He needed a slam dunk. He needed for some thug to point a finger at me and say, 'she tried to hire me to kill her husband.'

It would be all the jury needed to know. Then, everything else in O'Connell's case would fall into place. The circumstantial evidence would have a firm anchor.

Sean O'Connell would be on his way to being the next Attorney General.

And I'd be spending the next twenty years in prison.

26.

Lew didn't return until well after noon but, as he had predicted, the news was too electrifying to stay inside the courthouse. The news radio station reported that Joe Pettinari, a mob-linked 'enforcer' might take the stand as early as tomorrow as the prosecution's star witness. Pettinari claimed to have met with me in a Boston park ten days before George's death, where I offered him an envelope stuffed with cash, a photo of George, and a detailed schedule of his daily itinerary. Pettinari had turned down the job only because I had insufficient references to prove I wasn't trying to set him up.

When he arrived home, Lew looked like he had been kicked.

"Judge Richardson questioned him for two hours in O'Connell's and my presence," Lew said. "She was openly skeptical, she really drilled into Pettinari, right from the start. She told O'Connell he'd never practice law in the state if the guy turned out to be a manufactured witness. She gave O'Connell every chance to withdraw Pettinari before her examination. O'Connell was scared to death, but he said he'd put his career on the line that the guy was genuine."

"His story is that on June 16, he got a call from you – although you wouldn't give your name - asking him to meet you the next day in the park at Post Office Square. You'd be wearing a blue dress and would be seated by the fountain at exactly 5 p.m. He said you had gotten his name from a 'mutual friend' whose name you wouldn't reveal. Pettinari said he treated it as a serious inquiry because his number is hard to get."

"He says he scouted the park for an hour before you showed up and didn't see anything that looked like a set-up, but he was still suspicious. You showed up wearing a blue dress and a big pair of sunglasses, with a thick manila envelope and a file folder. He approached you."

"You gave him your pitch. You pulled out a photo of George and a typed copy of where he could expect to be at any given time over the next few days. The schedule showed what train he took in the morning and evening, where his office was located, and where he usually ate lunch. It showed the path he took between his house and the train station. Then, you showed him an envelope stuffed with hundred dollar bills and said it contained $10,000. You wanted it done fast and you didn't care if it looked like an accident or a robbery. You just wanted him dead as soon as possible."

"Pettinari said he told her he'd give it some thought but he needed the name of the person who put you in touch with him. You said the money was all the reference you needed. Pettinari said he told you that things didn't work that way. Unless someone could vouch for you, he assumed you were wearing a wire and this was all a set-up, with someone taking photos from across the park."

"You said, 'Isn't ten thousand enough?' and he said that you could get someone from Roxbury to do it for five hundred. The question was how you got his name and number. You finally said, 'I found your name in several news stories and used an internet people-finder service to get your number.'"

"Pettinari said he laughed and told you that unless you were willing to undress right there in the park to prove you weren't wearing a wire, he was out of there."

I asked Lew why Pettinari said he was coming forward now.

Lew shifted on his feet, indicating this was the uncomfortable part. "Pettinari is a muscle guy – an enforcer. He's got a long rap sheet and has gone to prison a couple of times. Yesterday afternoon he was arrested for extortion and assault. It was your typical shakedown and Pettinari always disabled any security cameras before he beat people up. A Korean grocer in Charlestown, though, saw Pettinari coming, called his nephew, and set up his cell phone on a shelf. Pettinari tore two cameras out of the wall and smashed the video recorders, then demanded a thousand dollars from the Korean. When he wouldn't pay, Pettinari started beating the crap out of him. The nephew had called the police who get there in the middle of it. Pettinari ran out the back of the store but was caught two blocks away. He claimed he was never there. The cell phone video showed otherwise."

"When they brought Pettinari in to be booked, he said he was prepared to give them something big in return for a walk. When your husband died, Pettinari immediately recognized George's photo as being the same one he had been shown a week and a half earlier – the one pulled off the PJ&B web site. He made a lot of notes about what happened that afternoon and put them away for just such an occasion."

"Judge Richardson looked at the notes and asked a lot of questions about details – the kind of dress you were wearing, for example. He said it was dark blue with a plunging neckline to show lots of cleavage – he obviously didn't use those words. She asked about markings on the envelope – it was plain manila – and the weather that afternoon. She asked him to describe the exact meeting location. After two hours, she pronounced him credible."

"But I wasn't there," I said. "I never met him."

Lew took my hand with both of his. "I believe you, Kat. O'Connell has set this up. He's got a real bad guy with all the right credentials. He's offered Pettinari the deal of a lifetime: memorize these facts and be able to tell the story consistently, and you'll get a walk on the extortion and assault charge. Officially, he gets pleaded down to misdemeanor aggravated assault. The way I figure it, they arrested Pettinari about two in the afternoon, O'Connell went to Judge Richardson at 7:30. O'Connell had three, maybe even four hours to rehearse the story and get Pettinari to write down the details. I've got about twenty hours to find the hole in that story and break him."

Through the afternoon and evening, the media drumbeat grew to a fever pitch. There was file footage taken in summer glory of the beautiful little park at Post Office Square where the meeting took place.

There was a mug shot of Pettinari: a scary guy if ever there was one. Definitely a man capable of murder and of lying on the stand. O'Connell had found his perfect witness. He couldn't be absolutely certain he could get me with the evidence he had, so he manufactured what he needed.

I couldn't go home – the evening news showed the media camped out in front of my house – and so I spent a second night as Lew and Phoebe's guest. I again stared at the ceiling, knowing Lew was downstairs in his office, thinking, calling, doing what he could to find the hole that would allow him to expose O'Connell.

It was probably four in the morning when an image popped into my mind.

Oh, my God, I thought. *I think I've got it.*

I raced out the bedroom door and shouted down the hallway. "Lew, Phoebe, wake up! Wake up!"

* * * * *

At 9:30 the following morning, court re-convened. O'Connell and his assistants sat at their table, smug and laughing. They had the case nailed. They weren't giving one another high fives, but I could sense the Champagne was already being chilled back in O'Connell's campaign headquarters.

O'Connell rose, buttoned his coat, and asked if he could start by recalling a witness, Rich Cordell, the second-in-command at the SEC's Boston office.

Cordell clearly had been prepped and was anticipating every question. This was also his and Jason Whitburn's victory. With a murder conviction from the Commonwealth in hand, they could easily have me indicted by a federal grand jury as George's accessory. Once I had served my twenty years at the women's prison in Concord, I would be shipped off to a federal pen for racketeering and violation of fifteen different securities laws. Whitburn was in court, his rookie mistake very nearly buried and his own future bright.

"On the evening of June 27th, you executed a search warrant at the defendant's home, did you not?" O'Connell asked.

Cordell said that was correct.

"And in the course of that search, you uncovered numerous financial documents, computer files, and other items related to your investigation of the defendant and her husband."

I noted that O'Connell had deliberately restricted himself to discussions of financial materials. One of Lew's early victories was to exclude anything taken out of the house that had to do with George's death since such material wasn't covered by the search warrant.

"We did," Cordell said.

"Among the items you recovered were charge slips and bank records for the defendant and her husband?"

Narrowed still further.

"Did you find a Bank of America debit card charge for an off-peak, round trip between Wellesley Hills and South Station dated June 17?"

"We did."

"And what time was that purchased?"

"The charge slip indicated it was purchased at 3:41 p.m."

O'Connell showed him the slip, asked him to verify it, and then asked that it be entered into evidence.

"You also recovered a Gateway desktop computer belonging to the defendant, did you not?"

"We did."

"Certain files on that computer had been erased. Is that correct?"

"It is."

"But you were able to recover those files?"

"We were."

"And those files included photos, taken outside of a hotel in Boston, of the defendant's husband and of her husband's mistress, Susan Booth?"

"They were taken with a cell phone camera and emailed to the defendant's computer. They bore a date stamp of June 17th and a time stamps of 5:45 p.m. and 5:50 p.m. The following day, according to the computer's event log, the photos were annotated by the defendant to describe what had happened the previous evening."

O'Connell took out the photos with their time stamps, asked him to verify them, and then asked that they, too, be entered into evidence.

"Finally, you also recovered from the defendant's computer, emails apparently copied from a computer in Ms. Booth's apartment?"

"We did. The most recent of those emails had been written the morning of June 17th."

The emails were entered into evidence.

"Based on this evidence, did you conclude that the defendant traveled to Boston on the afternoon of June 17 and stayed there into the evening hours?"

"I did."

O'Connell turned Cordell over to Lew for cross-examination. Lew patted my left hand as he rose from the defense table. Phoebe gripped my right hand tightly.

"Mr. Cordell, you stated in your previous testimony that you had been investigating the defendant and her husband for some time. Is that correct?"

Cordell said it was correct.

"We've heard two witnesses – Marcia Kelly from the ad agency and the defendant's brother-in-law mention that they had been contacted by the SEC as part of that investigation. The defendant's brother-in-law, in fact, indicated that it was a call from an SEC investigator that interrupted his giving the defendant a tour of the 'Rev 3' facility which the prosecution says gave the defendant time to find some pills. About how many people had you contacted or interviewed by June 17th?"

Cordell looked perplexed, and then looked to O'Connell for

guidance.

O'Connell jumped to his feet. "Your honor, these questions seem to have little bearing on my direct examination of the witness."

Lew quickly countered, "You honor, at the time he completed his first round of examination of Mr. Cordell, Mr. O'Connell said he reserved the right to recall Mr. Cordell to question him about the investigation's final days. You have my word that I have only one or two questions on the subject."

Judge Richardson said she would allow one or two questions.

"Fifteen or twenty," Cordell said. "We had contacted, interviewed, or scheduled interviews with fifteen or twenty people to give us background on the deceased and the defendant."

"Was Susan Perkins Booth one of the people you had contacted?

"We had contacted her and attempted to schedule an interview. She had not yet agreed to meet with us."

"No more questions," Lew said.

*****

O'Connell rose, buttoned his jacket again, and called Joseph Vincent Pettinari.

The huge man walked forward and the noise level in the room rose substantially. Pettinari stood a few inches over six feet and would have been even taller if he had a neck. I would guess he pressed the scales at north of 250 pounds, a considerable amount of it muscle. His face was not pretty. This was a man who had been in many fights.

It was his hands, though, that were the scary part of the package. They were half again as large as any pair of hands I had ever seen. They were like slabs of beef. If you were hit by those hands, you went down and stayed down.

Pettinari was sworn in.

"What is your profession?" O'Connell asked.

"I'm a bill collector," Pettinari said, grinning. "I'm a freelance bill collector."

"Would the people who employ you be what are commonly called gangsters?" O'Connell asked.

Pettinari nodded. "They're people in the loan and protection business. Some people might call them gangsters but other people…"

"Mr. O'Connell," Judge Richardson interjected. "Please remind your witness he is giving testimony in an extremely serious matter. Tell him to can the wise cracks."

"Do you work for gangsters, Mr. Pettinari?" O'Connell asked.

"Yeah. For gangsters."

"On June 16 last year, you were contacted by a woman who would not give her name, but who asked you to meet her in the park at Post Office Square at 5 p.m. the following day. Is that correct?"

Pettinari said it was correct.

"What happened when you met that woman at 5 p.m. on June 17th?"

"She offered me ten grand in cash to kill a guy. She said she wanted it done quick. She said she didn't care whether it looked like an accident or a robbery. She just wanted him dead. She had a photo of him. She also had a sheet of paper that showed me where he worked, what train he took to work in the morning, and where he usually ate lunch."

"Did you accept her offer?"

"Nah."

"Why not?"

"I figured it was a sting. I was pretty sure she was wearing a wire. I told her if she stripped down right there in the park I might do business with her."

"But she showed you the money?"

"Hundred dollar bills. An envelope stuffed full of them."

"And she showed you this photo?" O'Connell pulled a photo of George that had been on the PJ&B web site back when there was a PJ&B.

"That was him. That was the mug she wanted me to hit."

"Is the woman who tried to hire you to kill this man in court today?"

Pettinari looked around the room. His gaze settled on me. He pointed a stubby finger at me. "That's her."

There was a gasp inside the courtroom.

"Let the record indicate that Mr. Pettinari pointed to the defendant," O'Connell said.

*****

Lew took his time approaching the witness stand. Under his arm, he had a rolled sheet of photographic paper Phoebe had handed him.

"How did this woman say she found you?" Lew asked.

"Through some computer search thing. I didn't really understand it."

"How was she dressed?"

"Short, dark blue dress." Pettinari drew his fingers together on his chest. "Cut down to here to show lots of…" Pettinari glanced up at the judge, then cupped his hands above his ample midriff in that unmistakable symbol for women of a certain shape. "…Chest."

"She wore sunglasses?"

"Big ones. Dark, so you couldn't see her eyes."

"But you saw her face?"

"Well enough. But like I said, big sunglasses."

"How about her hair?"

"Brunette. Shoulder length."

"Legs?"

"Great legs. Went all the way to the top." Several people in the courtroom laughed. Judge Richardson banged her gavel.

"A real looker, then," Lew said.

"A honey."

"But she never gave you her name."

"They never do. At least not their real name." More laughter in the courtroom, but this time, more subdued.

"But she knew all about the deceased – his schedule, where he worked. That sort of thing."

"All there on that paper she tried to give me."

Lew took the rolled paper from underneath his arm and unfurled it into an 11"x18" sheet. We had called every copy shop in Boston starting at 6 a.m. until we found one that could make a large-size color copy in under an hour.

"Is this the woman you met?"

Pettinari looked at the photo. There was a look of surprise on his face. "Yeah, that's her. That's the dress." He stabbed his finger at the photo. "No question."

Lew turned to Judge Richardson. "Your honor, this is an enlargement of the cell phone photo introduced into evidence just a few minutes ago by the prosecution. You will note it is a photo of Susan Perkins Booth taken June 17 of last year at 5:50 p.m. The photo was taken outside the Hotel 15 Beacon, about a twenty-minute walk from Post Office Square."

The courtroom exploded.

I looked across at Sean O'Connell. His face was ashen, his mouth hung open.

27.

A recess was declared. Judge Richardson said she would see both counsels in her chambers. For an hour and a half, I sat in the courtroom, refusing to acknowledge the barrage of questions from reporters. The court bailiff came by and asked if she could get me anything to eat or drink. That was a first.

When Lew and O'Connell returned, I could see the DA's jaw clenched tightly. Lew, on the other hand, could barely conceal his smile.

He leaned over and spoke in hushed tones. "O'Connell wanted a continuance or a mistrial. Judge Richardson wouldn't give him either. He offered to drop or reduce the charges. I said I wouldn't have a murder charge hanging over your head any time he felt like re-filing and I didn't want you facing double jeopardy. So, the trial goes on."

Judge Richardson entered after a few minutes. We all rose.

The judge cleared her throat. "Before the recess, defense counsel had elicited an identification based on photographic evidence. The bench has ruled that the photograph, while substantially larger than the one previously entered into evidence, is identical in all regards to the state's exhibit. Does the defense want to continue cross-examination?"

Lew rose. "We have two final questions of the witness."

"Then you may proceed."

"Mr. Pettinari, based on your viewing the photograph taken on that date, do you continue to believe the defendant is the same woman with whom you met last June 17th?"

"Nah," Pettinari said. "The woman was younger. The one in the photo was definitely the one I met with." He indicated me with his chin. "This lady looks something like her, but the other broad was seven, eight years younger."

"My final question: when this woman left the park, where did she go?" It was a question no one had thought to ask Pettinari the day before.

"She went into that fancy hotel across the street from the park. Bond."

There was a red canopy for a bar called Bond facing the park.

"I believe the hotel you're referring to is the Langham. There's a bar, Bond, in that hotel."

"If you say so," Pettinari said. "The broad in the blue dress went through the door under the red canopy."

"Where she was employed as an assistant manager," Lew said. "No further questions."

"Does the state wish to re-direct?" Judge Richardson asked O'Connell.

"No, your honor. The state is through with this witness."

* * * * *

The trial continued. Or at least O'Connell made a game effort to continue the trial. The missing pills from Ritvin bottles at Paul's company were dutifully charted. The grainy photos from the mall were introduced. Cliff – minus any reference to our affair - was called to the stand to say I had put murder on an equal footing with divorce as a means of getting out of a marriage. A dozen more witnesses were paraded over two days.

But O'Connell's heart wasn't in it. Joe Pettinari had ensured that the jury would disregard anything short of a direct confession on my part. Lew swatted away the prosecution's witnesses like so many flies, dismissing their claims and offering counter-hypotheses, always pointing back to Susan Perkins Booth. The detectives had never questioned her and her finances were never put under a microscope. To the police, I had been the only suspect, something Detective Tucci tacitly admitted after half of hour of trying to change the subject.

When the state rested, Lew said he was prepared to go directly to closing arguments.

The following morning, O'Connell gave it his best. "I want you to consider this theory: the defendant was all too aware of her husband's illegal stock dealings just as she was aware of his mistresses. Caught in the bind that divorcing him would mean she would never see any part of nearly five million dollars he had stolen, and aware that an SEC investigation could mean heavy fines, she set out to kill him and steal the millions he had secretly banked."

O'Connell glared at Jason Whitburn with his next sentence. "Meanwhile because of bungling and ham-fisted SEC actions, the deceased's mistress, Susan Booth, had also become aware that her lover was under investigation. She, too, sought to gain control of her lover's secret accounts, and attempted to hire a 'hit man' to get the victim out of the way."

"But it was the defendant who gave her husband the Ritvin that ultimately killed him, and the defendant who emptied those accounts. We believe we have proven her guilt beyond a reasonable doubt."

At least the jury didn't laugh.

Lew's turn came. He pursed his lips and stared at the floor for a moment, as though uncertain of where to begin.

"Let me tell you a story," he said, finally. "Let me tell you a story of one of the most inept investigations ever conducted by any pair of law enforcement organizations. And how it trapped an innocent woman while letting the guilty party get away without as much as a hint of suspicion."

"This is a story of a bad man named George. George came from a good family but, somewhere along the line, he went wrong. He began violating the laws that govern how stocks are traded and the fiduciary trust that is the foundation of his profession. In about a year, he extorted payments, accepted bribes, and made illegal stock trades that netted him nearly five million dollars. All through their marriage, George cheated on his wife. When he began violating the law in earnest, he also set out on a new, more flagrant form of adultery, perversely selecting women who were younger versions of the woman he had married."

"Over time, the authorities became suspicious of George's stock dealings and George's wife, Kat, became aware of his philandering. Both Kat and the SEC began their investigations of George."

"George's last girlfriend was more than just suspicious of George. Susan Booth knew all about it. She either discovered it over time or, more likely, George boasted of it as men are likely to do. She gained his trust and knew his account passwords. She was his accomplice."

"Then, one day, the bungling SEC calls Susan and says they want to talk to her about George. Susan panics. The feds are going to take back all that money, just as George is starting to talk divorce from Kat. Oh, and let's not forget one more piece of information weighing on Susan: she's pregnant. Except that George isn't the father."

"Susan hatches a plan: hire a hit man to kill George. 'Kill him as soon as possible,' she says. But the hit man laughs at her. And so she hatches a second plan: Ritvin plus Viagra. She already knows he uses Viagra. Sometime on the morning of June 27th, she got him to ingest Ritvin, knowing they would meet later that day for a tryst."

"Knowing he would be dead in a few hours, she emptied his accounts and transferred the money to one that only she had access to. At 6:30 p.m., George showed up at her apartments. At 7 p.m., he was dead: death by poisoning. Death by sex."

"The police show up. But instead of wondering why George is dead in Susan's apartment, they immediately turn their suspicion on the wife. They never searched Susan Booth's apartment for Ritvin, or for a missing computer with all the secret account information. The police settled on a suspect and, with their blinders on, they never let go."

"Unfortunately, Susan Booth isn't on trial for murder today. She isn't even in court. She's just had some other man's baby. And she's counting the money she stole from George between the time she gave him the Ritvin and when he took the Viagra. "

"You, as the jury, can't convict Susan Booth today. But you can free the woman whose only crime was staying married to a bad man."

The jury filed out of the courtroom, had a final lunch courtesy of Suffolk County, voted a foreman, and voted unanimously to acquit on the first ballot. All this took one hour and forty-seven minutes.

27.

Susan Perkins Booth – 'Susie Perkyboobs' no longer fit with her mammary glands producing a quart of mommy milk each day – provided a 'proffer' statement to the SEC and the Boston police the day after my trial ended. She did so with an attorney and an agent at her side. The latter was negotiating for a movie or a book deal based on Susie's harrowing experiences.

Lew received a copy of the proffer, which he explained is a kind of 'this-is-what-I'd-tell-you-if-we-had-a-deal-but-otherwise-I-deny-everything' kind of statement, and shared it with me. The police were looking for a way to make nice given that I had been acquitted in record time and a 'malicious prosecution' civil suit often followed such quick decisions. However, given that I actually had committed the murder, I wasn't keen to press the issue and told Lew I just wanted to put the trial behind me.

Lew said the proffer statement read like the outline for a movie script and, after reading it, I had to agree it had certain cinematic qualities.

According to Susie, she had met George and immediately recognized him for the serial philanderer he was. She also saw a guy who threw money around with such abandon that it couldn't have really been his, or certainly not have been obtained by honest work. At first he said it was old family money. The first time he got drunk, however, he spoke in dark tones about how his father made it clear he was cut out of the old man's will because of his mother.

He then said the money came from bonuses at his job. But a little reading told her that investment banking firms showered their employees with money only once a year and not in cash. Also, George was not one of the rainmaking investment bankers. He was a fairly low-level analyst following unexciting companies.

Being ambitious and not especially ethical, Susie made it her business to find out the truth and to see if some of that money – or, preferably a lot of it – might be diverted her way. She used sex, a skill at which she modestly admitted she excelled, to get George to tell her everything. George got every conceivable sexual pleasure from an enthusiastic playmate as long as he kept talking.

In less than two months, between bouts of what she characterized as terrific sex because she was a young, nubile woman (I warned you there was a book/movie deal hanging on the outcome), George blurted out the name of every hedge fund from which he took bribes and every internet brokerage account into which those funds were deposited. Besotted with carnal pleasure, plus some recreational drugs with which he had no previous experience, he provided Susie with every password needed to gain access to those accounts, together with the names of the companies from which he had extorted payments for providing coverage.

Ever the one for research, Susie also figured out that George kept his girlfriends until their twenty-seventh birthday, and hers was just eight weeks away. The plan she developed was to give herself a five-million-dollar birthday present. He would dump her on schedule, but she would disappear with the money, leaving behind her dead-end job in boring old Boston. Her plan was to start in Miami, then work her way down to Rio and then over to the south of France, all in search of a wealthy husband. Susie recognized that five million wouldn't last forever, but it would provide that bridge to wedded bliss with the right, older gentleman. 'Right' was defined as someone with lots of money, no demand for a pre-nup, and a heart condition.

Then, two things happened in rapid succession. First, three Clear Blue Easy kits made it undeniable that she was pregnant. Alas, she couldn't say with certainty who the father was. George, of course, was her principal boyfriend, because boyfriends were ranked on the basis of the amount of money they were prepared to spend on her. However,

George was usually available fewer than three evenings a week. That left a lot of lonely nights and, as a result, a couple of potential fathers. She had no intention of keeping the baby but the pregnancy was new, she could wait a week or two before scheduling an abortion, and there was a possibility that she might be able to put the squeeze on multiple daddies to help pay for the procedure.

The second thing – and what really galvanized her into action – was the call from Jason Whitburn, my nemesis at the SEC.

On the phone, Susie said Jason called his request for an interview 'a routine check' and made it sound as though George was just having his credentials reviewed, like getting an oil change every 5,000 miles. Susie, of course, knew better. She realized her meal ticket to the carefree life was going to jail.

In her statement, Susie readily admitted she wasn't going to tell George any of this. Instead, she developed a new plan. Instead of waiting for her 27th birthday – by which time George would likely have sung like a canary, given how easy it had been for her to get the information – she would arrange for George to meet with an accident. An internet search for 'reputed hit man' and 'Boston' turned up numerous references to Joe Pettinari. A twenty-dollar payment to a locator service provided his unlisted number.

This led to the June 17th meeting in the Post Office Square park. Being a graduate of the Cornell School of Hotel Management, Susie prepared detailed materials worthy of a classroom assignment. To get the $10,000 cash payment, she returned a Piaget watch George had bought her (making it ironic that George was helping to fund his own death). To get the balance, she maxed out her credit cards getting cash advances.

Susie said her research showed that such a large amount should overcome any hesitation on Pettinari's part to take on the assignment, and she looked forward to reading of George's unfortunate death in a day or two. However, she had not counted on the meeting foundering on her inability to provide references, or the hit man's insistence that removing her clothes was the one way of demonstrating that she was not wired for sound. Though she didn't succeed in hiring Pettinari, she at least got one useful piece of advice that she filed away as an action item: that people in Roxbury might take on the assignment for far less money.

After she left Pettinari, Susie returned to the Langham, put the money in her locker and retrieved her overnight bag. She then went to meet George for a night of sex at the Hotel 15 Beacon. The fact that Susie had, only an hour earlier, attempted to hire someone to kill this man did not greatly bother her. Even as she was enjoying the dinner, the sex and the room service, she was making a mental catalogue of internet search terms that would yield a willing Roxbury resident.

Despite her best efforts, she had still not found a suitable solution ten days later when George showed up at her apartment for what was supposed to be four hours of bliss. George was just starting to get going when he clutched at his heart and went into convulsions.

Susie said she was at once both profoundly annoyed and elated. The elated part was easy to explain: George was going to die. Good riddance to the jerk. The annoyance was that he had chosen to depart this mortal coil in her apartment, leaving her to clean up the mess before she could go after his money.

As soon as the police and the EMTs left her apartment, Susie said she immediately went on line and checked the various brokerage accounts. To her dismay, they were all empty. She spent much of the night screaming in sheer frustration. Neighbors thought it was grief.

Susie said she checked the accounts several more times that night, just to be certain. Zero dollars.

The next morning, Susie determined that her lone ace in the hole was the one in her womb. Instead of an abortion, she made the decision that her child would be George's heir. As suspicion fell on me in the following days, she grew more confident this was a lucrative move. No one was more shocked than she when the Medical Examiner pronounced George to be shooting blanks in the progeny department.

Of course, just to be certain, Susie said she contacted two fertility specialists to determine whether one or two sperm might have sneaked their way around the cyst and fertilized the egg that became little Georgina. The specialists were unanimous: little Georgina should have been more accurately named little Ramóna (who had two shots at the title based on the probable conception date) or little daughter of the Guy at the Four Seasons Bar (one opportunity, but multiple shots, if you get my drift).

In confessing to soliciting Joe Pettinari - a crime for which she was angling for a suspended sentence based on her being a mommy - Susie was adamant about several things. First, she had never heard of Ritvin before George was autopsied and she had no idea of how to obtain it. She had nothing to do with George's death other than providing the sexual stimulation that shook the lethal cocktail into action.

And, in being willing to provide names and amounts of payments to George from three hedge funds that had thus far eluded the SEC, she stated categorically that she had not raided and re-routed George's five million dollar piggy bank, and demanded that the IRS and the SEC close all investigations into her finances.

Of course, no one believed her.

To Detectives Tucci and Halliday, fresh from having been embarrassed on the witness stand for their failure to have looked more carefully at Susie as a suspect, the proffer was a gold mine. Although it was neither admissible as evidence nor a confession, it provided a road map to solving the crime with a newer, better perpetrator.

All it took was a little imagination: Susie had probably met George at South Station that morning with a quick kiss and a Ritvin-laced cup of coffee, or perhaps joined him for lunch, where his salad was garnished with the drug. Everything else was already in place: she had tried and failed to hire Joe Pettinari to kill George. By her own admission, her computer would show that she had been trying to find an alternate killer. Procuring a couple of Ritvin tablets on the internet, or even at the right clubs, would be a piece of cake. The icing on that cake was that Susie was the only person in the world who could be absolutely certain that George was going to pop a Viagra tablet later that day, and knew without question that his heart was going to be getting a strenuous workout that evening.

It was all so plausible that, were it not for the fact that I had murdered George, I would have believed it.

Susie was arrested two days later.

Susie's statement also came too late to be of interest to Jason Whitburn. The Byzantine trades and trail of payments were of use only if George were on the witness stand to personally attest that he had provided information for cash and that Hedge Fund "Joanie" was really Jet Investments. Otherwise, it was all second hand and impossible to prove.

On the other hand, Jason heard his first admission that someone had knowledge of George's secret accounts and gave times and dates when they were accessed. As with the Boston police, it took only a brief leap of imagination to assume that Susie had emptied the accounts in the morning – using George's computer, which would have been stashed as Susie's to keep it away from my prying eyes - either before or after giving George the first part of his lethal half-and-half. After George was taken away by the EMTs, it would be prudent to toss George's computer off a bridge into the Fens, and then make certain that the transactions had cleared using her own computer.

The federal grand jury's indictment followed her arrest by Boston PD by a matter of hours. It was going to be a long, hot summer for Susie Perkyboobs.

*****

As Susie was baring her soul in her quest for fame and fortune, I was reveling in my freedom. Being found 'not guilty' brought all manner of benefits. Chief among these was that I could not be charged a second time for the same crime. I had gotten away with murder.

Because there was no murder conviction, the likelihood of a federal grand jury indictment was greatly diminished. The grand jurors read the newspapers: the brazen little hussy from the hotel had hired the hit man. She obviously had the money, too.

My accounts were unfrozen. More than a million dollars – those brokerage and IRA accounts that were caught in limbo when I tried to liquidate them months earlier - showed up in the mail. I even got the one-times-salary insurance payment from Pilgrim State Casualty. Lew also gave me a large check representing the balance of what I had turned over to him before my accounts were frozen, less his fee. But when I subtracted out what I had been told the fee would be – upwards of $400,000 – there was far too much money. According to the check from Lew, I had been charged only about $100,000.

"You spent nine months on the case," I said. "You were working for me exclusively."

Lew shrugged. "This may have been the most satisfying victory of my legal career. Don't forget that you were the one who realized that it was Miss Booth who tried to hire Pettinari. And Phoebe and I already have more money than we know what to do with. You paid for the out-of-pocket costs; the investigators, the research and the paralegals. Let's just say the rest is on the house."

I broke down and cried in front of him.

I put the house in Wellesley Hills on the market. It had too many bad memories associated with it. My putting the house up for sale made news, and there were offers almost immediately. Certain people want a house with 'history'. Some of those people aren't especially choosy about what the history is.

I also got back my passport. I was now free to leave the country if

I chose.

I had dinner with Paul and Jerry. Paul called me the day after the trial concluded and invited me to his house in Cambridge. I accepted gratefully.

Some good had come out of the trial, Paul told me. The head of R&D at a major biotech company with which Paul had not previously worked read about 'Rev 3' and the research that was getting underway there. The biotech company offered funding, which Paul didn't need. The head of R&D also offered an avenue of investigation that was slightly different than what Paul had envisioned but that might yield a usable drug more quickly, and with a ready corporate buyer in the wings.

But Paul also wanted to talk privately.

"George once admitted to me that you were the one who found his first big deal," Paul said as we sat in the conservatory of the big house after dinner. Jerry had slipped discreetly away to leave us alone. "He said he always felt like a fraud. He felt deep inside he wasn't very smart and his stupidity was proven by the fact that his wife had to be the one that brought him the opportunity that got his career out of neutral."

"I've spent a lot of time wondering why George went bad," Paul continued. He swirled a glass of port and looked at the liquid collect on the sides of the glass. It was very expensive port to judge from the patina on the bottle. "I have a hypothesis I'd like to share. I think my brother may have been looking for a dramatic exit. If not from life altogether, then from the life he had lived for thirty-six years."

I sat up straight in my chair. I had never heard Paul talk this way.

"Let me stress that this is only a theory," Paul said. "I don't believe George could have possibly thought he was going to get away with the insider trading or taking money from those companies. And, the hedge funds were a disaster waiting to happen. Whether or not George was bright, he had been in the business for more than a decade and he knew about the controls investment banking firms have in place and the checks the SEC runs on trades."

"There is also the pattern of self-destructive behavior," Paul said. "The cheating with younger women, for example, or throwing money around that anyone could see wasn't his own. That wasn't a mid-life crisis. That was a man who didn't care anymore."

"Like the guy who robs a bank and then walks out into the street with his gun pointed at the police?" I offered.

"Maybe," Paul said. "But George did it with a pot of stolen money and fortune-hunting women on his arm."

I took a sip of the port. It tasted as rich as it looked and emboldened me to ask the question that had formed in my mind. "Are you saying he was waiting for someone to kill him?" I asked.

"He wanted to be caught. He wanted to be put out of his misery," Paul said. "For thirty-six years, our father – who makes me want to believe in hell so that he can roast there for an eternity - is a bastard who delighted in telling us what rotten kids we were because we had the wrong mother. If you listen to that kind of crap long enough, one of two things happen: either you tune it out and go your own way, or else you internalize the drumbeat and start punishing yourself."

Paul topped off our glasses. "Rachael is clearly not a happy person. I tuned it out. George started flogging himself long before he met you. I believe that what happened to him last year was the inevitable culmination of dad's hatred for our mother, inflicted on his children when the mother was no longer there to absorb the blows. It was also George's ultimate get-even-with-dad move. Embarrass the old man in a way that can't be ignored. End up in prison at the very least. Besmirch the family name."

Paul leaned forward. "George came to me about a year ago. Swore me to secrecy. Confessed about the extracurricular women and hinted very broadly about the securities things. He told me he was miserable at home and I asked him why. His answer was revealing:

'You see Kat,' he said. 'Look at her. Now look at me.'"

"What did he mean?" I asked, not comprehending.

"He meant that you had reached your mid-thirties, and you were still attractive, and sexy. You were the woman of every straight man's dreams. Meanwhile, he was getting pudgy and his hair was thinning. He resented you. He resented that you were full of life and energy and he was getting middle-aged. He couldn't keep up, and he hated himself for it. And he may have hated you, too."

Paul continued. "When he told me he had started seeing younger women, I asked, 'Why don't you just get a divorce?' His response was, 'My way is better'. At the time, I thought he was talking about cheating as a way of getting even with you. I think what he was really talking about was getting caught and punished, getting that once-in-a-lifetime opportunity to laugh in dad's face. If he died in the process, it would be worth it if our father suffered a loss of face."

"Wait a second," I said. "George cheated on me with a string of twenty-six-year-olds, and stole five million dollars because he wanted to get even with his father? And he'd be willing to die just to make the point?"

Paul nodded. He rose from his chair and began slowly circling the room, touching plants as he went. "Revenge is a strange thing. And maybe – just maybe - he was looking for someone to kill him. A form of assisted suicide - like running out in front of the police. And, if he wasn't killed, he'd go to prison, and you'd lose everything."

"But he had stashed away five million dollars," I said.

"It made him a bigger target," Paul said. "And from what I heard at the trial, he certainly was living well those last few months."

"George wanted me to kill him?"

"Or catch him and punish him. It's just a theory, Kat."

I thought about it. God damn George. He decided to take out his unhappiness on me by sending me to prison until I was old and gray.

Then a thought occurred to me. I swallowed a couple of ounces of the port to get up my courage.

"Paul, when you and George had that heart-to-heart talk, did he ever say he was taking Viagra?"

Paul paused in his walk and took a long drink from his own glass. He stared out into the darkness beyond the conservatory glass. "George used to taunt me with his sexual exploits. 'I had these three women last week; how about you?' Even after he knew I was gay, he couldn't help himself."

A few more moments of silence. "Yes, he talked about Viagra as his stimulant of choice for keeping up with his girlfriends."

"Did you ever tell him about Ritvin?"

Paul smiled and offered me a toast with his glass: I had figured out a major clue. "He asked me about it – this 'super Viagra' cocktail. And, yes I did tell him. 'Just a pinch,' I said. 'You'll be rigid as a flagpole all night.' But, no, I never gave him any. I'd lose my license to keep pharmaceuticals."

"But you hoped he'd find some on the black market and overdose?"

Paul was silent.

"Is that why you talked to me about 'counter-indications' of Ritvin and Viagra at your father's birthday party? You were hoping I'd take the bait and… kill him?" I was too astonished to come up with more delicate language.

Paul smiled again. "No. But I wanted you to know what was possible. Ritvin was certainly on George's mind the afternoon of the party because he asked me – for about the fourth time – if I could get him some."

He shrugged. "I also knew Ritvin was one of the drugs that were already unpacked when you visited." He voice dropped to a whisper. "I didn't know if you had taken any and I didn't want to know. But after George's death, I personally went through several hundred bottles of drugs, wiped them all clean of fingerprints, and removed or added pills so that no one could ever prove that you had gotten Ritvin from me or anyone."

"But what if I had been convicted?" I said, my voice rising. "I could have gone to prison for twenty years."

Paul shook his head vigorously. "Kat, you were never going to be convicted," he said. "Lew Faircloth told me the case was all circumstantial, and he had a few tricks up his sleeve if things got dicey. If there had been any question, the police would also have gotten a very different deposition from me when they took my statement."

"Lew…" I said. "You spoke with Lew?"

Paul nodded.

A light bulb popped on. "You were paying for my defense."

Paul said nothing.

"That's why the total bill was so absurdly low. You were footing the bill."

"George wanted to be punished, Kat. He was a man who, thanks to his father, had long since passed his breaking point. You probably held him together those last few years, but it was going to happen eventually. You shouldn't have to pay for his breakdown."

It was my turn to be quiet.

"Kat, you're free," he said quietly. "You're thirty-six and, unless I missed my guess, you're now a fairly wealthy woman. You're also intelligent, attractive, and possessed of a drive and determination that will get you through any adversity. For eight years you were married – for whatever reason – to a deeply flawed man. In the final year of that marriage, he came apart. You've officially been cleared of any part in his death. You're free. Now go make the most of your new life."

*****

Before I could make the most of it, I had to have a conversation with Lew. I berated him royally for not telling me about Paul's bearing the cost of my defense.

"It was your brother-in-law's and my agreement," Lew said. "If I told you, the deal was off. Then you would have been paying the full freight. Although you would still have gotten a discount at the end. Beating Sean O'Connell really was the most satisfying conclusion I've had in a very long time."

"Paul said something cryptic," I said. "He said you had some tricks up your sleeve. He also said if your assessment of the case had been different, he would have given a very different deposition."

Lew nodded.

"What did he mean?"

Lew did not speak for a moment, weighing breaking a confidence versus helping me.

"Paul likes you a great deal," Lew said. "He thinks you were what that family needed, back when he thought saving the family was still possible. If I had told him that I thought there was a strong case against you – that the odds greatly favored conviction – he was prepared to swear that, on your father-in-law's birthday, he had given your husband several Ritvin tablets together with instructions for their use."

"He was going to take the fall?"

"Paul wouldn't go to prison. There wouldn't even have been anything to convict him of. The pills would have come from a friend, not from the company. Yes, Paul would have lost his pharmaceutical license, but he said it was no big deal. Once they had Paul's statement, the police would have assumed George simply OD'ed out of his own stupidity. End of case."

"He would have done that for me?"

Lew thought for a moment before answering. "He would have done it for his brother as well as for you. Paul cares for you just as he cared for George. He couldn't help George. He could help you."

28.

Which left me with everything I wanted in life except someone with whom to spend it and, maybe, a purpose. I had been given a second chance. The question was what I was going to do with it.

Growing up, I never chased boys. Not even when I was twelve and calling up Ronnie Lane, the cutest guy in class, was not only acceptable but a common practice. After I knew they were interested, I waited for them to come to me. If they didn't, it was their loss.

As you may have surmised, Warren had not phoned. I was upset that first day because his message had been so cryptic. I had a further right to be upset because I had been publicly called a whore by multiple witnesses, with half a dozen reporters scribbling notes and a court reporter taking down every word for posterity.

The next two nights after Warren's call I did not go near my home – the media circus surrounding Sean O'Connell's 'mystery witness' and all that. But when I did go home there was still no message. And he also had my cell phone number.

When he hadn't called after the trial was over, I guessed that the publicity had been too much. Everyone had their limits, and it had been my bad timing to meet Warren when I did. Six months later and Boston would have moved onto the next scandal.

It didn't make me hurt any less inside. It just made the pain comprehensible.

After agonizing over it for a day, I broke every rule I've ever lived by and called Warren's office. I told his assistant I needed an appointment. I was put on hold while she checked with him, and got to hear the Beatles' singing that yesterday, all their troubles seemed so far away.

How perfectly appropriate, I thought.

She came back on the line and suggested a 4:30 meeting. I told her I'd be there.

No one paid attention to me on the Wellesley Hills station platform or on the train. When the 'not guilty' verdict came in, I had been on the front page of the *Globe* and the *Herald.* The latter showed a photo of me walking out of the courthouse after the verdict with the single-word headline, *FREE!* Less than a week later, the city's attention was focused on the really important things, like who would pitch the impending Red Sox home opener.

The door to Warren's office suite was open, though the assistant was nowhere to be seen. He had probably sent her home for the day, the better to talk to me in private. I knocked on his door and he opened it, that engaging smile on his face. But behind the smile I could see in his eyes something else: an emotional distancing of himself from me. The last time he had greeted me – the Saturday morning before the trial opened – he had enveloped me in his arms and covered me in kisses. This time, there was only a smile.

To his credit, Warren didn't fumble with words or look at the carpet. Instead, he told me the truth, looking me straight in the eye. On the preceding Tuesday, his seven-year-old daughter had been ice skating. She had taken a bad fall, broken her foot and lost two teeth.

"Cheryl called me and asked for my help," Warren said. "She was half out of her mind with worry and guilt that she hadn't told Beth not to skate so fast. I told her it was part of growing up and that little kids occasionally break bones."

The two of them had stayed with her in the hospital emergency room, talking through the evening.

You can guess the rest.

"We've decided to give it another try," Warren said. "I don't know if it's permanent. The same issues that pulled us apart four years ago are still there. But Cheryl has a more realistic view of the world now than she did back then. And her point is that kids have a better chance of a normal life in a two-parent household."

I had twenty things in my head, ready to spit out the first time he gave me an opening. Really nasty things about being a coward and moving backward when the rest of the world moved forward, except not expressed nearly so dispassionately.

Instead, I held my tongue. I did ask, "And you give up your tax practice?"

Warren shook his head. "That's part of the 'realistic' view of the world. She understands that this is the part of the law that I'm passionate about."

What about being passionate about me? What about tearing one another's clothes off and making love until we were too exhausted to move?

I didn't say those things. And I didn't offer to be his mistress. I did ask if Cheryl knew about me.

He nodded. "I told her I had been seeing someone and that it had been getting serious."

'It had been getting serious.' How do you diagram that sentence fragment? Was that past conditional tense? Past imperfect, I decided. Like how I ended my marriage: murder imperfect.

"What happens now?" I asked.

He shrugged his shoulders and, for the first time, looked out the window when he spoke. "I'm moving back to the old house. It's too impractical for her to move to my place, with kid's stuff. I've got a slip for the boat..."

In the law, I think this is what they call a *fait accompli*. While I was getting off the hook for murder, Warren was getting engaged to his ex-wife. Finding a slip for the boat meant there was nothing temporary about the situation. It was time for Kat to exit, stage right.

"What do we do about my account?" I asked.

That was a question Warren was ready for. He slipped back into his business mode and pulled out a name and address.

"This will get you started," he said. "The one thing I caution you about is that the IRS is going to be watching you. They'll be looking for spending patterns that don't add up and for accounts that suddenly have large balances. If you want to use the Caymans money, do it from outside the country. Otherwise, it will probably be a year or even two before you're sufficiently 'old news' that they're no longer paying attention."

I thanked him. I know he wanted to give me one of those wonderful, long lingering kisses as a goodbye present, but I turned and presented my cheek instead. I didn't want to be 'the other woman' any more.

*****

I took the train back into Boston the next day to a place George had always derided as the most staid, unimaginative investment management firm in the city, Endicott Brothers.

In their main office in the financial district, it was still 1925. The wood was oiled walnut, the brass was polished to the highest sheen. The ceiling – three stories up – was covered with a mural of the Gods of Commerce making everything work just the way it should. Everything was hushed. The men wore suits with jackets and the women all wore heels.

When I gave my name to the receptionist, she wrote it on a sheet of paper where a runner took it to someplace where crass things like telephone calls were made. A minute later, the runner came back with a note: Miss Lewis would be down directly.

Miss Lewis turned out to be a twenty-something honey blonde in a crisp white blouse and dark skirt. She smile showed dimples but she took my hand in a firm, businesslike manner. We took an elevator to a high floor and went into a small conference room with a terrific view of the Common.

Once alone, she turned out to be all business. Ann Lewis, per her business card, delicately explained that Endicott Brothers maintained a correspondent banking relationship with numerous international entities, providing ease of access to funds from anywhere in the world.

To her credit, she never said, 'Say, aren't you the woman who was on trial for the murder of her husband?' or 'Huh, where did all that money come from?' Instead, she typed a string of numbers into a computer, waited a moment while a screen popped up, tapped a few more keys, and swung the computer monitor around where I could read it, making certain it was clear that she had not peeked. Not that she couldn't go back to her cubbyhole and tap out the same sequence of numbers and ogle my account all day.

"Is this the correct amount of what you believe to be in the account?"

I looked at the screen. It showed $4,727,663.90. Those T-bills had earned back a significant part of the $300,000 it had cost to set up the account in the intervening months.

"That looks correct," I said.

"Just push 'escape' to clear the screen."

My, we were discreet.

Miss Lewis opened a leather portfolio. On it was printed my name in gold leaf and that of Endicott Brothers.

"This is everything I think you'll need to get started," she said. There was an American Express card and a debit card, both of which, she said, were linked to the account. There was a check book, also in its own leather case. I also got two fountain pens, a listing of Endicott Brothers offices in the U.S. and abroad, and a cache of Miss Lewis' business cards. The latter, I imagine, were intended for me to hand out to my many friends with need for offshore accounts.

The last piece of paper she handed me was a wallet-sized card in laminated plastic.

"These are your account codes," she said. "You're welcome to come here any time to view your account or make transactions, but if you wish to do so from the privacy of your own home, this will guide you through the process. Some people choose to commit the codes to memory for enhanced security." That last bit was said without even a touch of irony.

We shook hands and I got another sample of that firm handshake everyone in the training program had been taught. It probably had a name like, 'How to Treat Rich People with Respect'.

I was surprised when she asked, as we stood by the elevator, "Do you have any plans, now that it's over?"

Wow, what a question.

Did I have any plans? Did I want to see the world? Did I want to build a gated estate? Did I want to join the board of some organization somewhere that cared more about my money than its pedigree?

"I'm still trying to decide," I said. "I'm not in a hurry."

*****

I accepted an offer on my house – it was amazing how quickly a 'notorious' property could sell even in a lackluster real estate market - and totaled up my likely net worth after the sale. Including the net proceeds from the house, my 'legitimate' assets were a bit over three million dollars. A year earlier, before I broke the codes on George's computer, I would have been happy with half of that amount in a divorce settlement. Now, three million was just the part of my net worth that, like an iceberg, floated above the water. Underneath it was another $4.7 million.

Paul was right. I was now a fairly wealthy woman.

I rehired my maid and told her to pack up George's clothes and personal effects. Anything she didn't want for her family was to go to Goodwill. I inventoried the house and its contents and discovered, not to my surprise, that most of what was in the house were just objects. I had no sentimental attachment to the furniture or the artwork. A bed was a bed. All blenders were fungible, and I had never been one for cooking, anyway. The cars were leased. George's BMW had gone back to the dealer months earlier. I made arrangements to return my Lexus.

Do you have any plans, now that it's over?

I knew one thing: I needed to get away.

My first act of conspicuous consumption was to buy a first class ticket to San Diego. Patsy Brandt and her family had sold their house on Abbott Road and moved to California while the Quant Four debacle settled itself.

It was mid-April and Boston was in the throes of one of those nasty storms where the rain/snow line kept shifting in some inconclusive meteorological battle in which commuters are the casualties. Patsy met me at the airport in San Diego. She looked tanned and full of energy. The California lifestyle definitely agreed with her. We hugged and it was like two lost souls finding one another. It had been nearly ten months since our last meeting – in her garden on the day George died and Quant Four's bet on copper went disastrously bad.

She had, of course, kept close tabs on the trial and was full of questions, all of which I was pleased to be able to answer honestly – well, mostly honestly - for the first time.

Patsy, Peter and the children were staying in a large, airy and sunshine-filled house in La Jolla. It wasn't on the ocean but was close enough that I could smell the salt air. Best of all, I could feel the sun. The house had been 'loaned' to them for the duration by a friend of Peter's.

"Technically, everything's tied up right now, Patsy told me over lunch. "Peter practically commutes to New York working on his defense. It's his full-time job."

"Did Peter manage to put anything aside – offshore, where the IRS and the SEC can't get at it?" I asked.

Patsy dropped her voice to a whisper. "That's the most carefully guarded secret in this family. Peter says it may be years before we can touch any of it – and that's if we get off on the conspiracy charges."

I knew exactly how she felt.

In one way, Patsy said, the end of Quant Four was the best thing that had happened to her and the children. "It was all unreal," she said.

"We were swimming in this ocean of money without any consequences. I never had to lift a finger and there was nothing that I could want that I couldn't have immediately. Life shouldn't be like that."

For Peter, Quant Four's collapse meant the end of impossible demands, what Patsy described as 'a tightrope walking act that had no end and no net'.

"He delivered these huge returns to investors for years, and Peter constantly prodded his clients to take money off of the table. The house in La Jolla is courtesy of one of those investors who listened. But the demands were insatiable: thirty percent a year, forty percent a year. He had pension funds that screamed at him because he 'only' made thirty-eight percent last year while some other fund did nearly fifty."

"Buying analysts became part of reaching the target," Patsy said. "Everyone in the industry was using the same computer models to buy and short stocks so there was no more upside. Somebody else was always there first. Getting a bunch of analysts to give you advance warning of what they were going to do became the business model. And, Peter says it wasn't just Quant Four. He says dozens of firms are still doing the same thing."

Now I knew why my money was in Treasuries.

I stayed with Patsy ten days, unwinding. I told her all about Warren and I think there was more than a little envy in her expression as she listened. I left nothing out. When I got to the part where Warren reconciled with his wife, her eyes moistened.

"Poor Kat," she said. But I had a feeling her heart was saying, *right decision.*

So I swam in Patsy and Peter's borrowed pool, ate their donated food, and contemplated my future. The one thing I was not worried about was money. My portfolio was generating considerably more than a thousand dollars a day, most of it untaxed.

What, exactly, did I want?

What I wanted, I could not have. I could not turn back the clock ten months and undo George's murder. I couldn't settle for a divorce and cross my fingers that the decree would be final before the feds closed in and took it all away. I could not have Warren back. I could not go back to living in Wellesley Hills and being the woman I had been for the preceding nine years.

What I had, though, was a clean slate.

There were many words that described the kind of person I had been, but the one that kept coming back, the one I kept tracing with my finger on the pool deck was *shallow*. For nine years, I had been someone who had no purpose in life other than to consume.

I did not want to go back to being that person.

One morning, I told Patsy it was time for me to leave.

"Where are you going?" she asked.

I shook my head. "I'm not really sure. It's time to go see who I am."

I was on the west coast and I had my passport. There was a travel agent in La Jolla who immediately suggested a Pacific cruise or two weeks at a super-luxury resort in Bali.

I asked if she had anything more educational.

The travel agent drummed her fingers and said, "Hmmmm."

Two days later, I was the fill-in fourteenth person on a two-week escorted tour to Egypt. My passport, which had never held an entry stamp from anyplace more exotic than Martinique, finally had one from somewhere that was really foreign, as well as a hurry-up tourist visa. We started in Cairo and Giza, flew to Luxor and saw Karnak and the Valley of the Kings, then boarded a boat for Aswan. Another flight took us to Abu Simbel.

It was probably on the seventh day, somewhere on the Nile between Edfu and Aswan, that I made the discovery that I was enjoying myself more than I could ever have imagined. We gathered for lectures in the evenings and I was one of the ones asking the most questions and taking notes. While most of the others in the tour group went shopping in the bazaars, I was the one back at the hotel reading up on the next stop or wandering ruins on my own.

I called the travel agent in La Jolla from Alexandria, the last stop on the tour. "As long as I'm in the Mediterranean, what else do you have?"

From Alexandria, I flew to Athens and joined a group exploring the Aegean Sea civilizations. For two weeks, a dozen of us chugged on a small ship from one Cycladean island to another, walking ruins of temples and learning to distinguish influences of Crete, Athens and Rome. I stayed on for the extension to the Peloponnese and had the pleasure to walk the site of Mycenae at dawn, with the sun rising over the Argolid Plain.

Damn it, I was learning. For the first time since college, I was actually applying my brain to absorbing something other than fashion or food. It felt good. I wasn't going to become a scholar. I wasn't going to contribute to a monograph on the rise of the Euboean League. But I was getting my hands dirty even as I filled my mind with new things.

The 'old' me didn't completely disappear. There were single men on the tour of Egypt. One of them was a nice man, a widower in his fifties who had lost his wife to cancer the preceding year. This trip was the one they had promised to take together, but her time ran out before they could go. He was taking the trip to keep a final promise to her. He was from Oregon and had never heard of me, for which I was thankful. He had two kids in college who no longer needed parental supervision. We buddied up and spent long evenings together.

I told him my husband had died of a heart attack, which was certainly true. When he asked if it had been a 'deep, true love', I didn't lie and say it had been one that ought to have gone on for another thirty or forty years. Instead I said it was a marriage that I had entered into with love and expectation of a family and a long life together. I told him that both George and I brought heavy baggage to the relationship and that we would have parted had George not died. I said I was taking a year or so to get my bearings, leaving out the part that nine months of that time had been spent awaiting trial for murder.

He told me about his loneliness and, if I had tried, I could have ended the tour an engaged woman. Instead, I collected an address and promised to visit Portland.

In the Cyclades, there was a guy close to my age, a New Yorker who had decided to 'chuck it all' after making a killing in real estate. He was cute but a little too full of himself. He was a much improved version of George, but not nearly a Warren. I also had a hunch he had done some quick research on me because one day his interest went from so-so to red hot. I avoided him for the rest of the trip. I didn't want a relationship based on morbid curiosity.

I finally succumbed to a need for closeness on that trip extension to the Greek mainland. Morrie was forty and had survived a car crash, walking away from an accident that was supposed to have killed him. A week later, he realized he was living with a woman he didn't love and working at a medical specialty he hated. He exited both relationships and found to his relief that his wife had felt pretty much the same way during the preceding twelve years. This trip was his catharsis. When he got back, he would still be a doctor with a practice, but would switch from dermatology to general medicine. It was a decision, he said, that would cut his income in half but make him feel like he was helping people for the first time since his residency.

Three days into that sojourn, I decided I really liked this guy. He lived in South Carolina, a placed I considered to be one of the outer circles of hell, so there was no long-term future. But he was funny and thoughtful and remarkably intelligent. We spent three nights together and I knew he got as much out of it as I did.

*****

It is June now, nearing the first anniversary of George's death. It's funny how I now think of it as 'George's death' and not, 'the day I killed George'. I don't deny that I killed him and I don't think for a second that it was some preventable accident.

But I am not the person who killed him. In George's death, a new Katherine was released (yes, having used up several of Kat's nine lives, I decided to retire the name). I'm trying to make the most of the new me.

I was damaged goods when I met George. I was the product of parents who could not confront the basic truth that one of them could not be faithful to the other. My father fooled around and my mother 'coped' by drinking herself insensate. I carried that damage into my first serious relationship – with Mark – by having so few expectations of him that after five years together we were no closer to marriage than the day we met.

George could have been my new start. Instead, following some tragic script written in an ancient language, I sought out and married a man whose infidelities echoed and exceeded those of my father. That I stayed married to him for eight years was not a badge of honor on my part. It was a symptom of a sickness. His murder was my release.

I don't believe in fate. There was no invisible hand that intervened and got me free of those murder charges (and, for what it's worth, Sean O'Connell placed a distant second in the Democratic primary). I am free because Lew Faircloth took my case and crafted a defense that left reasonable doubt in the mind of jurors. I have a second chance because I could afford a really good lawyer, and because George had a mistress whom the jury disliked (and without ever meeting!) even more than they disliked me.

I write this from a place that is not important to the story. After Greece, my new best buddy, that travel agent in La Jolla., put me on an archeological dig somewhere in the Mediterranean. It's the kind of place that takes on a small group of well-to-do, earnest amateurs, who pay a lot of money for the privilege of getting their hands dirty, eating the same food night after night for two weeks, and hearing remarkably intelligent scientists talk about the importance of it all. Our attendance, in turn, pays for the dig.

I came here six weeks ago. When my time was up, I asked the chief archeologist if I could stay on as a volunteer, doing the grunt works of sifting for pottery shards and cataloging the beads. Maybe it was because I offered to write a check, or maybe it was because I threw myself into the work during those two weeks, but the head guy agreed to take me on. No pay, no benefits except a place to sleep and three meals a day.

And yes, there is a guy. He's one of the staff archeologists. Tall and shy, with just a touch of Indiana Jones in his mannerisms. Lester – God help me, that's his name – works with me and I'm gradually learning to use the spectral analysis equipment and to interpret the ground-sending radar images.

What I've learned about Lester makes him all the more interesting. He's on a one-year sabbatical from a university in a city where I wouldn't mind living. He was engaged once, but the bride-to-be met someone with aspirations higher than archeology. Oh. And his family's name is on a couple of civic buildings in that city.

Maybe I'll be politely asked to leave tomorrow. Or, maybe I'll be here for a year and leave as Lester's fiancée. What I can say without a doubt is that I'm being useful and that I'm around people who are doing something where making money is not the measure of success. They don't care who I was. They don't pry.

I see Lester looking at me out of the corner of his eye sometimes. I'm not sure he knows what to make of me. I probably frighten him.

I'm taking it slow. I have a long time to make things work.